SUNNY DAYS ON THE BOARDWALK

THE BOARDWALK SERIES - BOOK FOUR

GEORGINA TROY

Boldw**oo**d

First published in 2021. This edition first published in Great Britain in 2023 by Boldwood Books Ltd.

Paperback ISBN 978-1-80426-087-6

Large Print ISBN 978-1-80426-088-3

Hardback ISBN 978-1-80426-089-0

Ebook ISBN 978-1-80426-086-9

Kindle ISBN 978-1-80426-085-2

Audio CD ISBN 978-1-80426-094-4

MP3 CD ISBN 978-1-80426-093-7

Digital audio download ISBN 978-1-80426-092-0

Boldwood Books Ltd
23 Bowerdean Street
London SW6 3TN
www.boldwoodbooks.com

To Rob, with love.

1

20TH MARCH

Jools rested her three latest paintings against the low windowsill in the upstairs living room to try and gauge if they were suitable for the fishermens' cottages. It was the first day of spring and a relief to feel heat in the sunshine after the long, cold winter. She tilted her head to one side. The pictures made up a triptych of the scene in front of her. She never tired of staring out of the living room window at the beach below, at the cliffs to the right of the board-walk, and the red and white painted lighthouse at the end of the short pier on the left.

She loved this room and so did her gran. It was where they chose to spend their time when they weren't working in Board-walk Books, the second-hand bookshop they ran from the large room downstairs that took up most of the ground floor of their cottage.

'Yes,' she said at last, satisfied that Oliver Whimsy and her friend, Lexi Davies, would approve the paintings they had commissioned her to paint for the three fishermens' cottages Lexi owned, situated up the hill from the boardwalk. They'd loved the pictures she occasionally sold in the local café and wanted three similar paintings, one for each property. And if they didn't like them, she could paint something else. She was slightly surprised that they had asked her instead of Lexi's artist father. Then again, things had been a little strained between the two of them since the autumn and she could understand the reasoning behind their decision.

Teddy, her grandmother's naughty Jack Russell, bounded into the room and immediately went to investigate the first painting. He gave it a sniff and turned sideways.

'Don't you dare wee on that painting, Teddy,' she bellowed, stepping forward to shoo him away and pick the three canvases up.

Jools heard the little dog's paws padding down the stairs. No doubt he would be going to the bookshop in the hope that Gran, or one of the customers, might have a treat for him. 'Greedy little devil,' she said with fond exasperation.

She carried the three paintings through to her room at the back of the cottage. She chose the smallest room to sleep in so that in the cooler days she could use the second largest bedroom as her studio. Her favourite place to paint was the tiny area outside the back of the house, or on the beach or the boardwalk itself. Right now, though, it was still too cold for her to attempt to paint anywhere but inside.

She stacked the paintings neatly against the wall, wrapping each one carefully before tying them with string to make them easier to carry. As Jools worked, she couldn't help thinking about Finn Gallichan and his imminent departure. They had only been on a couple of dates but she quite liked him, although muscular men had never been her type before now. She wished he wasn't going to be away for the next couple of months. They'd got on well and she was keen to see him again.

She slipped her arms through her puffy jacket and zipped it up before pulling her bright orange beanie over her short pink hair, picked up the paintings and went downstairs.

'I'm taking these to Lexi and Oliver,' she said to her grand-mother, who was waiting patiently as several customers looked through some of the thousands of books they had crammed into every nook and cranny in their small shop. She liked it when people took their time. It had been fairly quiet over the Christmas period, but things had picked up when the snow had melted and locals needed somewhere to go that was close by, warm, and didn't cost too much money.

'All right, my love,' Gran said, giving her a wink. 'You take your time, I'm perfectly fine here.'

Lexi closed the shop door behind her and began the short trek up to the cottages. She loved living on the boardwalk and on days like these, when there were customers in the shop and her gran's Parkinsons wasn't giving her too much trouble, she didn't think she could be any more content with her life. Apart from the thought of having to bid farewell to Finn. Part of her thought that if he liked her as much as he professed to, he would find a way to not have to leave the island. Then again, she reasoned, he was going away with the same close friend he went with every year. She wouldn't want to let down one of her friends, especially for a man she had only just become involved with.

Lexi's cottage was at the end of a short row and Jools knocked on the door, turning to gaze at the vista below of the boardwalk and waves crashing onto the sandy beach.

'Hi Jools,' Lexi said, waving her inside. 'You didn't have to carry these all the way up here, I could have collected them next time I drove down.'

Jools handed Lexi one of the paintings and followed her through to the small living area. 'Hi Oliver.' She smiled at the tall, dark-haired Scot her friend seemed to be falling in love with. *If she hasn't already.*

'I've been looking forward to seeing these paintings,' Oliver said, watching Lexi and Jools unwrap them and place them side by side on the sofa.

Jools's stomach contracted anxiously. She hated this bit. She always hoped that her clients were happy with the work they had commissioned but could never be certain that she had captured the vision in their minds. She waited as Lexi and Oliver stepped back and studied her work.

'Lexi said you were good, but I didn't realise you were this talented,' Oliver said in a tone of awe that made Jools blush. 'These paintings are wonderful.'

'Thanks very much.' Jools couldn't hide her delight at his praise.

'They're stunning,' Lexi said. 'I knew they would be though.'

'Do you think you could paint a landscape from a photograph?' Oliver asked thoughtfully.

Jools shrugged. 'I could if the picture was very clear. If you could email it to me, so I could enlarge it on my computer, that would be even better. Why?'

'Could you do a couple of paintings for me? A view from here, and maybe one of the mountains near my parents' home in Scotland. They'd love that.'

Jools nodded. 'No problem. How soon would you want them?'

'Not for several months. I'd want to present them to my parents for their next wedding anniversary but that's not until July.'

'That's plenty of time,' Jools confirmed. 'I'll email a quote and we'll take it from there, shall we?'

Oliver smiled. 'Sounds good to me. Thank you.' He grinned at Lexi. 'I always battle to come up with something they'll both like for their anniversaries and this year I'll be able to give them two presents I know they'll love.' He looked back at Jools, still smiling. 'Thanks very much.'

'No,' Jools laughed. 'It's me who should be thanking you. I didn't expect another commission today.'

'If you leave your bank details with Lexi, I'll arrange a transfer straight away,' Oliver said. 'There's nothing worse than asking people for something and then making them wait for payment.'

Jools couldn't agree more. 'Thank you,' she said. 'I'll do that.'

Later, as she reached the boardwalk, Jools noticed someone locking the door at the Isola Bella Gelateria. Her stomach flipped when she realised it was Finn. She had supposed he would be at home, packing to leave the following day.

'Hi, Jools,' he said, pushing the keys into his jacket pocket and walking towards her. 'How are you?'

'Fine thanks.' She motioned towards the closed gelateria. 'Is everything all right in there?'

He nodded. 'I was checking on a couple of things for Alessandro before I drop off the keys.' He looked down at his feet briefly before catching her eye once more. 'I'm leaving tomorrow.'

'Yes. I know.' All the excitement of her new commission disappeared at the thought of Finn leaving the island so soon.

'Can we go for a quiet drink somewhere tonight?' he asked. 'I know Alessandro wanted to give me a send-off and invite everyone, but I'd rather spend time just with you on my last evening. If you want to, that is.'

Jools wanted to very much but wasn't sure whether agreeing to go out with him was only going to cause more heartache when he left. She realised he was waiting for her to answer and, seeing the sad expression on his sweet face, didn't like to refuse. 'I'd like that,' she admitted. 'Where were you thinking of going?'

He visibly brightened. 'We could try that restaurant in St Brelade's Bay you were telling me about.'

Jools thought of the expensive place she'd mentioned the week before. Although she was touched he'd remembered her comment, she shook her head. 'No, not there.'

'Why not?' He looked hurt.

'Because it'll cost a lot and you should be keeping all your savings for your trip.'

'But I want to treat you,' he said, a disappointed expression on his face. He reached out and took Jools's hand in his. 'It's my last opportunity to spend time with you for two months.'

Jools struggled to keep herself from snapping that their parting was a choice he was making. Then she reminded herself that she would probably think badly of him if he let his friend down. 'Let's go somewhere quiet then,' she said. 'Maybe for a pub meal. There's a lovely place down in the bay. It's got closed off areas where we can chat privately.'

His face lit up at the suggestion. 'Sounds perfect. Shall I pick you up at around six o'clock?'

'That'll be perfect.' Jools liked to think that they would be able to part on good terms, although she suspected it was going to be a fine balance between spending a fun, friendly last evening with him and allowing herself to get too close.

He leant forward and gave her a quick kiss. 'I'd better get these keys to Alessandro before he thinks I've forgotten. See you later.'

Jools gave him a smile and continued walking the short distance to the bookshop. The brass bell jangled noisily as she entered. Seeing her grandmother deep in conversation with a lady, she smiled at an elderly gentleman approaching the counter with several books in his hands.

'Good morning,' Jools said, unsure if she recognised him. She knew most of the customers apart from those holidaymakers who came in the shop during their summer holidays. 'Did you find everything you were looking for?'

'I did, thank you. Although...' He hesitated and then shook his head. 'No, it's fine.'

'Was there something else you wanted me to find for you?' Jools knew that occasionally customers were embarrassed to ask for books they were hoping to locate.

The man seemed to consider for a moment. 'It's just that I'm new to the island. Well, new in the sense that I was born here, just before the Occupation, and have now returned to live with my daughter.'

Jools did her maths. If the man had been born just before the German forces occupied the island in nineteen forty, he must be in his early to mid-eighties. 'Is this your first time back to the island?'

He shook his head and smiled. 'Heavens, no. I've come back regularly since leaving in the seventies, but I've either lost contact with my old friends from the island or they've died.'

Jools couldn't help feeling sorry for him. He might be living with his daughter, but there was a sadness about him that concerned her. She thought back to a conversation she had had with her grandmother a couple of weeks earlier, about restarting the book group at the shop on the second Thursday of each month. She knew her gran would enjoy it and liked to think that Betty, who was in her nineties and the oldest resident on the boardwalk, would want to take part. Maybe, she mused, the man that Oliver and Lexi had helped before Christmas might also want to join? He lived up the hill but Jools knew that she could always borrow Lexi's car to fetch him if he wasn't happy catching the bus at night time. He and Betty seemed to have become firm friends since his first visit to the boardwalk. What was his name? she wondered. 'Barry,' she said quietly.

'I beg your pardon?'

She bit her lower lip, embarrassed. 'Sorry. I was thinking aloud.' She took the four books from the old man and laid them on the counter. 'I didn't catch your name,' she said. 'I'm Jools. My grandmother, Mrs Jones and I run Boardwalk Books.'

His face lit up in a smile that seemed to take years off him. Jools realised he must have been very handsome when he was younger and wondered what had happened to make him seem so sad. 'I'm Alan Hidrio,' he said.

'Nice to meet you, Alan. Gran and I were considering restarting a book group we used to run from the shop. Would that be something you might be interested in?'

'Yes, that's definitely something I'd enjoy being involved in. I used to attend a book group where I lived in Hampshire and was sad to leave my friends when I came back here.'

Jools smiled, happy to think that she had found another member of the group. 'We were thinking the second Thursday of each month from around six o'clock. Would that suit you? Or would later be better?'

He laughed. It was a deep rumbling that seemed unlikely coming from such a reed thin man but it made Jools happy to hear it. 'I'm free every evening of the week and therefore any time you decide will suit me just fine. I'd be delighted to meet up any Thursday.'

'That's good to know,' she said, a spark of an idea forming in her mind. 'Right, if you want to write down your phone number in this notebook,' she said, handing him a biro and turning the pad to face him on the counter. 'Then I'll contact you as soon as we've sorted everything out.'

'Thank you, Miss Jones. You've made an old man exceedingly happy.'

Jools rang up the cost of each book into the till and told him the total. 'I'm glad,' she said, as he handed her the money. 'I know that Gran will be delighted to hear she has a new member too.'

* * *

Later that evening, as she sat in the old, low-ceilinged pub, waiting for Finn to buy them drinks at the bar, Jools thought she heard Lexi's stepmother, Gloria, on the other side of the wooden partition dividing their tables.

She was about to stand and go to greet them when she heard Lexi speak.

'No, Gloria.' Her voice was calm but firm. 'I appreciate your offer to take out a loan to help Dad pay back the money you and he spent on his bungalow, but it's not necessary. I'm just happy that we've all made up now and can move forward.'

'That's very kind of you, Lexi,' Gloria said. 'But I know how badly your father has felt about what he and I did and how much pain we put you through. I told you that I was sorry for what I'd done and I meant it.'

'Yes, love.' It was Lexi's father, Jeff, speaking now. 'If we pay you back all the money we spent, you can buy back the cottage from Oliver and all three of them will be yours again. It's the least we can do, isn't it, Gloria?'

'It is, my darling.'

'No.' Lexi seemed determined to refuse their offer. 'I appreciate what you're suggesting, really I do, but I won't accept it.'

'But why?' Jeff asked.

Jools noticed Finn giving her a wave from the bar and smiled at him, hoping he didn't return to their table until she had heard the rest of the conversation. Surely Lexi wanted to buy back the third cottage? She'd been devastated when her father had sold all three to Oliver without telling her, and it was only thanks to Oliver's generosity – and the fact that he'd fallen in love with Lexi – that two of the cottages were hers again.

'No, Dad. I'm happy with Oliver.'

'I know you are, but what has that got to do with what we're discussing?'

'Thanks, but I'm happy with Oliver owning it now.'

Jools had to cover her mouth so they didn't hear her gasp. Lexi must really want to make things up with her father if she wasn't accepting his offer. She was relieved to know that the upset of the past few months looked like it was behind her good friend.

'Are you sure, Lexi?' Jools recognised Oliver's voice. 'I know how much the properties mean to you. I would understand if you wanted them all back, I really would.'

Jools held her breath waiting for her friend to reply. 'No,' Lexi said. 'I might love the properties but I love you even more and right now I'm happy to keep things as they are.' Jools heard someone move. 'I want you to cancel the loan, Gloria. I've got all I need and I want you and Dad to be happy. That's all I ask.'

'We are, sweetheart,' her father said.

Jools noticed Finn returning to the table with their drinks in his hands and two menus tucked under his arm. She realised he was staring at her, a confused expression on his face, and realised her mouth was open in shock at what she had heard. He put their drinks down on two coasters and sat. Opening his mouth to speak, Jools raised a finger to her lips to quieten him and then pointed to the partition. Finn frowned but was silent.

'I want you to be happy too,' Jeff said. 'And to make up for what I did.'

'Then, cancel the loan.' Lexi's voice was quiet. Jools could hear the smile in her voice. She closed her eyes briefly and then smiled at Finn, picked up her gin and tonic and took a much-needed sip.

A noisy group of about ten people came in, laughing and teasing each other, and marched over to the bar. The rest of Lexi's conversation was lost in their laughter and Jools was relieved her friend wouldn't realise that she was sitting so close and would have heard her and her father speaking.

'Shall we order?' Finn asked, sliding one of the menus over to Jools. 'It's busy in here tonight and if we don't do so quickly, we might end up having to wait ages.'

* * *

Half an hour later she and Finn were enjoying their cod, chips and pea supper as Jools told him all about her encounter with the older gentleman.

'He was so happy when I mentioned the book group,' she said, the memory of his delight bringing a lump to her throat. She swallowed before continuing. 'He seemed such a nice old man, too. I suppose his wife must have died, or something like that. He said he's come to the island to live with his daughter. I wonder if I know her?' Her mind wandered as she tried to recall whether she or her gran had picked up any gossip about one of the locals having their father come to live on the island. She realised Finn was speaking and shook her head.

'I'm so sorry, I was lost in thought then.'

'You don't say,' he teased. 'You're an incredibly kind person, Jools. Do you know that?'

'I'm no different to anyone else.' She felt awkward at his compliment. He was staring at her thoughtfully. 'What is it?'

'You don't like it when someone compliments you, do you?'

She gave a one-shouldered shrug. 'It's fine. I just never quite know how to react, that's all.' She took a sip of her drink, relishing the cool liquid in her mouth.

Finn's mouth drew back into a smile. 'I'm going to miss you when I'm away.'

'You'll be too busy enjoying your travels to think of me,' she teased. When she saw how confused he seemed by her comment, Jools placed her glass on the table. 'I'll miss you, too,' she admitted. Then, when Finn kept staring at her and moved slightly closer, she sensed he was going to kiss her. Jools liked him, but decided that tonight wasn't the time for them to get all mushy with each other. He was going away and she wasn't going to humiliate herself by opening up to him, only for him to end up meeting someone else on his travels. And she didn't want to look silly in front of people who might know her. 'Do you know any Hidrios?'

Finn frowned. 'Sorry, what?'

'I was thinking about that man, Alan, and his relatives. If I know them, maybe I can find out more about him.'

'Why are you so concerned about him anyway? It's not as if he's asked you for help, is it?'

'No.'

'Then why do you feel you need to get involved with his life?'

Jools sat back in her chair, shocked by his lack of empathy. 'I didn't say that I was,' she snapped, irritated. Was this how he behaved when he didn't get what he wanted? If it was then maybe he wasn't the man she had thought him to be.

'I'm sorry,' he said, looking shame-faced. 'That was wrong of me.'

'What? The intimation that I was over-stepping the mark with Alan, or your annoyance that I didn't want to kiss you?'

'Who said anything about kissing?' he said, voice rising enough for the people at the next table to turn and stare at them.

Jools opened her mouth to retaliate when she became aware of someone standing at their table. She looked up to see Oliver Whimsy glowering at Finn.

'Is everything okay, Jools?' he asked quietly, stepping closer.

She realised how her spat with Finn must have looked to

others and forced a smile. 'Yes, thanks, Oliver. We were only chatting.'

'It was my fault,' Finn apologised. 'I shouldn't have questioned Jools about something that was none of my business.'

'No,' Jools said, 'You shouldn't have.' She nudged him playfully with her elbow. 'But I shouldn't have over-reacted.' She turned her attention back to Oliver. 'We're fine. Thanks, though.' She peered around him, seeing Lexi, her father and Gloria on the other side of the partition. 'You're here with Lexi?' She didn't want to give away that she already knew he was – that she'd overheard them talking.

Oliver bent to reply. 'Lexi and her dad have made up, I'm relieved to say. We're here to get to know Gloria a little better.'

Jools smiled over at their table. 'Are things going well?' she asked quietly.

Oliver crossed his fingers. 'So far, so good.' He looked from one to the other of them. 'I'd better go and fetch those drinks I ordered from the barman. Have a lovely evening, you two.'

They thanked him and watched him walk over to the bar.

'I'm sorry,' Finn said again. 'And to answer your question, no, I don't know any Hidrios.'

Lexi giggled. 'We've just had our first argument.'

Finn pulled a face. 'Have we?'

'Yes.' She indicated her meal. 'Eat up or this delicious food will get cold and I can't bear waste.' She gave him a wink to show that she was teasing, and watched as Finn nodded and picked up his knife and fork and began to eat.

'Where are you looking forward to visiting the most?' she asked eventually. Jools had never travelled far from the island because she hadn't ever felt the need to do so. She was intrigued by people who said they had to get away from the place each year.

'India and Sri Lanka. I've been before a few times but my mate,

Buzz, hasn't been there yet. I'm looking forward to showing him places that enchanted me the most. Have you ever been?'

Jools shook her head. 'No.'

'Maybe we could go together some day?'

She couldn't miss the hopeful tone in his voice. She liked the idea that he wanted to go away somewhere with her, but didn't want to give him ideas. 'I don't think so.'

'Why not?' he asked gently. 'Everything about India is magical. The first thing I noticed when I arrived was the colours, and the scent of spices in the air is amazing. It's difficult to explain the vitality of the place without visiting.'

She was embarrassed to admit her lack of travel experience but felt comfortable enough with him to open up slightly. 'I've only ever been to the mainland twice. I've never been further than that,' she admitted.

Finn stared at her, his mouth open, as if he had been going to reply but was lost for words.

Jools giggled. She was used to that reaction. 'To an avid traveller like you, that must seem very odd.'

He shook his head slowly. 'Not really.' She could see he was trying to hide his surprise. 'Is it because you've never wanted to go away, or something else?'

She suspected that he might think her reluctance was due to not wishing to leave Gran behind, but it wasn't. Not totally. She took a sip of her drink and swallowed. 'I'm scared of planes. Well,' she shook her head. 'Not actual planes but being on one. Flying. I can't understand how something that heavy with the weight of all those people and luggage on it can fly safely.'

'Didn't you fly when you went to the mainland then?'

'I went on the ferry.' She waited silently for his reply, daring him to say anything contrary.

'Then we make a good pair.'

Jools burst out laughing, causing the group at the next table to turn their heads and stare at her a second time. 'How do you work that out?'

He grinned at her, a twinkle in his eyes. 'I'm frightened of the sea.' He tilted his head. 'Well, of being on a boat in bad weather. I'm not sure why. Maybe it's after watching *The Poseidon Adventure* several times with my dad when I was little. He loved that film for some reason.'

'But I still don't get how you think we make a good pair. You don't like boats and I'm too frightened to fly. You love to travel and I'm happy to stay here in Jersey. I'd love to know how you think that makes us compatible?'

Finn took her hand in his. 'Because, together, we can help each other overcome our fears. What do you say?'

'Is this a challenge?' she asked, aware that she found it almost impossible not to accept one.

He narrowed his eyes and smiled at her. 'Oh yes, this is definitely a challenge. So, what do you say? Are you willing to take it up?'

Jools stared at him thoughtfully. 'I can't see how you'll ever persuade me to go up in a plane, but I'm willing to let you try.' She laughed. 'At least I have a few months grace while you're away.'

He nodded. 'I was thinking the same thing.'

2

EARLY APRIL

Jools was relieved she had work to focus on since Finn's departure the week before. She had taken a few photos of the view from Oliver's cottage and emailed them to him so he could choose the one he liked best. While she waited for him to get back to her, she decided to give her gran a bit of a break from Teddy's pestering and take him for a walk on the beach.

'But no going up on those cliffs,' she said, thinking back to the drama the previous autumn when her friend Bella, and Megan – a celebrity who had been visiting the island – got stranded high on the cliffs and had to be rescued. Teddy had been too nervous since then to venture too close and for that, Jools was grateful. 'You're so full of energy,' she said as he trotted next to her down the granite stairs to the sand below the boardwalk.

She pulled a new ball she had bought for him out of her pocket and threw it for him to fetch. Jools laughed as the little dog bounded across the sand, oblivious to anything in his path apart from his determination to retrieve his ball.

As she walked on, she couldn't help thinking about her next painting. She was glad she had a couple of commissions because the money that she and her gran made at the bookshop would never be enough to keep the two of them. Although, thought Jools, their lifestyles were pretty basic.

She heard a yell and looked across the beach to see Teddy racing back to her, a blue ball in his mouth. 'No, little guy,' she said, as he reached her panting, his teeth firmly clamped into the rubber ball. 'That's not yours. Your ball is red.' She reached down and after a little persuasion involving a small bone-shaped treat as bribery, she was able to take the ball from him. 'Yuck. It's all gooey.'

She stood upright and tried to see whose ball Teddy must have stolen. Spotting a very blond man striding towards her with a strange-looking mongrel bouncing up and down in front of him, she decided it must be theirs. The man came closer to Jools and smiling, held out Teddy's red ball.

'I think this might be yours,' he said. Then laughing, added, 'Well, that little guy's.'

'Sorry about that,' Jools said as they swapped the balls. 'He can be a little naughty sometimes and thinks that every ball or toy he finds must belong to him.'

'He's the same,' the man said, indicating the woolly black dog jumping up and down next to him. 'Calm down, Jarvy.' He shook his head. 'Maybe we should throw their balls at the same time but in opposite directions. What do you think?'

'Good plan,' Jools laughed again. 'After three. One. Two. Three.' She threw the ball as far as she could in the direction of the lighthouse and watched Teddy racing after it. Then, turning, smiled to see the other dog doing exactly the same towards the cliffs. 'That worked well.'

'It did,' he said, turning to face her and reaching out his hand. 'I'm Marius, by the way and that strange looking nutty mongrel is Jarvis.'

'Is he yours?'

'My grandad's.'

Jools smiled down at the dog. He had a long body and very long thin legs. 'He's adorable.'

'You wouldn't say that if you had to listen to him grumbling when it's time for his daily walk on the beach.'

Jools laughed. 'I'm Jools, by the way. That little devil is Teddy. He belongs to my grandmother.'

The sea was quite far out and, without agreeing to, they both began walking towards the water's edge.

'Do you live around here?' Marius asked.

Jools pointed towards the boardwalk. 'Up there in the second-hand bookshop.'

'Lucky you. I've always wanted to live on the boardwalk. I've got a studio near Devil's Hole. If I can't live here, it's pretty cool there too.'

The mention of a studio pricked Jools's interest. 'Are you an artist then? Photographer?'

He shook his head. 'I started off working with oils but I'm a glassblower now.'

'Over here? I didn't know there were any.'

He nodded. 'There are a few of us now. Why don't you come up and see me working one day when you're free? I often do demonstrations for customers and holidaymakers.'

'That would be wonderful.' She had never seen anyone making something out of glass before and the thought of it intrigued her.

'The studio is open to the public a lot of the time.' He pushed his long fair hair out of his face. 'You can find the opening times online if you don't want a wasted journey.'

'Thanks, I'll look you up.' She realised she might have come across as a little stalkerish and winced. 'That is... I mean...'

He laughed. 'It's fine, Jools, I know what you meant.' He went to say something further but before he could, Jools spotted his dog running around his legs. A couple of seconds later Teddy appeared and growled at Jarvis.

'Hey, Teddy. That's enough now.' Teddy gave another growl, setting Jarvis off and the two of them snarled angrily at each other, hackles rising.

Marius frowned. 'We can't chat in peace with these two arguing.' He bent to clip Jarvis's lead on to the ring on his collar. 'It's probably time I got back to work anyway, and I must drop this one back to my grandad first. I hope to see you at the glassworks if you decide to drop by.'

Jools was sorry to see him go. She had been enjoying chatting to this stranger, albeit only for a few minutes. 'I'm sure I will get there sometime soon.'

'Good. I hope so.' He gave her a wave and she watched him walk back to the steps and up to the boardwalk. Returning her attention to Teddy, she picked up his ball and threw it as hard as she could across the beach. 'Go on, you little devil. Let's get rid of some of your excess energy before we return to Gran.'

Having thrown the ball for Teddy until her arm grew tired, Jools decided he must have had enough of a run to ensure he would want a snooze when they got back to the bookshop. She called him over and they'd reached the top of the steps to the boardwalk when she heard Sacha calling them from her café doorway.

'Hey,' Jools called back. 'Come along, Teddy. Let's go and see what Sacha wants.' She jogged to the café, Teddy running in front of her. 'Everything all right?'

Sacha gave her a hug. 'Thanks for coming over,' she said, her voice low. 'I can't leave this place just now. Jack is out with Alessandro somewhere and I'm running it single-handedly.'

The mention of Alessandro reminded Jools of Finn. The two worked together in Alessandro's Italian gelateria along the boardwalk which was still closed for the winter. 'Can I help?'

Her friend shook her head. 'No, it's fairly quiet right now. I wanted to tell you about your sales while I had a moment.'

'Sales?'

'I'm going to need four more paintings for the café walls.'

It dawned on Jools what her friend was trying to tell her. 'You mean I've sold four paintings?'

'That's right. One yesterday afternoon and a further three this morning.'

'Who to?'

'That's the odd thing. I don't know.' Sacha pulled a face. 'Both times a woman came in and made the purchase. When I asked her if she was going to put them up in her home, she told me she was buying them for a client but refused to divulge the client's name. Very mysterious, don't you think?'

It was, thought Jools, wishing to know who had liked her paintings enough to buy four of them and relieved to have brought in some money.

'Didn't she say where you have to send them?'

Sacha shook her head. 'Nope. She's going to come and collect them. I was wondering if you could bring the paper and cord that you wrap them in so nicely and maybe a couple of your business cards. I've run out of the ones I had in the café.'

'Yes, of course. I'll drop Teddy home and come back straight away.'

Sacha reached out and patted Jools's arm. 'Exciting to have a mysterious admirer, isn't it?'

Jools wasn't so sure. It was nice to have sold the paintings but why would someone want to keep their identity a mystery? It didn't make any sense. It wasn't as if her paintings were valuable and they were only beach scenes. 'I guess it is. I'm stunned,' she admitted. Then realising that her reaction had taken away some of Sacha's delight at delivering such exciting news, she added, 'Thrilled too, though. Thanks very much, Sacha.'

'No need to thank me,' Sacha said. 'I just hang them on my wall. I love them, so it doesn't put me out at all.'

Teddy nudged Jools's leg. 'I think this one is ready for some food. I won't be long.'

Her enthusiasm fired, Jools ran back to the bookshop with Teddy bounding along next to her. She opened the shop door and went to see if her gran was serving anyone. Disappointed to see that she was busy, Jools decided she would have to wait to share her news. She pointed to Teddy so that Gran knew he was back home and then hurried upstairs to fetch wrapping paper, cord to tie the paintings and her business cards. She dropped them on her small work station and realised she needed to choose four new paintings to replace the ones she had sold.

Moving canvases forward from the neat rows leaning against the walls of her small studio, she hastily worked through each one, trying to find those that complemented each other but showed different aspects to the vistas she had captured in oils. Finally satisfied, she tied the four together and returned to the café.

'What do you think of these?' she asked when she had unwrapped the paintings and leant them in a row against the counter.

'I love them. I was sorry to see the others go, to be honest, but I'm happy to have new views to look at.'

Jools laughed. 'You have the view out of your window.'

'True, but you paint these so beautifully and somehow interpret the beach, cliff and lighthouse in a different way to when I go outside and see what's in front of me.'

Jools didn't like to say so, but Sacha's comments delighted her.

It was good to know that someone who had spent most of her life living among such scenery found something new in her art. She had only expected people who didn't live nearby to find beauty in the paintings. It was mostly holidaymakers, wanting souvenirs of the island, who bought them.

'Good,' she said. 'I'll go and hang these now and then I'll wrap the others.'

'Great. You can go up to my flat if you need a bit more space.'

Jools shook her head. 'No, it's fine, thanks. I can use one of these tables. I'm used to working in confined spaces.'

She realised that their conversation was being overheard by two older ladies who were sitting at the window table. They noticed her looking and smiled.

'They're lovely,' one of them said. 'I wouldn't mind one in my flat.'

Sacha walked over to their table and picked up their empty plates. 'They're for sale, you know. All the paintings in this café are the creations of my friend, Jools, here. Her gran runs Boardwalk Books, the second-hand bookshop along the boardwalk. You can always pop in there when you've finished your drinks, if you're looking for something else to do.'

'We are,' the smaller of the two replied. 'Aren't we, Sal.' She looked back at Sacha. 'We love a good romance novel.'

'Don't we all?' Jools smiled. She thought of Finn once again. She had imagined their embryonic romance might lead to something more exciting. Never mind, she thought, forcing herself to focus on carefully taking down the paintings from the walls and wrapping them.

She was soon finished and bid the two ladies farewell as they left the café. 'Did I tell you I've suggested starting up the book club in the shop again, once a month, on a Thursday evening?'

'No,' Sacha said, looking pleased. 'Brilliant idea though.

There's not much for the locals to do in the evenings when everything is shut. They'll enjoy it, especially when winter comes around again. Most of the locals would enjoy an excuse to spend an evening in your bookshop. It's like a treasure trove for book lovers in there.' She narrowed her eyes thoughtfully. 'I could keep the café open later so they can pop in for something to eat before going to yours.'

'That would be wonderful,' Jools said, relieved that her friend liked the idea enough to want to keep her café open. 'I was thinking of arranging the book group for around six o'clock. Would that suit you? Or we could make it seven and they could come here to eat first.'

Sacha gave it some thought. 'Seven works better for me. It would give those who work all day time to come here on their way to the group. I keep the café open late on Friday evenings in the summer and it wouldn't hurt to have a reason to do the same on Thursday evenings. Yup, that's a green light from me.'

3

A couple of days later Jools was helping her gran in the bookshop when Alan popped in.

'I've been hoping to see you again,' she said, slotting a book with a bright royal blue cover back into its place after a customer had changed their mind about buying it. 'Gran's been speaking to the others who want to join the book club. I've spoken to Sacha and we've come up with a plan.'

Alan's face lit up as he listened to Jools explaining about the club and planned meals at the café. 'That's great news. I'll look forward to coming along and joining in.'

'Good,' Jools said going back to the counter and turning the page on her notepad. 'We're hoping to hold the first get-together on Thursday, meeting at the café first. Everyone can talk through suggestions for the first book we'll be reading as a group.'

'Perfect.' Alan smiled.

'Jools tells me we've got your number,' Gran said. 'I'll call you if we cancel for any reason.'

'It sounds wonderful.' He seemed happy. 'I'm looking forward to making new friends here. I was wondering,' he said, as she wrote his name on the list for Thursday. 'I've been searching for a book for a few years now and thought there was no harm in asking if you might have it in stock here.'

'I can certainly look for it for you.' Jools enjoyed tracking down books for customers. 'We don't have all of the books we stock on our system, I'm afraid. Gran forgets to add the new stock sometimes,' she said grinning at her gran, who was on her way upstairs, 'so although we do our best, our computer records aren't foolproof.'

'I'd be grateful for any help. I don't really expect to find a copy if I'm honest, but I live in hope.'

'We'll do the best we can to locate a copy for you. Can you tell me the title and author, please?'

'Thank you. The book is *Message for a Spy* by Dan Blake.'

Jools couldn't recall coming across the book before, but wasn't certain they didn't have it. 'I'll have a quick look on the computer now. Right, let me see what we've got here.' She searched for the title first and then for the author but nothing came up. 'I can't see it on here, but as I explained, that doesn't mean we don't have it.'

'It's fine. I don't want to put you to any bother.'

'It's no problem at all,' she assured him. 'I'm always happy to look. I'll keep an eye open and let you know if I find it.'

'That's very kind of you to take the trouble.'

'Not at all.' Jools could see he was trying to hide his disappointment as he went to look through a bookcase by the window, and felt sad that she couldn't help him. She wondered why the book was so important. It wasn't a title she had heard of but was clearly important to him. She decided she was going to do all she could to make it happen.

'Have you any thoughts about what we could read for the book club?' she called across the shop, hoping to take his mind off it.

He held an open book in his hand and looked at her thoughtfully. 'I'm not sure. Do you have any suggestions?'

Jools shrugged. 'I've found from experience that it's probably a good idea to choose either an award winning novel or a classic. The problem with classics is that most of the attendees will probably have read them.'

Alan closed the book he had been looking at and slid it back into its space before withdrawing another. 'I don't mind what you decide. I'll be happy to read anything.'

Jools always found that the first book choice to get everyone's attention was the most difficult to decide upon. As people got to know each other better and chatted more, they seemed happier to offer suggestions for the following weeks or months.

'I'll tell you what,' she said. 'Let's wait for me to confirm a few more names and we can all meet for a coffee one morning at the café. We can swap suggestions and then decide on a title that the majority are happy with.'

'Good idea,' he agreed cheerfully.

'Great. I'll chat to the others and try to find a mutually convenient time. Is there any morning that suits you best?'

Alan laughed.

'Did I say something funny?'

'Sorry.' He pushed the book he was holding back onto the shelf. 'It's just that right now I'm free every day and any time. I'll fit in with everyone else.'

'Well, that makes planning simple,' she said, smiling. 'I wish everyone were as easy as you.'

The brass bell rang, announcing a customer's arrival. 'Here you are,' said a voice Jools recognised. 'Mum asked me to come and collect you.'

Jools turned, surprised to see Marius standing in the shop. She realised he had not yet seen her. It was obvious that he was speaking to Alan as he was the only other person there apart from her. She looked from Alan's dark complexion to Marius's creamy blond hair and doubted they could be related.

'Why? Is something the matter?' Alan asked, frowning.

'No, but—' Marius seemed to sense her watching and turned sharply. 'Oh, Jools. Sorry, I didn't see you there.'

'You two know each other?' Alan asked.

'We met the other day. On the beach when I was walking Jarvis for you,' Marius explained to the older man before turning and giving Jools a friendly smile.

'Now it's my turn to ask how you two know one another,' Jools said, intrigued. Surely Alan couldn't be Marius's grandfather when they looked so very different. But Marius had said that Jarvis was his grandfather's dog. Maybe Marius was adopted.

'My father was Norwegian,' Marius said.

Jools's mouth dropped open for a couple of seconds. 'I'm really getting worried that you can read my thoughts,' she admitted. 'It's weird. Are you like this with everyone you meet?'

He shook his head, laughing. 'No. But since Grandad came to live with us a lot of people have given me the same look you just did, and it was obvious what you were thinking.'

'Norwegian, you say?' She was intrigued. She hadn't seen any men around the boardwalk who could pass for being his father. 'Does he live over here?'

She heard Alan groan and glanced at him, relieved to see he looked amused. 'Sorry,' he said. 'I forgot how everyone here knows everyone else and their business.'

'Not everyone,' Jools teased. 'I obviously didn't know that you two were related. That is, I didn't know your grandson until the other day, let alone his parents.'

'You wouldn't have come across my father,' Marius said, smiling at his grandfather when he indicated a book that he wanted to look at. Marius walked closer to the counter and lowered his voice. 'My mum met him when she went travelling and they married very quickly. Her family were furious.'

'We were.' Alan said, without looking up from the pages he was reading.

'There's nothing wrong with your hearing, is there, Grandad,' Marius laughed. He rolled his eyes heavenward and then focused on Jools once more. 'When they divorced my mum returned to the island but by then my grandparents had moved away to Hampshire. Which,' he said, giving her a nod, 'is probably why you haven't come across them before.'

'And you? I've not seen you around either.'

'Maybe you have but don't remember.'

Jools knew he wasn't someone she would forget in a hurry if she had ever come across him before. 'No, I don't think I have.'

'Probably because I've always lived out east, Gorey way. It's only in the last couple of years that I moved to Devil's Hole.'

They stared at each other and Jools wondered how anyone who liked someone as much as she had thought she liked Finn could possibly be as attracted as she was right now to this blond Adonis standing in front of her.

Alan coughed and Jools and Marius immediately looked at him.

'Yes, Grandad?'

The older man shook his head and tutted. 'I was asking why your mother sent you here to collect me. I'm perfectly capable of making my own way home.'

'I know that,' Marius said. 'But it's getting stormy out there.' He pointed to the window. 'The wind is picking up and there's heavy rain on its way over the channel.'

Jools and Alan peered out of the window.

'He's right,' Jools said, surprised. 'I've been so busy focusing on books this morning that I've forgotten to look outside.'

'He's always aware of the weather.' Alan rested a hand on Marius's shoulder. 'Especially how it affects the sea.'

'You are?' Jools loved watching the sea and the way it changed colour from a deep navy in the summer months to the darkest jade green during storms. Watching the sea took her mind away from anything bothering her.

'He's right,' Marius said. 'I can't help myself. I've always been fascinated by the sea.'

'I'm very proud of this boy,' Alan said, leaning forward. 'Not only is he a talented artist but he also volunteers for the RNLI. I wish he didn't but he refuses to consider changing his mind about racing out in bad weather and putting himself in danger.'

'Thanks, Grandad.' Marius pulled a face at Jools as if showing that this was a regular complaint. 'I love being involved in the RNLI and intend carrying on for as long as they'll have me.'

Jools was impressed at his bravery and those of his colleagues going out in all weathers to rescue strangers. She had always found those in the RNLI completely selfless and admired them enormously. The thought of Marius being one of those people though bothered her. 'Won't you even consider listening to your grandfather about this?'

'I'm afraid not. I love the adrenaline rush and helping people. I don't know why. Maybe because it's the opposite of what I do all day at work.'

She heard the chairlift bringing her grandmother down the stairs. 'Need any help, Gran?'

'No thanks, love.' Jools's grandmother entered the room and Lexi made way for the wheelchair that she seemed to be using more often these days. 'I heard you going on at this brave lad and had to come and put my two penn'orth in.' She smiled up at Marius. 'You do what you must, young man. My husband was in the RNLI and although I worried about him every time he was called out; it made my heart swell to know he was doing something that made him feel so valued.'

Jools noticed Marius's eyes light up. 'Thank you, Mrs Jones. I appreciate you saying as much.'

Alan shrugged and smiled at Jools. 'I think that's us well and truly put in our places.' He gave her gran a nod. 'You're right, of course, Mrs Jones. I suppose I just worry about the lad.'

'You're bound to be concerned.' Jools's gran picked up a biro and tapped the notepad on the counter. 'Now, young man, will you be wanting to join the book club too?'

Marius looked as if he had been caught red-handed doing something he shouldn't. He gave Jools a pointed look that seemed to ask her to help him out.

'I don't think he'll have much time to join in,' Jools said. 'Not with his work and volunteer commitments.'

'Hmm, I suppose not. Never mind.'

Marius clasped his hands together. 'We'd better be getting along, Grandad. Mum is waiting for me to drop you home and I've already taken a bit longer than expected.' He smiled at Jools and her gran. 'Nice to meet you, Mrs Jones and it was good seeing you again, Jools.'

As soon as they had left the shop, Jools turned to her grandmother. 'Do you want to arrange the book group's first meeting, or shall I?'

'I'll do it. You need to focus on your paintings, especially now you have a mysterious admirer.'

'The buyer is an admirer of my work, Gran, not me.'

Her gran's eyes twinkled in amusement. 'Maybe? Maybe not.'

'I can see you're in a troublesome mood today, so I'm going to love and leave you and get up to my studio while it's quiet.'

She grinned at her gran and left the shop and was only a couple of steps up the stairs when she heard her grandmother say, 'I thought that Marius was rather sweet on you. Did you notice?'

Jools wished her grandmother wouldn't say such things. She didn't notice Marius doing anything to give that impression. 'Stop it, Gran. He was just acting friendly, nothing more.'

4

———————

A few nights later Jools was woken by a shriek and leapt out of bed in panic. It took her a moment to gather herself and work out that the sound had not come from inside the cottage but from out on the boardwalk. She quietly slipped her feet into the fluffy pink slippers her gran teased looked similar to her pink spiky hair and, pulling on her fleecy dressing gown, went through to the living room. As she crossed to the front window, she felt something furry brush against her shin and tripped over Teddy, grabbing the back of a chair to stop herself falling.

'For pity's sake, Teddy,' she hissed, hoping that her stamping hadn't woken her grandmother. 'I do wish you wouldn't walk in front of me.'

She lifted him up to cuddle him, realising that he might also have been given a fright when hearing the noise from outside. 'It's okay,' she soothed, stroking his head and placing him back down onto the floor.

She pulled back the curtains and peered out of the large window overlooking the beach. She couldn't see anyone out there at first, but in the moonlight noticed movement near the entrance to the lighthouse at the end of the pier. Leaning as far as she could without her nose being squashed against the windowpane, Jools tried to see who was out there and if they were all right.

'Claire?' she said, realising that the person leaping up and down outside was Bella's mum and that she was with a man who looked as if he had fallen.

Trying not to make any unnecessary noise, Jools quickly discarded her dressing gown for her puffy coat, pulled on her beanie and swapped her slippers for trainers before running downstairs. She realised Teddy was following her and bent to kiss the top of his head. 'No, you can't come with me this time, little guy,' she said, running outside and along the boardwalk.

'What's happened?' she called in a loud whisper as she neared the figures by the lighthouse. 'Is someone hurt?'

Bella's mum stopped jumping up and down and the man, who she now saw was Tony, stood up. He took hold of Claire's hand and held it up for Jools to see.

She gasped. 'Oh no! Have I just interrupted a marriage proposal?' She closed her eyes tight in horror at ruining such an intimate moment. 'I'm dreadfully sorry. I thought someone was in trouble and came to help.' She cringed inwardly at her stupidity and wished she could turn back the clock.

Claire ran forward and pulled Jools into a bear hug. 'Don't be silly. I'm excited to share our news with someone. I didn't think anyone would be awake at two o'clock in the morning. But yes, you're right. Tony just proposed to me,' she squealed, making Jools wince and hope that Claire's exuberance didn't end up waking other villagers. 'We're engaged! You are looking at the future Mrs Tony Le Quesne. Isn't that exciting?'

'Very.'

'And you're the first one to congratulate us, Jools.'

Claire looked incredibly happy. Jools was genuinely pleased to see her friend's mum so much in love, but the last thing she wanted was to take away the specialness of the event from Bella.

'I think Bella should be the first one you tell,' Jools said. 'Can we pretend that this never happened and I'll go back to bed? Hopefully, I'll wake up in the morning and think it was just a dream.'

'You're absolutely right.' Claire grimaced. 'Bella should have been the first to hear our heavenly news.' Claire kissed Jools on the cheek and stepped back into Tony's arms. 'Tell me what you think of my beautiful ring first though, and then I'll let you get back to your bed.' She held her hand out for Jools to take a closer look.

Jools was fond of Bella's mum but couldn't help thinking how different she was to most mums. Always putting herself first and flitting from one exciting escapade to the next. She doubted Bella would be surprised that this was the next turn of events for her mother and hoped that her friend would be happy with what had happened.

'It really is beautiful,' she said honestly as the pretty diamond cluster glinted in the moonlight. 'Congratulations to both of you. I know Bella's going to be incredibly happy for you.'

'Do you really think so?' Claire asked anxiously. 'I know she likes Tony, but she's always worried about me being so impulsive.' She gazed up adoringly at her fisherman fiancé. 'But I think that this time I've made a wise decision.'

'You're not the only one,' Tony said, looking as though he had won the lottery. 'Please don't be concerned, Jools. We're both delighted to know that someone is happy for us. It'll give me the confidence to break the news to my own children in the morning.'

'And me when I tell Bella and Betty,' Claire said.

Betty. What was going to happen to her? Jools gave them a smile and began walking back home. Betty wouldn't be completely alone now she had the rescue cat that Jack had found for her a few months before, but she needed adult help occasionally. Claire couldn't stay living with her if she married Tony. The pair of them couldn't live together in Betty's small cottage, not with Tony's two children. She wondered if either of them had thought of that. Not, she reminded herself, that Betty's care was their concern alone. It was for all of them to ensure that the village's oldest resident was properly looked after, at least for as long as she chose to stay in her cottage.

Jools arrived home cold and troubled. She was happy that Bella's spirited mum had finally found a man she loved enough to want to settle down with, and especially delighted that he also lived on the boardwalk so they would be in Bella's life permanently. She hoped Bella would react well when her mum broke the news but couldn't be certain that would happen.

Jools took off her hat, coat and trainers and got into bed. 'Come on then, Teddy,' she said, patting her duvet when he whined at her bedroom doorway.

She closed her eyes and lay there thinking about Betty and how she could help keep an eye on her. Jools decided that she would speak to her friends and try to come up with a way of looking out for Betty without being too obvious. She was a very independent lady and would not take kindly to being made to feel that she needed help. There was no need to do anything yet though, not until Claire and Tony had told Bella about their engagement.

The sun was rising by the time Jools managed to doze off and the next thing she knew her gran was calling her to join her for breakfast.

'Urgh,' she groaned, wondering why the sun was blazing through the window. She rubbed her eyes with her palms and slowly opened them. Having forgotten to draw her bedroom curtains, she was surprised that the daylight streaming in hadn't woken her earlier. Jools yawned and stretched, throwing back her duvet and covering Teddy before realising that the movement at the end of her bed was the dog. Jools giggled and pulled the covers away from him.

'Come on, sleepyhead. I don't know why you didn't wake me. You usually can't wait to get up and be fed.'

She walked to the bathroom and showered. She was shampooing her hair when she remembered what had happened several hours earlier. 'Claire,' she whispered, wondering if she had broken her news to Bella yet. They saw each other most days and she hoped that by the time she bumped into her friend she would already know about the engagement. If Bella brought up the news and told her, Lexi, and Sacha then she could be excited for Claire openly.

Dressed and her hair almost dry, Jools joined her grandmother in their tiny kitchen and sat opposite her at their small table. 'These scrambled eggs look and smell delicious,' she said, picking up her knife and fork and starting to cut into them. 'Thanks, Gran. You always make the best breakfasts.'

Her grandmother finished her mouthful of food and stared at her.

'What's the matter?' Jools asked, confused. 'Have I done something wrong?'

'I was just wondering where you went to in the middle of the night. Were you meeting up with that Marius boy?'

Jools sighed. She didn't want to share Claire's news before she was certain that Bella had been told but she could see that keeping it to herself was now going to be impossible. 'Gran, firstly, he's not a boy. Also, I'm almost thirty and don't need to sneak off to meet boys in the middle of the night.'

'Then can you put me out of my suspense and tell me where you went?'

Jools ate another mouthful of her breakfast while she considered her reply. 'I can but you have to keep it to yourself until I say otherwise?'

'Intriguing.'

'Gran. I need you to promise. I know how you can forget yourself and end up sharing...' she tried to think of another way to say 'gossip'. 'Local news to your friends. It really is vital that you keep this to yourself. At least for now. Do you promise?'

'Yes, of course I do.' Her gran looked unimpressed with Jools's request. 'Now, what is such a secret that I'm not allowed to share it?'

Explaining what had happened the previous night, while trying not to get worked up by her grandmother's growing delight at the news, Jools repeated her insistence at the end that the information needed to be kept top secret until Bella had been informed.

Her gran didn't bother to hide her glee at what Jools had shared with her. 'Will you stop nagging me and go and do your painting?'

Two hours later, Jools stepped back from the painting she had begun working on for Oliver. For some reason she couldn't seem to get the lighthouse as she wanted it to look. The sunshine on the side of the building wasn't quite right and despite trying to rectify the painting several times she was only making it look worse. 'Damn thing,' she grumbled, deciding that she needed to take a break to clear her head. She went downstairs to the shop. 'How's it going in here this morning? Had many customers come in?'

'A few.'

Jools noticed an amused glint in her grandmother's eyes. 'You haven't told anyone about that thing, have you?'

'I said I wouldn't.' Her grandmother scowled. 'And I haven't. Why don't you pop along to Sacha's café and fetch me one of those delicious coffees she makes and a slice of her Victoria Sponge.'

Jools knew her gran was getting irritated with her for fretting about Claire's news and wanted her out of the shop for a while. She was only too pleased to walk to the welcoming café overlooking the small bay. Sacha's cakes were the tastiest she had ever come across and she enjoyed treating her gran to the odd takeaway from the Summer Sundaes café.

'Fine, I'll go and get some treats for us.' She grabbed her jacket and purse and left the shop, hoping that Bella wouldn't decide to call in during her absence. Despite her grandmother's protestations that she could keep a secret, Jools had known her to feel compelled to share news when she really wasn't supposed to.

'Is everything okay?' Sacha asked, as Jools entered the café.

Jools watched her friend as she finished pouring frothy milk into a tall latte glass, adding a tot of espresso coffee. 'Yes, why?' she asked guiltily. She wasn't used to keeping secrets from either of her three best friends and wished, yet again, that she had not been so quick to go and find out what was happening at the lighthouse the night before. 'Just a little tired, maybe.'

Sacha frowned. 'You're sure?'

'Perfectly sure.' She began to lose her resolve to withhold the secret news but then decided to change tactic to divert her friend. 'Maybe I need a sugar boost,' she suggested, liking the idea. 'I've come to get a takeaway for me and Gran.'

Sacha raised a finger. 'Won't be a second.' She placed the latte onto a saucer, added a spoon and took it to a customer with a large slice of carrot cake on a plate. A minute later she returned. 'Now.

Let me guess? Two cappuccinos, a slice of Victoria Sponge and some chocolate fudge cake? Am I right?'

Jools grinned. 'You are, as always.' She opened her mouth to add how tasty Sacha's cakes were but before she could utter another word the door opened and Bella marched in. Jools tried to act nonchalant. Not that she was sure how she usually behaved when she knew something she shouldn't.

'You're never going to guess what my mother's gone and done now?' Bella looked from Sacha to Jools. 'Hey, do you two already know about this?' she asked, narrowing her eyes slightly.

'Know what?' Sacha picked up her knife and sliced into one of the cakes.

Jools tensed under Bella's scrutiny. She hated lying to her friend so simply said, 'I'm here to buy a mid-morning snack for me and Gran. Why?'

Bella, seemingly satisfied that neither of them knew what had happened, clenched her fists and rested them dramatically on her slim hips. 'She's only gone and got engaged.'

'What?' Sacha gasped. 'She hasn't. Has she?'

Jools wasn't sure what to say and was trying to think of something when she realised Bella was staring at her again. 'You already knew,' she said, an accusatory tone to her voice. 'How? It only happened in the middle of the night, or so Mum said.'

Jools was mortified to have been caught out and could feel her face reddening. 'I only know by accident,' she explained.

'Go on.'

Jools noticed Sacha pulling a worried expression behind Bella's back. 'I, well, that is, I heard a shriek outside last night when I was in bed. I thought someone was being hurt.'

'So, you went to investigate?'

Relieved her friend seemed to understand, Jools nodded. 'That's right.'

Her relief was short-lived when Bella glared at her. 'And you didn't think to tip me off about it?'

Jools was stunned by Bella's response. 'I thought it was your mum's place to tell you news this important, not mine.'

'Oh, did you? Thanks for nothing.'

'Hey, steady on, Bella,' Sacha soothed. 'I don't think Jools has done anything wrong here.'

'She's supposed to be my friend,' Bella argued. Jools could hear the anger rising in her voice.

She hated falling out with her friends. 'Isn't it good news though? I thought you liked Tony?'

Bella shrugged. 'That's got nothing to do with it.'

'I would think it has everything to do with it,' Jools argued. 'What's so bad about them getting married?'

Bella glanced at Sacha and Jools could tell she was hoping their friend would back her up.

'Hey, don't give me that look, Bella. I'm not getting in between you two, I've got customers to look after.' She smiled at two people entering the café and, Jools thought, looked relieved by the timing of their arrival.

Jools watched Sacha pull her small note pad from her apron pocket and pick up a pen. 'Please keep your voices down,' Sacha whispered before going to speak to the couple who had just come inside.

'Well?' Jools said quietly. 'I would have thought you'd be pleased for your mum. She's never been married before and she's obviously happy with Tony.'

Bella frowned at her. 'Of course I'm happy for her. I just think it's a bit quick, that's all. And it's not as if she's just marrying Tony, is it? She's about to become a stepmother. Hell, Jools,' she hissed. 'It's not as if she has bugger all experience when it comes to looking after children. What if she messes these two up as well?'

'As well as what?'

'Me, obviously.'

Jools wondered if Bella's anger was due to shock that her mother was finally settling down, rather than being the second person to find out.

'Look, I am sorry I didn't tell you, but it wasn't my place. I promised your mum that I wouldn't. Surely you understand?' She rested her hand on her friend's, hoping to soothe any hurt she felt. 'We all know Claire was a hopeless mother. Have you thought that maybe she knows that too? Could this be her way of getting a second chance at motherhood by helping Tony bring up his two children?'

Bella didn't speak for a few seconds and Jools could see she was mulling over what she had said. She hoped her friend understood where she was coming from and calmed down. 'I don't know. Maybe.' Bella sighed heavily. 'I'm being childish. I suppose I'm just envious that she decides to settle down and be a mother figure when I'm too old to need one.'

Jools nudged her friend and smiled. She was relieved that their irritation with each other seemed to be evaporating. 'Don't be daft. We all need our mothers. It's just, in our case, those mother figures have been our grans. Try to be happy for Claire. Who knows, getting involved in her wedding might be the perfect way for the two of you to bond properly.'

'Urgh,' Bella groaned.

Jools giggled. 'Would that be such a bad thing to deal with?' Bella shook her head. 'Then, what's wrong?'

'It's just that I was hoping it would be me and Jack who got engaged sometime this year, rather than my mother.' She straightened the wristband of one of the cotton gloves that she wore to keep her hands soft and unblemished for her part-time job as a hand model. 'What a selfish cow I am.'

Sacha walked back to join them and patted Bella on her shoulder. 'What rubbish. There's nothing selfish about you. You've just had a bit of a shock, that's all. You'll get used to the idea of Claire getting married soon. You just need a little time.'

Bella smiled at each of them. 'Thanks, girls. I can always rely on you to help me when I need you to.' She turned to leave.

'Hey, where are you going?' Sacha asked.

'To tell Lexi, of course. I can't have you two knowing my mum's news and not her.'

Jools laughed and waved at her friend before turning back to Sacha. 'Well, that went more smoothly than I had expected.'

Sacha sighed. 'Maybe, but it was a little tense there for a moment.'

'Just a little.' She noticed the time. 'I think I should be getting back to Gran soon. You know how impatient she can be.'

'She's not the only one,' Sacha teased, turning to face the coffee machine and starting to make the first of their cappuccinos.

5

EARLY APRIL

'If I see one more wedding magazine, I'll lose my mind,' Bella grumbled to Jools one morning. Jools was working in the book-shop while her grandmother met with a couple of friends for coffee and a catch-up. Shortly after her departure, Bella had arrived and Jools now gauged that her friend had been moaning about her mother's wedding planning for almost an hour.

'She never stops going on about fabrics,' Bella continued. 'And whether she's going to wear a veil or simply have a few fresh flowers in her hair. Tony's daughter, Jessie, is to be a flower girl, or bridesmaid, or something. She wants me to be maid of honour and Tony's son, Alfie, is to be the page boy. They've asked Jack to be best man and now that he's signed at that model agency, he's got to keep spaces in his diary for them, so Mum and Tony will have to take that into account when deciding on the date.'

Jools still found it strange to think of Jack modelling. He was certainly handsome enough but always seemed too relaxed, enjoying helping Tony on his fishing boat and Sacha in the café and surfing in his spare time, to want to commit to bookings with a modelling agency.

Jools lifted the top book on the small pile she was holding and pushed it into the gap in the shelf where a customer had removed it from earlier. She realised she had zoned out while Bella was talking but needed to say something. 'What's wrong with all that? It seems a pretty standard way for brides to behave as far as I can tell.'

'Not for my mother though.' Bella leant her elbows on the counter and lowered her face into her hands. 'I thought she would want an informal affair. A beach wedding with guests wearing flip flops and everything relaxed and fun. Not this performance. It's so unlike her, Jools. Do you think she's doing it this way because she thinks that it's what Tony would like?'

Jools could see where Bella was coming from. It sounded very unlike the Claire she knew and liked. 'Maybe. She probably thinks others are expecting their wedding to be more formal?'

'It's possible, I guess.'

'Have you considered sitting down with her and asking her? Maybe she needs someone close she can share her worries with.' The more she spoke, the more convinced Jools was that this was the case. 'How involved have you been so far with her planning?'

Bella stood up straighter and shrugged. 'I've been waiting for her to speak to me about it. Why?'

Jools pushed another book into place on the shelf. 'She might be hoping for you to take the lead in some of the planning.'

'You think?'

'I don't know, but it's possible.'

Bella stared thoughtfully out of the shop window. 'You could be right, I suppose. It must be stressful planning something like this alone.'

The brass bell jangled and they both stared at the bookshop doorway.

Marius walked in and stopped. 'Am I interrupting something?'

'Yes.' Jools said matter-of-factly.

Bella smiled. 'Ignore her. You're not interrupting anything at all.' She stepped forward and held out a gloved hand for Marius to shake. 'And you are?' she asked, giving Jools a suspicious look over her shoulder.

'Marius. I'm a friend of Jools.'

'One that she's kept very quiet,' Bella whispered to Jools. 'So am I,' she said louder. 'I'm Bella, by the way.'

'Pleased to meet you, Bella.' He stared at her hand, no doubt, Jools thought, wondering why Bella was wearing gloves on such a pleasant day. He seemed to realise what he was doing and shook it.

'Bella's a part-time hand-model,' Jools explained. 'That's why she wears those gloves all the time.'

'They're a pain,' Bella said. 'But it's something I have to do to keep my hands looking perfect. I also sell antiques.'

Marius's eyes widened slightly. 'Ah, yes. The Bee Hive at the blue cottage along the boardwalk?'

'You know my shop?' Bella looked impressed. 'Has Jools been giving you the lowdown on us all then?'

Marius smiled. 'Not quite,' he replied, appearing awkward. 'She was explaining about her three best friends and what you all did, although I don't recall the hand-modelling bit.'

'Was she now?' Bella grinned, giving Jools a wink. 'Funny how she's never mentioned you. What do you do for a living, Marius?'

Jools took another pile of books over to the bookshelves and began putting them back neatly, leaving Bella and Marius to get better acquainted. She wasn't sure why Marius was at the shop again. A part of her hoped that it was because he was attracted to her, but the thought made her feel guilty. Finn might have chosen to continue with his travel plans after they had begun seeing each other but she had never been one to act in a disloyal way. Would it be fair of her to give Marius a chance? If Finn liked her as much as he professed, surely he wouldn't be on the other side of the world right now with a friend. He hadn't even sent her so much as a post-card yet, she thought miserably.

'Oh, I don't know,' she said, sliding the last of the books into a gap in the middle of one of the shelves, deciding not to think about Finn for the time being.

'Pardon?'

Jools realised that Bella had asked her something. 'Sorry, I missed that?'

Marius was staring at her, slightly amused. 'You said you didn't know something and we're curious to know what that might be.'

'Yeah,' Bella said. 'Spill.'

Jools frowned. 'I hadn't realised I'd spoken,' she said, irritated with herself.

'Well, you did,' Bella said. 'So why don't you tell us what's bothering you and maybe we can help.'

Marius caught Jools's eye and they stared at each other briefly. 'If it's something you'd rather share privately with your friend then I can leave the two of you alone to chat.'

Jools realised she had to change the subject and quickly. She had no intention of discussing her thoughts with either of them, especially not Marius. 'No, don't be silly. I was only trying to come up with a few suggestions for the book group.' She didn't like lying but in this instance it couldn't be helped.

'I love a challenge.' Bella leant against the bookcase and crossed her arms. 'Now,' she said, rubbing her chin. 'Let me think.'

Marius laughed. 'I don't think that my taste in books is going to be suited to your group.'

Jools was intrigued. Any man who loved books had a head start in her affections. 'Why? What books do you prefer?'

'Sci-Fi.'

'Ah, yes, you could be right about that.' She wasn't ready for him to leave yet. 'Do you have any idea what your grandfather enjoys reading? Maybe it'll give us a clue where to start with selecting a few books.'

He frowned and stared at the floor as he gave her question some thought, then looked up at her, smiling. 'He enjoys adventure stories and anything to do with the Second World War. War, itself really. Biographies too, sometimes.'

His suggestions didn't immediately bring anything to mind, but she was grateful he'd made an effort. 'Thanks, Marius. That's a great help,' she said, fibbing to him for the second time in several minutes. It dawned on her that he hadn't mentioned his reason for popping in. 'Sorry, I never asked if I could help you?'

'With what?' He looked confused.

'Well, why you came here this morning. Was there something you wanted?'

He stared at her silently then glanced at Bella. 'No, it's fine. It can wait.'

'If you're sure?' Jools felt disappointed but wasn't sure why. 'Hopefully, I'll get up to Devil's Hole soon to see you glass blowing.'

'I can come with you if you like?' Bella said. 'We could see if Lexi and Sacha are free. I'm sure they would enjoy something different.'

Marius smiled. 'I'd be happy to show you all around my workshop if you're interested.'

'We would be,' Jools said quickly, happy to have something to look forward to away from the boardwalk, Bella's mum's wedding issues and her paintings, which she really needed to press on with as soon as her gran returned. 'We'll see you very soon then.'

'Great.' Marius beamed at her. 'I'll look forward to it.'

She watched him leave the shop and as soon as the door closed, Bella giggled. 'I think there's something you've been keeping from me. Again,' she added pointedly, but with a teasing tone to her voice.

'Such as?'

'Why have you never mentioned that gorgeous man before? He's funny, hot and very obviously interested in you. What's going on, Jools?'

Jools knew her friend well enough to be aware that if Bella wanted an answer to something she would persist until she got it. 'There's nothing much to tell.' Bella pulled a doubtful face. 'I promise. We met on the beach when our dogs took a dislike to each other and then again here when he came to collect a customer, who happens to be his grandfather.'

'Go on. There must be more.'

Jools shook her head. 'There isn't, not really. He's an artist, like me, but he now focuses on glass blowing and invited me to go to his studio and watch him working. That's it. Really.'

'I don't think it is. I think he likes you rather a lot but isn't sure whether or not to say something.'

Jools frowned. 'I don't think so, but we won't argue about that now.' She didn't want to continue the conversation. 'I've still got to come up with some ideas to put to the book group. You can make yourself useful and help me brainstorm while you're here.'

* * *

That evening, Jools sat with the book group and surveyed the members. Gran was in her element, sipping coffee and making notes on her ever-present notepad. Alan was chatting quietly to Barry, the man Oliver and Lexi had helped when he fell over on the headland at Grosnez just before Christmas. Like Alan, he was recently widowed and new to the boardwalk, slowly making friends. Her gaze moved to Betty. She might be in her mid-nineties and rather frail now, but she was straight-talking, extremely caring and determined to stay living in her cottage for as long as she could.

Jools had hoped Lexi might join them but she was away with Oliver for a few days, meeting his parents and sister for the first time, at his family home in the Highlands.

'It's kind of you to set this up for us,' Barry said. 'Such a pleasant way to spend an evening and it's exciting to have something to do each month.' He gave a little laugh. 'To be honest, I don't really mind what book we choose. I'm just happy to have something to focus on and to be able to meet up and discuss it.'

'I'm the same,' Alan agreed, giving Barry a nod. 'These good people have made such a difference to my life already, just by being so welcoming at their interesting little bookshop.'

Sacha placed a mug of hot chocolate down in front of Betty. 'And what about the café?' she asked, giving Alan a smile. 'I hope you're looking forward to coming here for a bite to eat before the meetings.'

'We are,' Alan said.

'Yes,' Barry agreed. 'We've been chatting about meeting for weekly suppers here with Betty just before Jools told us about the café staying open. We're delighted with the idea. We don't want to wait to get together every four weeks and can look forward to coming here every Thursday evening.'

Sacha took Barry by the shoulders and bent to give him a smile. 'I was joking, but I am happy to know you want to come here to eat. I love meeting new friends and it's been fun getting to know you these past weeks.'

'Likewise,' Barry said, patting her hands.

Watching the interaction between those sitting at the tables Sacha had pushed together on their arrival, seeing them make friends and find interests they loved, made Jools's heart soar.

'Right,' her gran said, looking up from her notepad for the first time in a while. 'Now we all appear to have our drinks, I think it's time we chose a book to read.' They watched her expectantly, waiting for the options. 'I want us to feel free to suggest whatever we wish, but my initial thoughts are, *Mrs Dalloway* by Virginia Woolf, *North and South* by Elizabeth Gaskell, or something more recent such as, *Wolf Hall* by Hilary Mantel, or *Fatherland* by Robert Harris.'

Jools had read all of her grandmother's suggestions so didn't really mind which one they chose. After half an hour's discussion everyone conceded to Betty's wish to read *Fatherland*. 'I've not read it before and I've heard that it's very good, although I'm a bit alarmed at the thought of there being another outcome to the Second World War.' She shuddered. 'What we went through back then was bad enough, as far as I'm concerned.'

'We have a couple of copies in the shop, if any of you wish to borrow them,' Jools said. 'Just pop in tomorrow and I'll hand them out.'

'No need to worry about me,' Alan said proudly. 'My passion might be collecting second-hand books but I also have a tablet that I read on. I find it's much lighter to hold when I go to bed.'

'I'm the same,' Betty said. 'I never thought I could take to one of those, but Tony's little girl persuaded me and she loads any books I need onto it.'

Jools felt comforted to know that Betty was being so well looked after by Claire's new little family. She looked from one happy face to the other, reminded why she had always loved living on the boardwalk. She couldn't imagine such a close community feel elsewhere and, apart from when a local got too involved in others' lives, it really was a happy place to live.

'Wonderful,' Gran said, slamming her biro onto her notepad like an auctioneer banging down a gavel. 'It's good to be organised. Happy reading, everyone.'

6

DEVIL'S HOLE

Jools heard Lexi chatting to Bella outside her window and gasped. She was supposed to have met her five minutes ago and had forgotten the time. She quickly wiped her paint brush on a nearby rag and, after dipping it in walnut oil, left it to dry on a small rack. She pulled her old paint smock over her head and draped it over the back of a chair before running to open the window.

'Sorry, I won't be long,' she shouted, closing the window before her friends argued with her. 'Bugger it.' She rushed into the bathroom and washed her hands. Then, her fingers still damp, pushed them through her hair to make it stand up and look as if she had bothered. She dabbed on a little lip gloss and a touch of mascara. 'It'll have to do,' she said to her reflection before going into her bedroom to change her clothes.

As she rushed to her wardrobe to find something to wear, Finn's postcard, which had arrived in the morning post, fluttered off the top of the bookcase. She bent to pick it up, reading the words she knew by heart.

We've arrived in Sri Lanka and I'm working on overcoming my fear of the water. I've been taking swimming lessons in the sea, and although I can't say that I'm perfect yet, I'm much more confident in the water. I hope you are proud of me. Have you booked or taken a flight anywhere yet? Looking forward to showing you my new skills when I get home in the spring.

Finn. xx

She placed the postcard back on the bookcase and hurriedly changed.

'I'm here,' she said a couple of minutes later as she closed the shop door behind her. 'Sorry about that.' Realising Sacha was missing, she said, 'Were we supposed to meet Sacha at the café?'

Lexi retrieved her car keys from her jacket pocket. 'We're going to go ahead,' she said. 'She's running a little late and will come and join us if she can. If not, it'll just be the three of us.' She pulled back her sleeve to check her watch. 'We need to get a move on if we're going to watch that chap of yours doing his glass blowing. I gather he only does it for the public for a couple of hours on certain days.'

The thought of missing watching Marius working did not sit well with Jools. 'Come along then,' she said, starting to walk towards Lexi's car parked further along the boardwalk. 'And,' she added pointedly, 'he's not my chap.'

'That's not the impression Bella gave me when she told me about meeting him in the bookshop the other day.'

They reached the car and Jools got into the passenger seat, turning to face Bella in the back and glaring at her. 'Really, Bella? What exactly were you saying to Lexi, and to heaven knows who else?' She turned to face the front when Lexi started the engine and clicked her seatbelt into place. 'It's bad enough living with

Gran and having her making up intrigue about me without you doing it as well.'

'Rubbish,' Bella argued. 'I've never heard your gran saying anything untoward about you. And, if you must know, I didn't say anything other than what I saw for myself. The chemistry between you two was palpable.'

'Palpable?' Lexi laughed. 'You make it sound like it had its own heartbeat.'

Jools grimaced. 'That sounds rather random if you don't mind me saying. As far as us having chemistry, I didn't feel anything of the sort. You know I'm seeing Finn and I'm not the type of person to mess anyone around.'

She heard a harrumph coming from Bella and knew she was about to hear more.

'If he's chosen to go away and leave you for a couple of months, he risks you meeting someone else while he's gone. Which is what you've done, as far as I can see.'

'But nothing's going on between Marius and me, if that's what you're insinuating.'

'Maybe not,' Bella said. 'But that doesn't mean it shouldn't or won't. I could tell he likes you, whatever you might think. And,' she said pointedly, 'I know you well enough to pick up that the feeling was mutual. Stuff Finn and his fickleness.'

Lexi guffawed. 'What is with all these new words today, Bella? You swallow a dictionary, or something?'

Jools was relieved that Lexi seemed more focused on their friend's vocabulary than her own feelings towards Marius, but her relief was short lived.

'That said though, Jools, it does make me think that maybe you're keeping something from us.' Lexi indicated right and then glanced at Jools and gasped. 'You *do* like him!'

'I don't,' Jools argued, furious that her face was going red and that Lexi wouldn't miss it.

'You do. There's nothing wrong with it,' she said, more quietly. 'I mean, you and Finn only saw each other a couple of times before he went away, so it's not as if it was a great romance and that you're letting him down in any way.'

'You see?' Bella cheered from the back seat. 'That's exactly what I was thinking.'

Jools knew her friends had her back and wanted the best for her and she loved them for that but she was not in the mood for anyone's interference right now, regardless of how well-intentioned it might be.

'I do like Marius, okay? I admit that. But I barely know him, and, regardless of what you might think, I don't know how he feels about me, or if it's something I want to pursue. I like Finn, too.' She sighed. 'Why is it that I don't find anyone attractive for ages and then two men come along that both take my fancy.'

'Yes, well, it does seem to happen that way.'

'What?' Jools stared at Lexi. 'Do you like someone other than Oliver?'

'No,' Lexi said, shaking her head and turning down a narrow country lane. 'But I was seeing Charlie when I realised I had feelings for Oliver.'

Bella giggled. 'You had one date with him. It had hardly begun before you both put a stop to anything more.'

'Two dates actually, but you're right,' Lexi said. 'We did agree on the first date that there would be nothing between us and that we'd rather be friends.'

Jools sighed. Her friends weren't being much help but at least they'd stopped quizzing her about her feelings for Marius. Spotting the granite buildings on either side of the narrow road that would take them to the Devil's Hole car park, she said, 'In there,' trying to keep her excitement under control.

After parking, they walked up to the buildings, which were attached in a U-shaped three-sided courtyard. Jools had looked up Marius's glass blowing business on the internet and discovered that his business was one of three, the others being a pub called The Priory Inn, popular with tourists, and a local candle maker. She spotted the sign to Marius's studio and waved for the others to follow her.

'Blimey,' Bella giggled behind her. 'Someone's keen.'

'Shush,' Lexi said. 'I think we've teased poor Jools enough. Come along, let's get in there. I've yet to meet this mysterious man of hers.'

Jools decided to ignore them. She knew they meant no harm and were probably excited that she was interested in something other than her painting and the bookshop for a change. She didn't blame them. It had been almost two years since she'd found anyone interesting enough to want to spend time with them.

'In here,' she whispered, stepping into the warm studio where a furnace burned fiercely at the back of the room.

'You're here,' Marius said, stepping towards her and holding his hands up. 'I won't give you a hug, or anything. I'm all hot and mucky.'

Jools heard one of her friends mutter something to the other. 'You've met Bella,' she said, tilting her head to the door to indicate her friends as they followed her inside. 'This is Lexi.'

'The one with the fishermens' cottages?' He gave Lexi a thousand-watt smile and raised a hand in greeting. 'Great to see you all here. Thanks for coming.' He walked to a work station near the furnace and sat on a worn wooden stool.

'What are you making now?' Bella asked as they moved closer to watch him work.

'This will be a seascape when it's finished.' He glanced at them and smiled when they didn't reply. Jools wasn't sure how he could depict a seascape in glass. As if he had pre-empted their confused reactions, he pointed to an area to his left where various items were displayed on shelves. 'Like those commissioned pieces I made yesterday.'

Jools and her friends looked at the row of five glass pieces, each in a rough square shape, made of pale blue and white shades of glass moulded together to produce a picture of the sea. Each one stood on a basic wooden stand, held up by two small metal holders.

'They're beautiful,' Jools said, wishing she could buy one, unsure whether to ask.

They returned their gazes back to Marius, watching him work. He looked almost angelic with his pale blond hair. Each of them stared in silence, fascinated by the process.

'It's quite mesmerising, don't you think?' Lexi whispered.

'It really is.' Bella answered, her voice filled with surprise.

Lexi wasn't sure if she was more intrigued by Marius or the creation he was working on. She had never thought of how she must look when she was completely focused on her painting and wondered if it was anything like Marius as he concentrated on his glasswork. He seemed so absorbed and calm, as if he had forgotten anyone was watching. Flickers of light from the furnace brightened his already pale hair and she wished she could take home one of his exquisite seascapes to keep on her bedroom windowsill.

When he had finished, he placed the piece on the side to cool and turned with a smile. Jools sensed he was used to people's awestruck reactions. He stood, indicating the other glass objects displayed at the front of the room. 'I make various things, as you can see. Vases, Christmas decorations, jewellery, and anything a client wants to commission that it's possible to make.'

The girls moved slowly along the displays, taking in the glorious range of colours. 'How do you make the different shades?' Jools asked.

'Various metal oxides are added to the glass,' Marius explained, leading them over to several containers with glass rods standing in them. He lifted one with a blueish violet tint. 'For example, this one is made by using cobalt oxide.' He lowered it and then took out a red rod. 'Gold chloride is used to make the red glass.'

'I love that colour,' Bella said.

'Does it work the other way around?' Lexi asked, intrigued.

He seemed confused for a second and then gave her a knowing smile. 'If you mean can red be used to make gold, then unfortunately not.'

Jools noticed beautiful, sunny yellow rods in the next container. 'How about that colour?'

'That colour will have been created using cadmium sulfide.'

'It's all so clever, don't you think?' Bella said.

Jools and Lexi nodded. It was very impressive and Jools could understand why a painter would want to turn his hand to glass-making instead. 'I can see why you love your work. Being able to create something this tactile must be very satisfying.'

'It is,' Marius nodded. 'I never mind having to work. I'm very lucky to be able to make a living doing something that I'm passionate about.'

His phone rang and Marius quickly checked his watch. 'That'll be a call that I'm expecting, hopefully about a new commission.'

'We'll leave you to get on then,' Bella said, eyeing Jools, who nodded her agreement.

'Thanks very much for giving us a demonstration,' she said. 'It was fascinating. Hard work too, by the look of things.'

'It was really interesting,' Lexi said, leaving the studio after Bella.

As Jools went to join them, Marius rested his hand on her arm. 'Would you mind waiting for a moment? I shouldn't be long. I'd like to put something to you.'

Jools wasn't sure what she would say if he asked her on a date, but turned and widened her eyes. 'Sure, no problem.'

He wiped his hands on a cloth and ran to the answer the ringing phone.

She waited for him to arrange a meeting with someone later that day and watched while he jotted down some notes.

'Sorry about that,' he said, returning to her.

'What is it you wanted to ask me?' She was intrigued but didn't want to come across as too interested. *Play it cool*, she told herself.

'I've had a query from a client about an exhibition she wants to put on.'

Jools wasn't sure why he was mentioning this to her but was intrigued. 'Go on.'

'She's a local dignitary who wants to use two different elements to depict the coasts of the island, specifically the wilder north coast. She wants me to create the glass exhibits and for another artist to complement each of my pieces in a different format. There are nine altogether. I thought of you and your paintings and wanted to know if you'd mind me giving her your name and contact details?'

Mind? Jools was almost breathless with excitement at the opportunity. 'Not at all.' She smiled, trying her best to remain calm and act professional. 'But surely that's something you could do? You used to paint using oils, wouldn't you want to do it?'

He shrugged. 'I know it probably sounds mad, but I don't want to spend my time painting any more. I'd rather stick to glass blowing. Anyway, don't you think it would be fun doing something like this with another person?'

'I do,' she said, relieved he hadn't reconsidered. 'Please let her know where to contact me.'

'Great. Thanks, I will.'

'No,' Jools laughed. 'Thank *you*.'

'There's just one stipulation,' he said sombrely. 'One of the pieces has to be a fantastical creature coming out of the sea.'

Jools wasn't sure what he meant for a moment. 'Like a mermaid, you mean?'

'I think she was hoping for something a little darker, like a siren.'

'Siren?'

'Apparently it's a mermaid who entices sailors onto the rocks with her singing voice.'

Jools shivered. 'Why on earth would she want pieces of art representing something so horrible?'

'I've no idea, but she's willing to pay us for it.'

Jools shrugged. 'Then if that's what she wants, that's what she'll get.' She made a mental note to look the creatures up on the Internet as soon as she arrived home. 'It'll be different to anything I've done before,' she added thoughtfully. 'Though I suppose they are connected to the sea, so it isn't too far from my usual subject.' She heard Bella calling for her from outside. 'I suppose I'd better get a move on.' She smiled at him. 'Thanks for thinking of me, I appreciate it.'

'No problem at all.' He walked over to the studio door and opened it. 'Do you think you'd consider coming out for a bite to eat with me sometime? We could chat a bit more and swap ideas for our exhibits. Lunch one day next week, maybe?'

'I'd like that,' she said, deciding that lunch wasn't a proper date, so she wasn't doing anything she shouldn't as far as Finn was concerned. 'I'd better not hold you up any longer.'

She left the studio and joined her friends. Both were grinning at her and waiting for her to tell them what she had been chatting to Marius about.

'Well, you took your time,' Bella teased.

She explained about Marius's phone call. 'He's giving my name to a client of his who wants two artists to take part in an exhibition she's planning,' she said, getting into the car. 'Wasn't that nice of him?'

'Nice?' Lexi s smiled, starting the car. 'I think it's amazingly generous.'

'Oh, and we're going out to lunch one day next week.'

7

BOARDWALK EASTER EGG HUNT

'I don't think there are enough young children on the boardwalk to warrant all this work,' Jools said, hiding another chocolate egg behind a box of cheap books beside the bookshelves. 'Gran, did you hear me?' she added when her grandmother didn't answer.

'I did.'

'Well, don't you agree that maybe this is a lot of unnecessary work every Easter?' She scanned the packed room and tried to spot another place where she could hide an Easter egg.

'No, I don't. You and your friends loved the annual egg hunt, didn't you? Even when you were too old to take part, I seem to recall,' she added, before Jools was able to reply. Gran gave her a knowing look. 'You're just overtired. I know you were painting late into the night.' She narrowed her eyes. 'Don't bother to deny it. I saw your light on when I went to the loo at around three this morning.'

Jools giggled when she saw her grandmother's expression, one eyebrow raised as if daring her to deny it. She had a point.

'It's only fair that we carry on the tradition for the young ones and give them the chance to enjoy it as you and your friends did.'

'We did have a lot of fun,' Jools conceded. She realised she was being selfish and lazy. 'I suppose we're also making memories for the little ones.'

'My sentiments exactly.' Gran grinned. 'Now, stop your grumbling and get on with hiding those eggs. We still need to plant the ones outside.' She pointed to a space between two large tomes that would be the perfect hidey hole. 'Make sure they're high enough so that Teddy can't reach them. We don't need the local dogs getting ill because we've placed the chocolate too low.'

Jools nodded. She remembered well enough because it was her grandmother's greatest fear each Easter that one of the dogs would be ill. She recalled when she was small how her grandmother's terrier had eaten a chocolate egg and had to be rushed to the vet. Neither she nor her grandmother had forgotten their fright and then relief that he was fine.

'Have you had your lunch date with that boy yet?'

Jools wished her grandmother wouldn't refer to the men in her life as boys. 'Not yet, Gran.'

She picked up a large shopping bag filled with various-sized Easter eggs and took them out to the boardwalk. Her heart leapt as she spotted the door of the gelateria was slightly open, a light on inside. Could Finn have returned? She hurried over to the ice-cream parlour, stopping at the door, unsure whether to go inside. What if he was back and didn't want to see her yet? She shook the thought from her head. Why wouldn't he? It was probably her guilt at her attraction to Marius making her think that way. *Marius.* Why hadn't he been in contact? It was probably a good thing if Finn was home from his travels. Humming from inside the gelateria distracted her. She wasn't going to find out anything by standing on the doorstep. Pushing open the door, Jools entered the cold room. 'Hello? Finn?'

'Ahh, Jools,' Alessandro said, stepping through a door at the back of the shop. 'You are looking for Finn?'

Jools nodded. 'I saw someone was here and thought he might be back on the island.'

Alessandro placed some paperwork onto the counter and shook his head. 'He is still away,' he said in his lilting Italian accent. 'I expect he will be back in the next week, maybe? I'm sure he will call on you at the bookshop as soon as his plane lands.' He gave her a sympathetic smile. 'You have heard from him at all?'

'I've received a postcard but nothing else. I was hoping he might send some photos of the places he's visiting, but I suppose he's having too much fun with his friend to think of it. I'm not sure when he's back exactly.'

Feeling a little embarrassed by her uninvited arrival at the Isola Bella Gelateria, Jools smiled. 'I'm supposed to be hiding these Easter eggs for the annual Boardwalk Easter Egg Hunt,' she explained. 'It's an annual tradition. I'd better get on.'

Alessandro raised his eyebrows. 'Traditions like those are always fun. I miss some of the traditions my family had in Italy,' he said wistfully.

'It must be very different living here,' Jools said, realising for the first time that Alessandro had fitted in seamlessly despite being new to the island. 'You must miss your family and friends in Rome.'

He nodded. 'I do, but not all the time. I love living here near Sacha, especially when everyone is so...' he frowned thoughtfully.

'Eccentric?' Jools joked.

He frowned. 'Sorry? I don't understand.'

She shook her head and giggled. 'A lot of us have odd characteristics, you know, strange little ways.'

He laughed. 'There are always...' he hesitated. 'Eccentricities in communities. I think they are the ones who give the place character.'

'You're right, they do,' Jools agreed. She heard a woman's voice outside telling her child if they didn't stop grumbling they would not be taking part in the Easter Egg hunt. 'I'd better get on and sort these out.' She raised the shopping bag. 'Gran will be unimpressed if I don't hurry up and get back to the shop. It was good to chat to you though.'

'Yes, it was nice to see you, Jools. I'm sure Finn will come to see you as soon as he returns.'

Jools smiled and left to carry on hiding the chocolate eggs. She needed to find places that weren't too obvious so that parents passing with their children didn't start collecting them until the hunt began.

As she hid the final egg, Jools carefully folded her empty shopping bag and slipped it under her arm. It was a relief to finish. As she walked slowly back to the bookshop she thought of Marius and wondered why she hadn't heard from him. Maybe he was waiting for her to contact him. Unless he was inundated with work at his studio. Smiling, she decided that was probably what had happened.

At the bookshop, she pushed open the front door and walked through to see her gran.

'Ahh, there you are. I thought you might have come home via Sacha's café.'

'No. Why?'

Her grandmother finished writing a note on the pad in front of her. 'A smartly dressed woman called for you while you were out. She said something about the glass blowing chap. Marius, isn't it?' Jools nodded, intrigued to discover what she had missed. 'He gave the woman your name and number so she could contact you about a painting of a siren?' She wrinkled her nose. 'I think that's what she said. Do you know anything about it?'

So, Marius had given her details after all. 'I do,' she replied happily. She could see confusion in her grandmother's eyes. 'What's wrong?'

'Siren? Not like the one old man, Le Brun, winds up every Liberation Day?'

Jools thought of the red and black painted war siren the retired baker insisted on winding up every May the ninth to acknowledge the anniversary of the island's liberation from German forces after the occupation during the Second World War. Each year, he was given a warning by the current Constable of the parish which he continually ignored.

'No, Gran,' she said. 'This lady wants a mermaid-type creature for some reason. Sirens tend to be malicious, so I'm not sure why she wants a painting of one on her wall, but who am I to judge? It's paid work and that's what I need to remember.' She spotted a business card on the counter. 'Is that her card?'

Her grandmother reached out and picked it up, gazing at the details for a moment before handing it to Jools. 'She seemed very pleasant, if a bit quiet. I didn't recognise her.'

Jools was used to her grandmother's suspicions about strangers – anyone who lived away from the village – and how she only trusted people she had known a long time. Jools wasn't sure why this was but assumed it might be due to spending part of her childhood living under Nazi rule. She supposed if her earliest memories were of fear, and learning to be wary of others, it was bound to have had a deep effect on her.

'I'll look forward to meeting her,' Jools said. 'Maybe I'll find out why she's chosen that particular subject for a painting.' She always enjoyed the discovery. Usually, her clients wanted a memory on their walls of a particular view they loved, or one that brought back happy memories, or maybe a pet that they treasured, or a portrait of someone they loved. Jools mostly enjoyed painting landscapes, especially those of the view from her window over the sandy beach and out to the channel. Lots of clients favoured paintings of the red and white painted lighthouse on the pier, which Jools usually enjoyed working on.

'I'd better give her a call, I suppose.' She turned and left the room, wanting to call from her mobile when her grandmother wasn't listening. Jools knew her grandmother's nosiness was something she couldn't help, and most of the time she didn't mind her listening, but she didn't know who this woman was. Jools usually picked up quite a lot from a person's voice. She liked to know who she was dealing with as much as possible before starting to work on a painting, believing it helped her understand what the client was expecting. She ran upstairs to make the call.

'Don't be too long,' her grandmother shouted after her. 'The Easter Egg hunt will be starting in twenty minutes.'

Half an hour later, Betty finished her brief speech and declared the hunt open. Jools estimated that there must be about fifteen children shrieking with delight as they ran off in different directions to look for the chocolate eggs. Gran was feeling tired and Jools decided to accompany her back to the bookshop and make her a cup of tea. When Gran was weary and needed to use her wheelchair, Jools made an effort to spend more time in her company. Gran always insisted it wasn't necessary, but she was the only family Jools had and spending time with her was something Jools made the most of.

Laughter filled the air and footsteps ran up and down the boardwalk. Jools smiled and followed her grandmother into the shop. 'It always makes me smile to see them having so much fun.'

'Noisy though, isn't it?' Gran said. 'I always forget how ear-splitting their excitement can be.'

'I'll quickly go and make you a cup of tea before they remember they can come in here and find more chocolate.'

'That will be lovely. I'm rather parched.'

Jools left her to watch the shop from the counter and returned with the tea in her grandmother's favourite blue and white china cup and saucer, which she placed on the counter.

'You haven't told me what your new lady client said when you called her.'

Jools took a sip of her drink and thought about the brief call she had made. 'She said she would leave it up to me to decide how I paint the picture. She wants the siren to look as if she's rising from the sea in front of the boardwalk.' Jools recalled the woman's soft tone. 'She's going to email a picture of a woman whose face she wants me to depict in the painting. I thought that a little odd if I'm honest,' she said. 'I probably wouldn't so much if she had asked for a mermaid but she made a point of saying it had to be a siren. I don't imagine she can be too fond of the woman she wants me to paint.'

'Maybe it's some sort of private joke?'

'I suppose it could be.'

'What about payment?' Gran asked. 'Did you discuss that?'

'Yes,' Jools laughed. 'We did. She's paying me two thirds before I begin and the balance when she sees the final painting.' Jools knew how much her grandmother worried about her, especially when it came to asking for money. She wished she wouldn't fret so much. Her gran was still concerned about the first few times Jools had sold her paintings. Back then she'd found it difficult to accept that people were happy to part with money for the work she had produced. That was years ago. 'I really don't have a problem discussing payment, Gran. I wish you'd stop worrying on that score.' She gave her grandmother a brief hug. 'When I've received the first payment, I'll begin sketching my draft and work out exactly what I'm going to paint.'

'I wonder why she wants you to do this for her?' Gran said thoughtfully before taking a tentative sip of her tea.

'We'll probably never know,' Jools replied.

Before her gran could ask anything more, the shop door burst open and crashed against the wall in the tiny hallway before several children ran into the bookshop, yelling and pushing each other, their excitement filling the small space with noise.

'Steady on, you lot,' Gran bellowed. 'Calm down and be a little quieter or you'll have to leave. I don't want any damage done to my books.'

Several of the children whooped in delight as they discovered some of Jools's hidey holes and retrieved the foil wrapped chocolate eggs. Satisfied with their discoveries, they left to continue their adventure, running out of the shop door.

'Oof,' Jools heard, and turned to see Marius, red in the face, pushed back against the wall. 'They're a little over-excited, aren't they?' He grinned at Jools and she relaxed, glad he wasn't hurt.

'Come in,' she said. 'I'll make you a cup of tea by way of apology.'

He laughed. 'Thank you, I could do with one.' As he made to walk forward, two more small children ran past him. 'Shall I close the door, or are there more to come?'

Jools giggled and tipped her head to indicate that there was one more child searching intently among the bookshelves. 'Over there.'

Marius walked into the shop and smiled at the serious little boy, who looked about five or six. 'Am I allowed to help him look?'

'Please do,' Gran said. 'I have a feeling he has little intention of leaving unless he's certain he's found the very last one.'

Marius seemed almost as excited as the child. 'Come along,' he said to him, conspiratorially. 'Let's search together, we might find more that way. I'll search in the higher places and you can look down low.'

The child nodded enthusiastically. 'Thanks. My sister says she'll find more than me.'

'Then we'll have to prove her wrong, won't we?' Marius shot Jools a surprised look. 'This is serious business, obviously.'

'It certainly is,' Jools laughed.

She swapped an amused glance with Gran, then watched her grandmother stare silently at Marius as he helped the little boy in his quest for more chocolate eggs. She was probably wondering whether he was more suited to her than Finn was.

'Yes,' the little boy yelled as Marius triumphantly held up the two eggs he had found. He opened his bag and waited while Marius carefully placed them inside.

The brass bell jangled and a woman entered the shop. 'Good morning, Mrs Jones,' she said. 'Hi, Jools. Is my Billy here?' She noticed her son and shook her head. 'His sister has been back home for nearly twenty minutes. I knew he would still be looking around somewhere. He's a determined little devil. Billy. Come along now, that's enough.'

'He's been helping me, Mum.' The boy pointed to Marius.

'Thank you,' she said flirtatiously. 'I hope he hasn't been annoying you.'

'He's been no bother at all,' Jools said, glad the little boy was finally going home and that she could spend some time with Marius.

As soon as the woman and her son had closed the door behind them, Gran said, 'Why don't you two go and have a chat upstairs in the living room? I'll be fine here.'

'Thanks, Gran.' Jools was looking forward to telling Marius about her new client and waved for him to follow her. 'Shall we go?' she suggested. 'We can sit in comfort there and I can tell you all about my phone call.'

Marius followed her up the stairs and after Jools brought up mugs of tea they sat down on the chairs nearest to the window overlooking the sea.

'This is an incredible view,' Marius said, gazing out of the window to the calm waves rolling gently towards the beach. 'You're so lucky to live here, Jools.'

'I know,' she said. It was something she thought to herself each time she stared outside. 'I wanted to thank you again for sending that lady to me.'

'She contacted you then. I'm pleased.' He smiled at her. 'She seemed a little...' he hesitated. 'Odd, but I suppose it's all business.'

'I thought you said she was nice?'

'She was, but maybe a little strange. I'm not sure exactly why I think that. It was more a feeling that I picked up from her.'

Jools shook her head. 'She seemed perfectly fine when I chatted to her.'

'Good,' Marius said. 'That's all that matters.'

They chatted for a while before it dawned on Jools that she hadn't asked why Marius had come to the shop. She did not imagine he had really meant to join in with the hunt. 'Did you want something?'

He nodded and grinned at her. 'Remember that lunch we discussed?'

Jools nodded. 'I thought you might have forgotten about it.'

'Not at all,' he laughed. 'I've just been busy at the studio with a large commission that came in a couple of days ago. I was hoping you might come for a quick bite with me today.'

'Now?'

'Yes,' he said, smiling. 'We could chat about our exhibits. Are you free?'

She liked the idea, very much. 'I'll go and check that it's alright with Gran.' She saw that he had finished his tea and, taking both mugs into the kitchen, she washed them and left them on the draining board to dry. 'Let's go back downstairs.'

'Gran?' she called as she entered the shop. 'Do you need me for anything?'

'No, sweetheart. You go and spend some time with this lovely young man of yours. You could bring me back a slice of cake if you're going to Sacha's café.'

'No problem.' Jools waved for Marius to follow her back through the shop. 'I won't be too long,' she said to her gran. 'And I've got my mobile if you need me.'

As soon as they were outside, Jools apologised. 'I'm so sorry, I do hope Gran didn't embarrass you back there?'

Marius's step faltered. 'How would she have done that?'

Jools felt her cheeks heating up and wished she hadn't brought up the subject. 'You know, when she said about you being my young man. She's always doing that sort of thing and it's so embarrassing.'

'Always?'

Blast it, Jules thought. 'No, not always. But it is the sort of thing she does. I don't think she realises how awkward it is.'

Marius's hand grazed hers before he took hold of it as they walked. She turned her head to look at him and saw he was giving her a kind smile. 'Your gran is just looking out for you, Jools. Nothing more. You shouldn't be embarrassed, it's sweet.'

If she hadn't already liked him a lot, then she certainly did after his comment. 'You're right. She does worry about me. She's getting on in years and she's not as healthy as she used to be.'

'I'm sorry. It's difficult worrying about those you're close to, isn't it?'

She gazed out to the rolling waves and swallowed the lump in her throat to stop herself from getting upset. She rarely allowed herself to think of a future without her gran and didn't relish doing so now. 'It is.' She cleared her throat. 'Right, please don't let me forget to take home a slice of cake for Gran, she'll only send me back out again.'

'I won't.'

As they entered the café, Jools spotted Sacha giving her an approving look. She loved her friend, but hoped Sacha wouldn't make it obvious that she was happy to see her with Marius. The last thing she wanted was for him to think she never had lunch with a man – even if she didn't.

Sacha pointed to a table at the back of the room and gave Jools a wink.

'I think she wants us to sit here,' Marius said.

Once seated, Jools leant forward and lowered her voice. 'I'm paying for this lunch.'

'No, you're not. I asked you out and I want to pay.'

Jools shook her head. 'No. This is my thank you for finding me a new client. If you don't agree to let me pay then I'm going to buy Gran's cake and return to the shop.'

Marius pushed the sleeves of his worn grey sweater up his arms and shook his head. 'You're pretty determined, aren't you?'

'She is,' Sacha said, handing them both a menu. 'I'd give in and do what she wants if I were you. It'll save a lot of time in the long run.'

Marius looked up at her before turning his attention back to Jools and grinning, his blue eyes twinkling in amusement. 'Fine, I'll do as you suggest today. But it's my turn next time.'

Next time?

8

9TH MAY – LIBERATION DAY

Jools woke on Liberation Day with the usual sense of excitement and pride that the anniversary of the liberation of the people of Jersey had come around once more. She could only try to imagine the sense of fear her grandmother and her contemporaries must have felt, living under Nazi rule for five long, tortuous years, until the British Forces liberated them on the ninth of May, nineteen-forty-five. Each year, everyone had a day off work, and most of the shops were shut. Those who'd lived most of their lives on the island and considered it their home, raised flags, put up bunting, queued to ring their parish church bells and celebrated with their families in whatever traditional way they preferred. There were services, parades, bands playing, parties and a re-enactment at Liberation Square of when the British soldiers landed and raised the Union Flag on the Pomme d'Or Hotel balcony, as they did in 1945.

The residents of the boardwalk held their own street party each year. Jools always looked forward to the event, spending the days before helping her grandmother put up bunting across the front of the bookshop and along the bookshelves inside. They always enjoyed themselves, but took a few moments to think of those who had gone before them and suffered the most during the Occupation. Most years the weather held out and the sun shone on the islanders as they marked the anniversary with their families and close friends.

Jools looked out of her bedroom window and smiled. Today, it seemed, the sun was going to brighten their day as she had hoped it would.

'Have you checked if Sacha needs any help to bring out all the food?' Gran called up from the shop. 'I know she's got Jack and Bella helping, but he keeps going away to be photographed since that photo of his went... what did you call it?'

'Viral, Gran,' Jools answered. 'It's called going viral.' She put in the silver Jersey flag earrings her gran had bought her a couple of years ago. 'Sacha's expecting me soon but I'm going to help hang bunting across Betty's cottage with Claire first.'

She straightened her thin cotton sweater over her jeans and slipped her trainers on before walking downstairs to join her grandmother. 'What do you think?' she asked, giving her grandmother a twirl. Then, putting her fingers behind each ear, added. 'Like my earrings? I thought today was the perfect day to wear them again.'

If she was honest, she hadn't been sure when to wear them, they were so distinctive – a red cross on a white enamelled square – but didn't think anyone would be surprised to see the Jersey flag being sported in such a way today.

Gran narrowed her eyes and leant forward. 'They look perfect.'

'Great. Then if you don't need me for anything else, I'll get going. I'll be back to accompany you to the party after I've been to the café.'

Jools left the shop, smiling and waving hello to various villagers as she hurried to Betty's tiny cottage. Claire was standing outside, chatting to Betty, who was sitting drinking a cup of tea as she watched everyone finalising the celebratory preparations.

'I'm not late, am I?' Jools asked, suddenly unsure.

'No, love,' Betty reassured her. 'We thought we'd wait out here and take in all the excitement.'

Claire disappeared into the cottage, stepping out a moment later with an armful of cotton red, white and blue bunting that looked several decades old. Jools smiled. She much preferred the older flags; they gave her a nostalgic feeling when she looked at them.

'The stepladder's just inside with a hammer and a few nails.' Clarie inclined her head towards the door. 'If you wouldn't mind fetching those, we can get this sorted.'

Jools did as she asked and a few minutes later, stood on one of the higher rungs of the ladder holding one end of the bunting asked. 'Does this look central to you?'

'Perfect,' Betty said. 'Just give that nail a couple of bangs and hang it up. No need for too much ceremony.'

Jools was relieved. She wasn't very handy when it came to DIY and didn't know how securely she'd hammered the nails in.

'Here, can I do that for you?' asked a voice she was getting to know well. Jools smiled to herself, happy to hear Marius's cheerful tone. She turned and grinned at him. 'Thanks, but I'm managing better than I expected.'

He held onto the stepladder and studied her work. 'It looks great.' He smiled at Betty and Claire and held out his hand. 'Hi, I'm Marius,' he said. 'I'm a friend of Jools. She suggested I pop down to join in the celebrations if I got the chance.'

Jools could sense Betty's eyes on her as she carefully stepped down the ladder. 'There.' She looked up, aware they were waiting for her to say something about Marius's appearance. 'That does look okay. What a relief.' Facing Betty and Claire, she feigned surprise. 'What?'

Betty took a sip of her tea and shrugged. 'I don't know about Claire, but I was wondering who you are and how you two met?' she said, turning her attention to Marius.

Jools watched as his eyes widened slightly and he took a small step back before laughing. 'We met while we were walking dogs for our grandparents,' he explained. 'Then Jools came to my studio with two of her friends to watch me working.'

Betty frowned. 'You're an artist, too?'

'He works with glass,' Jools explained. 'He's very good, too.'

'Hey, thanks.' Marius stepped up to her and gave her a kiss on the cheek. 'I'm glad you like my work.'

Claire folded the stepladder and took the hammer and remaining nails from Jools. 'Why don't you two go and have some fun. We'll no doubt see you later when the celebrations really get going.'

'You're sure you don't need me for anything else?' Jools asked, eager to spend a little time in Marius's company, even if it was only walking along the boardwalk to the café.

'You've done all that we needed,' Betty said. 'Off you go now.'

Jools bent to kiss Betty's soft cheek. She opened her mouth to speak when the chilling sound of a siren made her jump. Betty's hand flew to her chest and Claire shrieked. Marius's mouth opened in shock as he glanced around him.

'What the hell is that?' He looked as if he thought they should run for shelter.

Betty rolled her eyes heavenward. 'That's old man, Le Brun,' she shouted above the din of the siren. 'He does this every year. I know it's coming but it always gives me such a fright when it does.'

Jools, comfortable that Betty wasn't too upset, took Marius's hand in hers and, waving at Betty and Claire, led him away towards the café. 'It'll be quieter in there,' she shouted, walking quickly, looking forward to getting as far away from the noisy shrieking as possible.

'How long will it last?' Marius asked, laughing as he broke into a run.

'Too bloody long for my liking.'

Once inside the café, Jools gave a sigh of relief. They could still hear the siren, but at least now it wasn't quite so deafening.

'That sodding noise,' an older man grumbled as he led his wife into the café behind them. 'I'm sure he needs permission to set that ruddy thing off like he does.'

'Stop moaning, Cyril and sit down,' the woman – his wife, Jools presumed – instructed. 'You know why he does it. Have some compassion, for once in your life.'

Jools and Marius walked up to the counter and waited until Sacha had finished dealing with a customer. 'How are things going?'

'Hi there, you two.' Sacha rested her palms on the counter and smiled. 'It's been incredibly busy,' she said as Jack walked out of the kitchen carrying three cooked breakfasts. 'Then again, it usually is on Liberation Day. Can I get you anything?'

'I was wondering if you needed any help,' Jools said. 'I know you've got the party food to prepare and take out.'

'All done, thanks. Well, it's all made. Why don't you both take a seat and I'll bring you something to eat and drink to keep you going.'

'Just a tea for me,' Jools said.

'Coffee for me, thanks,' Marius replied without taking his eyes off Jools. She tried not to read too much into it.

They found a spare table near the back of the room and sat down.

'Tell me the old man's story,' Marius said. 'I have a feeling it might be a sad one.'

'Why would you think that?' Jools asked, intrigued to know.

Marius shrugged. 'Because that is one hell of a racket and although it gives everyone a fright, he does it every year and no one tells him to stop. I figure there must be a reason why you're willing to leave him to it.'

He was right. 'I think initially he might have set off the siren to simply mark the anniversary, but Gran told me that when he had been married man about two or three years, his wife had a few drinks, which wasn't something she usually did, and went for a swim. No one realised she had gone until it was too late and poor Old Man Le Brun found her lying in the surf. She had drowned and I don't think the poor chap ever got over it.'

'That's so tragic,' Marius said. He looked towards the window as the chilling wailing slowed and finally ceased. 'What a terrible thing to have happened. I can see why he's allowed to carry on. It would be too cruel not to let him.'

'I think so, too. He never married again or had children. Poor man.'

They sat silently, staring out of the window at the bright sunshine against the waves. Jools couldn't help thinking how devastated Old Man Le Brun must still be by the loss of his wife to mark the anniversary of her death in such a public way.

'What's the matter with you two?' Sacha said, arriving at their table and placing their drinks in front of them.

'I was telling Marius about Old Man Le Brun.'

'Aw, it's terribly sad, isn't it?'

'It is.'

'We let him mark the day and once it's done everyone feels free to celebrate properly.'

'Does he ever join in?' Marius said.

Jools nodded. 'He does, actually. I don't think he did for a long time, but someone years ago persuaded him.' She thought of the wizened old man and how he seemed to forget his troubles when the party on the boardwalk began.

'As soon as you've finished those drinks,' Sacha said, 'come and find me and we'll start taking the food out to the trestle tables. Jack's just setting them up with Alessandro.'

'I can go and help them, if they need me to?' Marius offered.

Sacha shook her head. 'No, you sit there while you have the chance. You'll probably not have a second's peace as soon as you go outside. You're new and the villagers will have spotted you and Jools chatting so will be interested in finding out more about you.' She grinned. 'I hope you thought to bring some business cards,' she said, giving him a playful wink. 'You never know, you might manage to drum up a little business for yourself.'

* * *

Half an hour later, Jools and Marius carried out the last of the trays of food from the café.

'Right, I'd better go and get Gran and I'll see you back out here,' Jools said, smiling at Marius.

'Great,' Jack said, overhearing. 'If you've got nowhere to be, you can come and help serve this lot with me and Alessandro.'

'Sure, no problem.'

Jools knew she had better hurry back to fetch Gran before the Constable of St Helier gave his speech about Liberation Day and declared their street party open. Gran would never forgive her if she missed any of the fun, but by the time she neared the shop the door opened and Gran was being pushed outside by Marius's grandfather.

'I'm not late, am I?' Jools asked.

'No, dear.' Gran smiled at her and raised her hand to indicate the friendly man Jools knew Marius was extremely fond of. 'Alan and I thought we would let you young ones enjoy yourselves and spend the afternoon here with everyone.'

Jools wasn't sure she was happy to let her gran celebrate the party without her. 'Are you sure? We usually make the most of today together.'

'Perfectly.' Gran waved her away. 'Go and have fun. I'm sure Marius is there somewhere.' She peered around Jools and gave a satisfied nod. 'I thought so. There he is with Jack and that lovely Italian boyfriend of Sacha's. Right, off you go now, sweetheart. Enjoy yourself and don't worry about me.'

'I'll not leave Mrs Jones by herself,' Alan reassured Jools. 'She's determined to show me all the stalls and talk me through the celebrations, so we'll be fine. No need to worry.'

'If you're sure,' Jools said, wanting to make completely certain that Gran wasn't testing her in any way but meant what she said.

'I am. Now off you go.'

Jools bent to kiss her and gave her a smile. 'Fine,' she said. 'See you around, no doubt.'

She left them to their fun and walked back to Marius. How odd to think that her gran and his grandfather had made friends. Jools was relieved to see that the older man seemed more relaxed and happier than he had done the first day she met him. He seemed kind and she was pleased to see him settling down and making friends with the villagers. She smiled to herself. If he was a friend of Gran's, then Gran would make sure the other villagers took him under their wing and included him, just like they had done when Betty decided Barry was her friend. Wondering where Barry might be, Jools turned towards Betty's cottage and was relieved to spot her sitting on the bench outside her front door laughing with the older man, his faithful little dog sitting happily at his feet.

Speeches made, music rang out over the tannoy and a band of four girls, a little younger than her, took their place on the small stage and began singing a stream of forties' songs that even Jools began tapping and singing along to. She reached Marius and he slipped his arm around her waist.

'Are you sure those are the right lyrics?' he teased.

Jools giggled. 'No. Not all of them anyway. But the tune is catchy.'

'Come along,' Marius said, his hand finding hers.

'What?'

He pulled her gently away from the trestle table. 'You're going to dance with me.'

Jools shook her head, horrified at the thought of dancing in front of the crowd of onlookers. 'Oh no. I don't dance.'

'Why not?'

'I don't know how.'

'What, at all?'

'I can move to songs that I know, if that's what you're asking,' she said, shaking her head and pulling back from him. 'But I can't jitterbug, or whatever this music is for.'

Marius laughed and pulled her into his arms. 'This isn't jitter-bugging. Anyway, I can't do that either. I meant we should dance. You know, just move to the music which I know you can do because you've just admitted as much.'

Jools glanced over his shoulder at other couples enjoying the music in front of the makeshift stage and shook her head. 'No, I can't.'

'Give it a go,' he said gently. 'One dance. Then, if you don't enjoy yourself, we'll leave it. Deal?'

She groaned, knowing she would seem miserable if she did not at least try to have some fun. 'Fine. Come along then.'

She let him pull her by the hand to the middle of the dance area and stood giggling at him as he attempted to dance like the others were doing. Then, Marius pulled her into his arms and within seconds they were laughing and dancing as well as they could manage to the lively music and Jools was having the best fun.

'See, I knew you'd enjoy it if you gave it a go.' Smiling, he raised her hand in his so she could step underneath, then caught her and held her tightly for a few steps before doing the same thing again.

'I am,' she laughed, as he spun her around once more.

By the following dance she had forgotten all about being self-conscious and gave in to the music. As they danced around the others, Jools spotted her grandmother watching her and clapping along. She couldn't recall feeling so liberated and light-hearted in a very long time. Marius whirled her around and around the floor until the music was slowing and the song coming to an end. As it finished, she relaxed into his arms and hugged him, and over his shoulder found herself staring at Finn.

Her heart skipped a beat. She wasn't sure whether it was surprise at seeing him standing there so unexpectedly, or because she was pleased to see him – or whether she felt guilty that he'd caught her having so much fun with another man.

'What's the matter?' Marius asked. He stopped swaying and turned to find the focus of her surprise.

Finn tore his gaze from her and frowned in Marius's direction before looking back at Jools. Her stomach clenched anxiously. Finn didn't look happy as he stepped forward.

'Who's he?' Marius asked, his voice low.

'I'm her boyfriend,' Finn said, rather territorially. Not waiting for Marius or Jools to reply, he added, 'Hi, Jools. Did you miss me as much as I missed you?'

Jools was unable to answer for a moment. She knew she owed Marius an explanation but wasn't sure she needed to explain to Finn. She was still angry with him for going away in the first place, and for not keeping in touch with her as much as she had expected. Worst of all, she realised that she didn't know what she was supposed to do next. She hadn't had a boyfriend in such a long time and now, here she was, in front of everyone she knew, standing between two men who liked her. Contrary to all the romance novels she had devoured over the years, having two men competing for you wasn't something she had ever expected to happen to her. Now that it was, she decided she didn't like it very much at all.

'Finn,' she finally managed. 'You're back.'

Finn frowned at her again and looked as if he wasn't sure whether she was joking. 'Er, obviously.'

Marius tensed, his arms dropping from around Jools. 'I'll leave the pair of you to catch up.'

Jools turned to look at him, unable to miss the confused expression on his handsome face. She had hurt him, that much was obvious. She wished she could take a moment to speak to him in private and explain a bit about her relationship with Finn, but knew that now wasn't the best time. She did need to speak to Finn. 'I'll come and find you in a bit,' she said, her voice barely above a whisper. 'Sorry about this.'

'It's fine.'

She could see that it wasn't and the realisation comforted her slightly. Before, she hadn't known which of the two men she preferred but seeing them together, and Finn's territorial reaction to her compared with Marius's gentle retreat to give her space to deal with whatever was happening, made her realise that Marius was the one she would be happiest with.

Stepping forward, she said to Finn, 'I think we need to have a chat.'

He nodded. 'I've got the keys to the gelateria,' he said, holding them up. 'I was supposed to be back a couple of days ago to help Alessandro open up, but I was delayed due to an airline staff strike. I need to go there now and give him a break. I thought you might come with me and we could chat in between serving customers.'

Jools hadn't realised the Isola Bella gelateria was open already. It made sense that Alessandro had re-opened his business in time for today's celebrations. She knew from Sacha that Liberation Day was one of the busiest days of the year for the café especially after a long, quiet winter when few visitors came to the island and the only customers were the hardy locals. She presumed it would be the same for Alessandro's ice-cream parlour. 'Yes, of course.'

She accompanied him the short distance to the ice-cream parlour, manoeuvring their way through the throngs of villagers dancing, singing and chatting excitedly as they ate and drank the food Sacha had put out. Jools waited by the doorway for Finn to speak to Alessandro and for the handover to take place.

'Ah, Jools, have you come for a gelato?' Alessandro asked, spotting her. 'Tell Finn that you are to have one for free.'

'Thanks, Alessandro, but I've just come in to have a quick chat with him when he's finished serving the customers. That's all right, isn't it? I don't want to disturb him while he's working.'

Alessandro smiled. 'It is fine. You must be excited to see each other again after so long.' He patted Finn on the back and gave her a sweet smile. 'I must go and find Sacha now. I said I would help her and I've been away longer than I promised I would be. I shall see you soon, Jools.' He went to walk out of the door, then stopped and turned. 'It is good to have Finn back here, no?'

'It is,' she said, wishing she felt as happy about it as Alessandro obviously did.

She watched the locals having fun on the boardwalk and hoped that Finn would soon finish serving before everyone realised the Isola Bella was open and came in for gelatos. Jools noticed Marius chatting to Jack further down the boardwalk and her heart sank to think that he had so readily stepped away from her on Finn's arrival. Maybe he didn't like her as much as she had thought. She heard Finn joke with the customers and wish them well for the day. After watching them leave, she walked over to speak to him at the counter.

Finn washed his hands and dried them. 'I don't know how I get so mucky doing this,' he smiled. 'It's not as if I scoop the ice-cream from the cartons with my hands.' He walked around the counter to her and took her hands in his. 'Jools.'

'Finn,' she said, wishing he wasn't choosing now to act flirtatiously.

'Have you missed me as much as I missed you?'

How could she possibly answer such a question without hurting him? Jools decided that now was not the time to tell him she wasn't sure they actually had much chemistry. The poor man had travelled thousands of miles back to the island. The least she could do was wait a few days before confessing that she didn't want to continue seeing him.

'Jools?' He looked confused.

'Sorry,' she said, embarrassed to be caught thinking about finishing with him when he had only just returned. 'I don't know. How much did you miss me?' she asked. 'Not enough to send me more than one postcard, I noticed.'

It was his turn to feel awkward, she realised as he grimaced. 'I know. I'm a useless article,' he laughed. 'Or at least that's what my mother told me when I arrived back on the island.'

'I thought you might text me.'

He shrugged. 'I'm sorry. I wasn't sure how much it would cost to use my data from across the world. And I meant to upload my photos onto Instagram but couldn't recall my log in details.'

Jools had the sense he wasn't being totally honest but wasn't sure whether to push it. It wasn't as if she'd wasted time waiting for him to contact her. 'It doesn't matter,' she said. 'Did you have a lovely time? That's what I really want to hear.'

'I did,' he said, a wistful note in his voice. He seemed to lose himself in memories, then shook his head as if to snap himself back to the present. 'It was awesome. My mate and I met up with other travellers and a group of us moved around to various places together for a while. It was rather good,' he said, his voice trailing off, and she knew she had to ask.

'Finn, did you even take any photos?'

He looked confused for a moment and then shook his head. 'My mate took a few but I'm hopeless at that sort of thing.'

'But you just said you were going to post your pictures on Instagram?' She could see a pattern taking shape. He was being evasive for some reason and she wasn't sure why. 'Did you even take your mobile?'

He nodded. 'I did but lost it,' he admitted. 'I think I left it on the plane out of Jersey. It was freeing to be without it, if I'm honest. I couldn't help thinking that it must have been how my dad felt when he went travelling in the eighties.'

Jools wondered for a moment how it must feel to not be at the other end of a phone, to be completely out of contact; no calling, emailing, or messaging through social media. She liked the idea and could see how Finn might have enjoyed the freedom of truly being away from home and the people back on the island.

'I'm glad you had a wonderful time,' she said.

'How about you?' he asked, his voice changing slightly. 'Is that chap I saw you dancing with someone I should be bothered about?'

What should she say? 'His name is Marius and he's a new friend. He kindly instigated a commission for me, which was lovely. His grandfather also comes to the bookshop and Gran's roped him into joining her book group. They're both lovely.'

Two teenage girls ran into the ice-cream parlour. 'Have a good look and let me know which flavours you want,' Finn said, stepping back and taking Jools's hand in his, pulling her gently back behind the counter. 'I'm glad that he's just a friend,' he said. 'I've missed you, Jools. I was worried that you might meet someone else while I was away. I know we didn't part on the best terms and we'd only really seen each other a couple of times.'

Jools opened her mouth, wanting to explain her feelings for Marius, but before the words would form, she realised she didn't completely understand what they were. There was no point upsetting Finn unnecessarily. Let him settle down and get used to being on the island again and maybe she would remember why she had liked him so much.

'I want the strawberry with some of the chocolate,' the taller of the two girls said with a giggle.

'And I want the peach,' the other one said, nudging her friend and batting her eyelashes at Finn.

Jools decided to let him get on with it. 'I'll catch up with you a bit later,' she said, moving away from the counter.

'Great.' Finn raised his hand in a wave. 'I'll speak to you soon.'

'Sure,' she said, walking from the gelateria out into the sunshine, aware that whatever her afternoon would entail, it was not going to include dancing with Marius again.

9

She stepped outside onto the pavement and her eyes hadn't had time to adjust to the bright sunshine when she slammed into someone.

'Oof.' Jools groaned as her chest connected with someone much taller than her.

'Hey, you OK?' said a female voice. 'Oh, it's Jools, isn't it?'

Jools shaded her eyes with her hand and squinted at a beautifully sleek woman smiling down at her, wishing she had also thought to wear sunglasses. The woman looked familiar and was holding hands with Charlie, the hotel manager, who Jools knew only vaguely.

'Hi,' she said, desperately trying to recall the woman's name, aware that she had met her several times.

The woman gave a tinkling laugh. 'It's Portia,' she said. 'Surely you haven't forgotten me already. I was only here a couple of months ago. I'm Olly, Oliver Whimsy's friend from London.'

Mortified, Jools closed her eyes and shook her head. 'Sorry, Portia. It's been one of those days and I'm not really thinking straight.' She gave Portia her friendliest smile. 'I didn't realise you were back on the island. You've come at the right time though.'

'So it seems.' Portia took in the scene around her.

Jools followed her gaze, enjoying the infectious happiness of the people around her. 'Everyone's making the most of their day off work, as well as the great weather.'

'As they always do on Liberation Day,' Charlie said, with the assurance of someone who had always lived on the island.

'It was Charlie who insisted I fly back to Jersey for this event,' Portia explained. 'He said it would be fun, and it is.' She leant forward. 'To be honest, I had no idea about the Occupation, but Charlie, being a good Jersey boy, has kindly filled me in on some of what happened. It must have been horrendous. I can see why the islanders still celebrate their liberation after all these years.'

'Yes, so do I,' Jools agreed. 'Some of them, like my gran, can still recall what it was like to live through those tough years, so it means a lot, especially to them, and it's our history of course.'

'I see that Jack and his friend are selling drinks over near the café,' Charlie said. 'Shall we go and get some?'

Realising that her throat was very dry, probably from the stress of having to face Finn, Jools nodded. 'Great idea.'

As they began to walk, she realised that the friend of Jack's that Charlie had referred to was Marius. Jools cleared her throat, not wishing to explain what had happened earlier to Charlie and Portia, and accompanied them to the stall.

'Hi there,' Marius said, giving Jools an uncertain look.

She suspected he was unsure whether she had come to speak to him personally or was simply there with her friends. She hated not being able to talk to him privately but daren't risk Finn coming out from the gelateria and spotting them. He would probably jump to the conclusion that she had run straight from there to Marius and things were awkward enough already. It was a new experience for her, and one she didn't like at all.

'We've come to buy some drinks,' she explained, aware that even to her ears her cheerfulness came across as forced. 'It's thirsty work being out in this glorious sunshine.'

Jack finished serving a customer and turned, beaming when he saw them. 'Portia, you're back. I didn't know you were on the island. How've you been?'

'Great, thanks. We're only here for today though. I've come over to see what the celebration is about and to take Charlie back home with me. We're flying to London first thing tomorrow morning.'

'We? Isn't the hotel open yet then, Charlie?'

Charlie smiled. 'Actually, Portia has persuaded me to hand in my notice so I can spend some time living with her in London to see how it goes.'

'Really?' Jack looked as surprised as Jools felt at hearing this news. 'Good for you,' he said. 'I hope you'll both be very happy.'

Charlie had been the manager of the Sea Breeze Hotel for about three years and had always seemed to enjoy his work. It was a shock to hear that he was leaving when summer was on its way and Jools couldn't help thinking how quickly his relationship with Portia had progressed. Still, their affection for each other was obvious and they seemed very much in love. What did she know about these things? She was hardly an expert where romantic relationships were concerned. She recalled hearing about Portia's heartbreak when her fiancé had died and was delighted that she had found someone who made her happy.

'I'll bet it's going to be exciting swapping this place for London,' she said. 'I think it's romantic.'

She noticed Marius giving her a sideways glance and wanted desperately to take his hand in hers, reassure him that she wasn't messing him around and did have feelings for him. Did he have feelings for her? She wished she wasn't so confused.

They gave Jack their order and he poured drinks and handed them out. 'Have you seen Lexi and Oliver yet, Portia?' he asked. 'They were supposed to come down today.'

'We popped in to see them last night and share a takeaway.' Portia laughed. 'They're so loved up, they've probably forgotten the time.'

Jools was happy that one of her closest friends had finally found the man she suspected she would marry. Lexi's life hadn't been the easiest, especially in the past few months, with her father going behind her back to sell her beloved cottages, but it had all been resolved. Oliver was an impressive man, not only attractive but worldly and charismatic. She wouldn't have placed him with Lexi if she had met him without her friend, but they seemed to gel perfectly. Her yin to his yang, she supposed.

She felt a hand slip into hers and give it a gentle tug. Turning, Jools saw that it was Marius. She glanced over her shoulder and saw that Jack, Charlie and Portia were deep in conversation and allowed Marius to pull her slightly away to stand against the metal railings.

'Sorry,' he said as he let go of her hand. 'You don't mind, do you?'

She shook her head, her fingers feeling the loss of his. 'No.'

'I know the situation is difficult with your boyfriend coming back so unexpectedly but I wanted to speak to you while we had a moment.'

'I'm glad,' she admitted. 'I didn't want you to get the wrong idea about me and Finn. I'm not the sort of girl to get close to someone when I already have a partner.'

'He's not your partner then?'

Did she spy a hint of hope in his expression? 'We had a few

days out together,' she explained hurriedly, in case they were interrupted again. 'I liked him, but we'd barely started anything before he went away with his friend. It was a prior arrangement,' she added before he could ask. 'I know I need to speak to Finn and clear things up, but I'm not very good at confrontation.' She thought of all the times she'd been direct and sorted out issues when her friends had needed her to. 'Not when it concerns me, anyway.'

'Right. I think I see. Does that mean that you're interested in giving us a go then?'

Jools felt a jolt of excitement. 'Yes,' she admitted. 'I'd like that very much.'

'That's great.' He beamed and bent to kiss her.

Jools leant back, hating the look of surprise on his face. 'Sorry. I don't mean to give you mixed signals.' She shook her head. 'I'm rubbish at this romance lark.'

'It's fine,' he said. 'What were you going to say?'

She struggled to reply, not wishing to ruin the moment more than she already had. 'Before we, um, I suppose, see each other again, I want to clear everything up with Finn. I want everyone to know where they stand. He seemed a bit shocked to see us together, so I'll need to take things carefully.' Marius was staring at her. She wasn't sure whether he understood, or was happy with what she intended doing. 'Are you all right with that?'

Marius nodded and then gave her a reassuring smile. 'You do what you have to,' he said, leaning forward to give her a light kiss on the cheek. 'I'll wait to hear from you when you've settled things with Finn.'

'Thank you,' she said, aware that he and Finn had reacted in different ways. If she had been confused about her feelings for either of them before, then today had shown her clearly who was the better of the two men.

'I'll let you get on,' Marius said, stepping away. 'I'd better get back to helping Jack. Have a fun afternoon.'

'Will do.' Jools watched him walking away. He was doing exactly as she had asked, so why did it make her sad? Jools took a deep breath. She needed to stop feeling sorry for herself. As soon as she'd sorted things out with Finn, she could see how things panned out with Marius.

'Hey, what are you doing standing here all by yourself?' Sacha nudged Jools gently in the ribs. 'This is supposed to be a fun day and you look sad. Want to share?'

Jools shook her head. How typical of Sacha to notice that she was miserable. She needed to get a grip. After all, there was no rush. She and Marius had all summer to get to know each other and she wasn't going to be mean to Finn, especially so soon after his return. She forced a smile and linked arms with her lovely friend.

'No, I'm fine. Thanks though. I was just thinking.'

Sacha frowned, looking unconvinced. 'Anything I can help with?'

Jools laughed. 'Nothing at all.' Another band struck up a tune and several couples walked onto the dance floor and began jitter-bugging and jiving. 'Why don't we join in and show these people how not to dance.'

'Ha-ha, speak for yourself, Miss Jones. I can deliver a passable jitterbug, even if you can't.' Sacha pulled her towards the dance area in front of the temporary band stand.

'Can you?' Jools asked, surprised, wondering when Sacha had found time away from the café and Alessandro to take lessons.

'No, of course I can't,' Sacha giggled, flicking her sun-kissed blonde hair back from her shoulders. 'But I'm going to give it a good try.'

After a lot of laughing, a few stumbles and a growing audience of other dancers, similarly lacking in expertise, Jools was relieved that her hopeless dancing was less obvious to the audience. She noticed Portia tugging Charlie's arm, trying to persuade him to dance. When he refused, Lexi grabbed her hand and together they did their best moves to the fun, forties music.

'You lot are rubbish,' Jack mocked as he and Bella joined them on the dance floor.

'Charming,' Jools giggled.

'Why don't you show us how you do it then, clever pants?' Sacha gave her twin brother a shove. 'Go on. Let's see how brilliant you are at this dancing lark.'

'Fine, I will.' Jack and Bella took a moment to build momentum and soon he was flinging her over his shoulder, executing acrobatic lifts and twirls that stopped everyone in their tracks.

'What the hell?' Jools stared in awe at their musicality and movement. She tilted her head at Sacha. 'Did you know they could do this?'

Sacha shook her head. 'I heard there were dance classes at the parish hall in preparation for today, but had no idea this is what Jack and Bella had been learning.'

'Well, I, for one, am impressed,' Portia laughed. 'This is incredible. I'm jealous now that I didn't think to learn a few steps. It looks enormous fun.'

Sacha grinned. 'My brother has always been a bit of a show-off. I have to admit that I'm amazed.'

As the afternoon drew into evening, Finn finished his shift and closed the gelateria, waving at Jools as he left. It had been a long, and for the most part fun, day and she was tired. She had checked on Gran and accompanied her back to the bookshop a couple of hours earlier, and she and Bella had made sure that Betty and Barry had something to eat and were happy chatting back at

Betty's cottage. Jools wasn't really in the mood to think about anything serious. She had seen Marius a few times but had mostly spent time with her girlfriends, only saying a quick goodbye when he left to take his grandfather home to his mother's where she was cooking a celebratory evening meal for the family.

Jools watched Finn push the parlour keys into his pocket as he ran over to join her. 'Had a good day?'

'Yes, thanks. It was great fun, but it usually is.'

'Drink?'

Jools nodded and they began to walk to the stall that Jack was once again looking after. 'I never forget, though, why we mark this anniversary, or the people who suffered during the Occupation.'

'Nor me,' Finn said. 'It makes you think, doesn't it? I mean, about how you might cope if you couldn't leave the island and see family members or friends. Or what it must have been like to have German signs and money instead of the local currency.'

'Or what it was like to nearly starve,' Jools added. 'It's no wonder people like my gran and her contemporaries still feel the pain of those times. And know how lucky they were to survive it all.'

She heard suppressed shouting coming from below the board-walk. Stopping, she leant over the metal railing to see what was happening and saw Claire, pushing Tony away.

'I hate you, Tony. You know I wanted us to get married sooner rather than later and now you're saying you won't do it until you're sure that Bella is in agreement. Really?'

Jools leant back, wincing. She didn't want her friend's mother to catch her eavesdropping on her argument and also didn't fancy knowing something else about Claire and Tony's relationship before Bella.

'You okay?' Finn asked, frowning as he waited for her to re-join him.

'I heard a commotion and was worried something might be wrong, but it's all fine. Nothing to worry about,' she said, hoping that was indeed the case.

They walked slowly in silence for a few seconds.

'Bloody hell,' Jack said, when they reached the drinks stall. 'You two look like you've just received bad news.' His face blanched. 'You haven't, have you? I mean, if you have then, hell. Sorry, I wasn't thinking.'

Finn laughed. 'No, mate. We were just talking about the Occupation and how difficult it must have been to live through it all.'

Jack puffed out his cheeks. 'That's a relief. I thought for a moment I'd really put my foot in it.'

Jools grinned at him. 'You can make up for it by giving us a couple of beers.'

'Cheap at the price,' he said, turning to open two bottles and handing one to each of them. 'We're closing soon as it's getting rather chilly, but Sacha has been given a special licence to serve food until ten o'clock in the café if you're both hungry.'

'Thanks,' Jools said, unsure whether she wanted to sit with Finn and broach the subject of their relationship – or whatever it was between them. Although Marius wasn't pushing her to do anything she wasn't ready for, Jools was aware that if she spent time with Finn, she might give him the wrong idea.

'Sounds good,' Finn said, taking a drink from his bottle and smiling at Jools.

'I won't be able to, I'm afraid,' Jools said quickly. 'I promised Gran that I'd go home and join her for something to eat, so I can't be too long.' It wasn't true but she knew that Gran was always happy when she was at home for supper. 'I've had rather more to drink than I should have and I think I've had too much sun. It's given me a headache.' The last bit was true. Her head was beginning to thump at the temples, but it could have been due to the excitement of the day.

'You must be careful,' Jack said. 'I know it's only May and we've not had much sun for the last few months but it's stronger than you think.'

'Even for you?' Finn teased. 'The surfer dude?'

'Yup, even for me.'

Jools doubted that was the case. She noticed Jack giving her a brief, questioning look. He was always ready to defend his sister's friends and she suspected he was backing up her story with his comment about the sun.

'I was hoping we could spend a few hours together this evening,' Finn said more seriously.

Jools tried to push away her feelings of guilt and shrugged. 'Sorry. Maybe tomorrow,' she said, hoping her headache would be gone and she might have cobbled together a speech to let him down gently. 'We'll catch up then.'

Finn nodded. 'Sure. No worries.' He finished his beer and kissed her on the cheek. 'I can see Alessandro over there. If you don't mind, I'll go and chat to him and see you in the morning, or whenever you're free. Have a good evening with your gran.'

'Thanks.' Jools finished her beer, wondering whether she was being contrary to feel put out that he was almost as eager as she was to end their evening together.

10

After a restless night's sleep, not helped by Teddy jumping up and snuggling down on her bed at some point in the early hours, Jools woke with a thumping headache and an overwhelming sense of dread. She pushed herself up and leant against the headboard, staring at the grey light coming through her thin curtains. Rain drummed against the window and something metallic clattered along the boardwalk before slamming against the railings. Teddy hated storms, which explained his appearance in her room.

Jools stretched and kicked back her duvet, careful not to cover the little dog as she stepped out of bed and walked to the window. She pulled back the curtains and leant on the windowsill to stare at the stormy, jade green, sea. What a contrast to the weather the day before, she thought, not minding too much. Jools loved the warmer sunny days but also enjoyed hearing strong winds as they swirled around her home. It made her feel cosy and cocooned, but rarely were storms as bad as this one seemed to be.

She flinched as sea spray hit the glass. There was a high tide as well as a full-blown storm.

'No going outside for me for the next couple of hours,' she murmured to Teddy as he stretched and yawned. 'No playing on the beach for you either.'

She grabbed her dressing gown and made her way to the bathroom for her morning shower, leaving the dog to go back to sleep.

Half an hour later, dressed and carrying two cups of tea in her grandmother's favourite china, Jools made her way downstairs to the bookshop.

'Here you are, Gran.' She placed the teacups on the counter. 'I don't know why you're bothering to sit down here this morning. I can't imagine anyone braving this weather.'

'Thanks, love.' Her grandmother picked up her cup, blew on the steaming liquid, then placed it back on its saucer. 'Not everyone will realise how treacherous the boardwalk is during high tide in bad weather,' she said. 'We locals know, but holiday-makers won't realise that stones can get swept up by the waves. I don't want to be closed if anyone needs to race in here.'

Jools nodded. Her grandmother was right. There probably would be customers popping in at some point during the morning. 'If you'd rather sit upstairs and watch the storm, I can stay here and serve anyone who comes in. I know you love to watch the storms, especially bad ones like this one seems to be.'

'No, lovey. I'm perfectly happy down here.'

Jools gave her grandmother a hug. 'I'll be upstairs, painting in my studio. If you need me, just yell.'

She carried her cup of tea up to the room where she painted during the summer. She preferred to be outdoors, but on days like this, when the weather was dreadful, nothing could beat its cosy warmth.

After pulling on a paint-smeared cotton tunic with two large pockets at the front to protect her clothes, she set to work. She'd completed the first painting for Oliver and was now working on the siren painting for the exhibition. It was different to her usual subject matter and she expected it to be harder to get right.

Jools studied the lithe figure of the mermaid-like creature rising from the bay. As she had discovered from her research, the creature had a beautiful human face that with a few tweaks took on a more sinister appearance.

'I think that's about right,' she said to herself, absent-mindedly chewing the end of her paintbrush. 'Eugh.' She grimaced at the sour taste. 'That wasn't clever.' Taking a sip of her cooling tea, she focused once again on the painting. She hoped she'd done enough to satisfy her customer, but could always make the face more frightening if required.

She picked up her palette and, choosing a pale turquoise and a touch of white, mixed the colours until they were the shade she needed. Then, losing herself in her work, Jools lost track of time, as she always did.

When the shop's bell jangled, Jools glanced at her watch and saw that she had been working for over three hours. She smiled. Gran had been right about holidaymakers wanting to take refuge in the shop. She was always right, Jools mused, filled with love for her grandmother.

She'd started to add a final touch of paint to the side of the siren's tail when she heard a cry, followed by Bella's voice downstairs. Jools tensed, straining to hear what Bella was saying, but all she could pick up was the sound of someone sobbing. *Claire?* She put down her palette and paintbrush and pulled off her tunic before running downstairs.

'What's going on?'

Bella looked up and rolled her eyes as Jools entered the room. 'Sorry for all the noise.' She indicated her tearful mother with a sideways nod. 'Mum has got it into her head that something has happened to Tony.'

'Like what?' Jools asked, concerned.

Claire sniffed, smiling at Jools's gran who had pulled a tissue from the box she kept behind the counter and handed it to her. 'It's just that he always calls me by eleven to see how I am.'

Jools glanced out of the window. It was no longer high tide, but the sea was still rough and the weather stormy.

'Maybe he's just busy,' Gran suggested. 'He's probably loading fish from the nets, or whatever it is that fishermen do, and forgotten the time. I'm sure he'll phone you as soon as he's able to.'

'Yes,' Bella said, giving Gran a smile. 'That's probably it.' She put her arm around her mother's shoulders. 'Why don't we leave Mrs Jones and Jools to get on with their work and go to my place and have a nice cup of tea.'

'We had a row last night and I told him I hated him,' Claire sobbed.

'Mum, why would you say something so mean?' Bella frowned. 'Tony's so kind and he adores you, we can all see that.'

'I know. Oh, poor Tony. What if something's happened to him?' Her comment brought on fresh tears and Bella pulled her into a hug.

'Calm down, Mum. He'll be fine.'

'You listen to that daughter of yours,' Gran soothed. 'Go and have a nice cup of tea. I'm sure Tony will contact you as soon as he's free to do so.'

Claire blew her nose and, after giving each of them a searching gaze, nodded. 'Okay. I suppose there's not much else I can do anyway.'

'That's a good girl,' Jools heard her grandmother say as she felt her phone vibrate in her pocket. She took it out to see who was calling. It was Marius. She didn't like to answer the call when they had guests but wanted to speak to him. They hadn't had a chance to chat properly after Finn's arrival the day before and, although they'd spent some time with her friends and had fun, they hadn't been alone.

'Marius or Finn?' Bella whispered.

'Marius.'

'Take the call, love,' Claire said. 'I would if it was my Tony wanting to speak to me.' The thought of her fiancé led to more tears.

Jools smiled her gratitude and moved away for a little privacy. 'Hi,' she said, keeping her voice low as she pressed her phone to her ear. 'How are you?'

'Good, thanks,' Marius said. 'I thought I'd see if you were free to meet up sometime today. I know the weather is awful, so I thought I'd come down to yours. If you don't mind.' When she didn't answer immediately, he added, 'Tell me if you'd rather I didn't. I just thought it might be nice to have a quick chat to see where we stand. If you want to, that is.'

'I'd like that,' she admitted. 'What time were you thinking of coming down?'

'I thought... hang on a sec. I've just got a message and need to check it.' Marius mumbled something and then, his voice filled with urgency, said, 'Sorry, Jools. Got to go. I've had a shout from the lifeboat station.'

'A what?'

'It's what we call it when we have an emergency. I have to go.'

Before she could say anything further, Jools realised that Marius had ended the call. Her stomach contracted and she glanced out of the window and then at Claire, the sense of foreboding she had felt since waking increasing.

'What is it?' Claire asked.

'Um, that was Marius.' Jools didn't want to alarm Claire further.

Claire gasped. 'Isn't he in the RNLI?'

How did she know that? Jools didn't want to say yes, but knew she couldn't lie. 'He is.'

'I can tell by your face there's something you're not telling me.'

Jools frowned and walked over to Claire, resting her hand on the trembling woman's arm in an attempt to reassure her. 'I don't know anything.'

'But you know he's been called out, don't you?'

Jools wished Bella's mother wasn't so insistent. 'Yes, he's been called out. But that's all I know. It could be anything. Swimmers being caught out by the tide,' she said, aware that scenario was pretty unlikely given the wildness of the sea.

'It's Tony's boat,' Claire murmured. 'I just know it is. And to think that we were going to be married.'

'Mum, please try to get a grip?' Bella pleaded. 'There's no need to get hysterical when you don't even know if it's Tony's boat that's in trouble. Right, you're coming with me. We're going to go back to my place and you're going to calm down.' She took hold of her mother's shoulders and began pushing her gently out of the door. Looking over her shoulder at Jools and her gran, she said, 'Sorry about this.'

'It's fine,' Mrs Jones said. 'Perfectly understandable. We'll let you know if we hear any news.'

'Thanks, we'd be grateful.'

'Do you want me to call in on Betty?' Jools asked.

'Barry's with her,' Bella said, opening the door and easing her mother outside. 'Chat later.'

Jools went and closed the door after them. 'Do you think Claire could be right, Gran? What if Marius's shout was for Tony's boat?'

Her gran shook her head slowly and sighed. 'We'll just have to hope it isn't and that they rescue whoever is in trouble sooner rather than later.'

But what about Marius's safety? Jools turned to look out at the raging storm. Yesterday, when the sun was shining and the sea a calm pale blue, she'd thought she had all the time in the world to sort out her relationships. Today, it was becoming clear that she was wrong to make assumptions. Why hadn't she followed her instincts and been straight with Finn? Poor Marius, she thought, her heart aching fearfully. What if he never got to know how much she liked him?

'He'll be fine, lovey,' Gran soothed. 'He's trained well and knows what to do in these situations. Try not to fret about the boy.'

If only it was that easy. 'I like him though, Gran,' she admitted. 'What if something happens to Marius and I don't get the chance to let him know?'

'You mustn't think that way,' Gran said. 'You have to be positive. Things usually turn out right in the end and we must hope and pray that's the case this time.'

Gran was right. Marius knew what he was doing. All the RNLI volunteers did. Jools had heard about the intense training the crews undertook.

She took a steadying breath. 'I think I'll go upstairs and carry on with my painting,' she said finally. 'Unless you need me for anything?'

Her grandmother gave her a reassuring smile. 'That's a good girl. There's no point in staying down here and staring out of that window. It won't bring him back any quicker. You go and work on that painting. The sooner it's finished the quicker you'll be paid and can get on with something new.' She raised an eyebrow. 'I'm sure you'll be happier to focus on a more appealing subject than the one you're working on now?'

'I will,' she admitted, forcing a smile.

She left her grandmother and walked slowly up to her studio. She wasn't sure how she was going to be able to focus on her work, with the howling wind acting as a constant reminder of the storm, but she was going to give it a good try. It was better than feeling utterly useless, just sitting and waiting to hear from Marius again.

11

Jools tried hard to concentrate but couldn't stop her mind from wandering. It didn't help that the howling wind confirmed her suspicion that the stormy weather was worsening. She thought of Marius, out in the violent waves with the other volunteers, and knew that all she could do, apart from pray, was trust that he had enough experience to stay safe.

'Focus,' she said, dabbing her paintbrush into a marine blue on her messy palette. She might not be able to do much for Marius or the others, but she could surprise him when he returned with what she had achieved. She raised the brush and had started to add more colour to the darkening sky when her phone vibrated in her pocket. Almost dropping the paintbrush, she quickly placed it on the small chest of drawers she kept for her artist utensils and retrieved her phone. The brush rolled onto the painted floorboards and bounced, leaving a trail of blue on the wood.

'Bugger,' she grumbled, her hand fumbling to answer her phone. It took a moment because she had paint on her hands. Frustrated with herself, Jools angrily wiped her fingertips on her tunic and peered at the paint-smeared screen, unable to see who was calling. 'Marius?' she asked as she finally connected to the call.

'No. Is me, Alessandro.'

Alessandro? He never called her. She tried not to panic but could tell by his voice that something was wrong. 'Is Sacha all right?'

'Yes, she is OK. She is worried about Jack. She asked me if you wouldn't mind coming to the café to talk to her.'

'No problem. I'll come immediately,' Jools reassured him, relieved to have her mind taken off her own worries. 'I'll be there in a couple of minutes. I'll just let Gran know where I'm going.'

'Thank you. And Jools?'

'Yes?'

'Please, she asks that you do not tell Bella where you're going, or why.'

'Okay.' Jools ended the call, confused by Sacha's request. They usually shared things with Bella, but if Sacha wanted her to say nothing she must have a good reason. Jools pulled off her tunic and put on her thick puffy jacket with the hood. She would soon find out what was going on.

'I'm off to see Sacha, Gran,' she said, downstairs. 'Do you want me to bring anything back? A cappuccino and cake, maybe?'

Her grandmother grinned at her. 'You know me too well, lovey. Yes, that would be just the ticket. Thanks.'

Jools braced herself before opening the front door. The thunder of waves was incredibly loud but at least she was in little danger of being hit by flying stones now it was no longer high tide. She pulled her up hood against the rain and ran towards the café. By the time she reached the café door the spray from the waves and almost horizontal rain had soaked her jacket and everything below it, including her trainers. It was going to be uncomfortable sitting down in wet jeans.

She stepped inside the warm café, relieved to see only a few of the tables were occupied by some of the hardier locals. Two were deep in conversation, sitting at a window table, the glass steamy as they watched the storm raging outside and intermittently ate their food.

Jools scanned the room and spotted Sacha sitting at a table by the back wall. As she neared her friend, Jools noticed that her cheeks were wet and her eyes swollen. Alessandro was holding her hands in his. They looked up as she reached their table.

'What's happened?' Jools managed to ask. Her heart thumped rapidly as she waited for one of them to share what must surely be dreadful news. 'Are you both okay?'

Sacha took her hands from Alessandro's and, taking a crumpled tissue from her sleeve, blew her nose. 'Sorry,' she said, clearing her throat. She went to say something further, but fresh tears began streaming down her face and she covered her eyes, shaking her head slowly.

'Alessandro?' Jools looked at him. 'Tell me.'

He sighed heavily. 'Jack,' he said, his voice barely above a whisper. 'Sacha, she discovers that her brother is on the boat with Tony. Jan, from up the hill, came in for a cup of tea earlier. Her husband was down at the Lifeboat Station when the May Day call came through and confirmed that it was for Tony's boat.'

It took Jools a second to connect Jack with the stricken trawler. 'Oh, right.' She pulled out a seat next to her friend and after taking off her wet jacket, slipped an arm around her friend's shaking shoulders. 'Do we know for sure that it's Tony's boat? Could they not simply have pulled into one of the coves away from the worst of the storm?'

'I wish that was the case,' Sacha said in between sniffs.

Jools's heart sank. 'And you know for certain that Jack's on it?'

Sacha nodded. 'He asked me to let Bella know when he left.'

Jools couldn't understand why Jack didn't send Bella a text. As if Sacha had followed her train of thought, her friend added, 'He couldn't find his phone. He probably left it at Bella's the last time he was there.'

Jools wasn't surprised. Jack was always busy, going from one place to the next, leaving things behind as he focused on the next project. She pictured Bella trying to comfort her mother earlier. 'Were you able to get a message to Bella?'

Sacha shook her head. 'No, not yet. I can't bring myself to do it. Alessandro bumped into her and Claire earlier. He said that Claire was already distraught about Tony. Apparently, they had a row last night and she's saying it's all her fault if he dies and she doesn't see him again. I don't know how they'll cope with knowing Claire was right about it being Tony's boat, never mind that Jack is with him. Claire needs Bella to be strong and I can't imagine that happening when she hears that Jack's missing too.'

Jools admitted that she was probably right. 'But if we keep this from them, then they'll be upset. They have a right to know, don't they? However much it might upset them.'

'Yes. Or, maybe no. Oh, I don't know,' Sacha said, giving in to sobs.

Jools wished she could be more helpful. She was worried and upset about Marius but at least he was trained for emergencies and was on the safer of the two vessels. She wanted to do the right thing by her friends, but couldn't decide what that might be.

The three of them looked up when the café door opened. Lexi and Oliver hurried inside. Jools waved, relieved to see them. 'We're over here.'

'We heard what's going on,' Lexi said when they reached the table. 'We thought we'd come and see if there's anything we can do.' She tilted her head at Oliver who was standing with a hand on her shoulder.

'Yes, just say the word.' He didn't seem to notice his wet hair was dripping onto his jacket.

'Thank you for coming down,' Sacha said, drying her eyes on a tissue. 'Get those wet coats off and I'll make some hot drinks.'

Lexi shook her head. 'You'll do nothing of the sort. We can make our own drinks, can't we, Oliver?'

'I'll do it.' He pulled out a chair for Lexi to take a seat next to Alessandro. 'I'll leave you to catch up and go and make us something.'

Jools watched Lexi and Oliver smile at each other. It was obvious that they were very much in love and it warmed her to see her friend with a man who seemed to reciprocate her feelings. Once he'd gone, she explained to her friends what had happened, including their quandary about whether to let Bella know that Jack was on the boat with Tony.

'I think they should be told,' Lexi said with certainty. 'We all know what it's like to hear bad news, but wouldn't it be worse if we were the last to know?'

Jools and Sacha exchanged glances.

'I agree,' Jools said, glad that her friend had come to this conclusion so quickly. 'I don't mind going to speak to Claire and Bella. You've got the café to look after, Sacha, and everyone knows to contact you here when Jack and Tony are rescued.'

'Oliver and I could go, if you need to get back to your gran,' Lexi offered. 'Or we could come with you to Bella's?'

'Thank you. I'd like that.' Despite putting on a brave face, Jools was only just staying calm. If Bella and Claire became hysterical, she might crumble and join them.

'Then that's what we'll do.' Lexi took Jools's and Sacha's hands in hers and gave them a gentle squeeze.

'I will need to drop off a takeaway cappuccino and slice of cake to Gran on the way though,' Jools said. 'She won't like missing out on her treat.'

Oliver returned with his and Lexi's drinks and a hot chocolate for Jools. 'I thought you could do with one of these,' he grinned. Then looking at Sacha, added, 'I've slipped the money behind the counter.'

'There was no need to do that,' Sacha said.

'It wouldn't feel right if I didn't.' Oliver carried a chair over from the nearest table and sat next to Lexi. 'Have you decided what the next step is then?'

'Yes,' Lexi said, warming her hands on her mug of hot chocolate. 'You and I are going to accompany Jools to Bella's and fill her and Claire in on the current situation.'

They finished their drinks and Sacha insisted on making up the takeaway for Jools's grandmother. 'It's on the house,' she argued when Jools insisted on paying for it. 'Please. I want her to have this. It's the least I can do if you're going to speak to Bella when it should be me.'

Jools knew better than to argue when Sacha was determined about something. She gave her friend a tight hug, then picked up the bagged cake and the cardboard cup of cappuccino and dashed to the bookshop in the rain with Lexi and Oliver.

'Here you go, Gran,' she said when they arrived, pulling a tissue from the box under the counter to wipe rain from the lid of the coffee cup. Not wishing to concern her grandmother, Jools decided not to tell her about Jack until she returned. She knew how much her gran loved Jools's friends and all the 'young ones' as she called them, who she had watched grow up and had probably babysat for at some point. 'I won't be too long.'

Her grandmother frowned. 'Is something the matter, love?'

Jools didn't like to lie but didn't want her grandmother

worrying before they'd heard any news. 'We're popping over to Bella's to check if Claire's calmed down yet. Hopefully, I won't be too long.'

'All right, love. You take your time. Thank you for bringing refreshments, it's just what I need for a stormy afternoon.'

Jools went to stroke Teddy's head as he sulked in his small bed in a corner of the shop. She knew how much he hated bad weather and hoped she would be able to take him to the beach for a run around tomorrow.

The three of them left the bookshop and ran to Bella's cottage where Jools banged on the front door, willing her friend to hurry and let them inside out of the driving rain.

The door opened and Bella frowned, seeing the three of them standing there, before hurriedly stepping back and waving them inside. 'What are you doing here? You look like you've been swimming fully clothed.'

'It feels like we have been,' Jools said, shaking to rid herself of the worst of the drips. 'It's lovely and warm in here, Bella.'

'The log burner's going full pelt today. What a difference in the weather to yesterday.' Bella held out her hand to take their wet coats. 'I'll hang these up and move the coat stand closer to the fire. Give them a chance to dry before you go back out there.'

'Thanks,' Jools said, shooting a concerned glance at Lexi. Did Lexi want her to break the news to Bella, or did she want to do it? She wasn't sure, but they had to tell her gently. At least Claire wasn't in the room, Jools thought with relief. It would be much easier to tell Bella without her mother descending into hysterics again.

Lexi took off her coat and handed it to Jools, who hung it up next to her own, while Oliver shrugged off his dripping jacket.

'We've come here to talk to you,' Lexi said, taking Bella by the hand and leading her towards two big armchairs placed in front of the log burner to make the most of the heat.

Bella looked at Oliver and then Jools as she sat down. 'What's happened? Do you know something about Tony?'

Jools shook her head. 'Not yet,' she said, sitting on the arm of Bella's chair.

'What then?'

Lexi, sitting opposite, leant forward. 'We do know the RNLI are out helping Tony's fishing boat.' Jools was relieved her friend was giving Bella the good news first. 'But we've just heard from Sacha that Jack went out with him this morning.'

'What?' Bella stared at Lexi. 'You mean on Tony's boat?'

Lexi nodded. 'That's right.'

Although Lexi's tone was calm, Jools saw the colour drain from Bella's face before she jumped up. 'Jack is on the boat?' she cried. 'Not my Jack?' She burst into tears and began pacing the floor.

Jools leapt up and rushed to her. 'Try not to panic,' she said, gripping Bella's arms. 'Marius and his crew are extremely well-trained. They've done this loads of times before.'

Bella panted, her eyes darting in different directions before finally settling on Jools. 'Then why are they not back yet?' She wrenched away. 'Surely if they're going to save them, they would have done it by now. They've been out there for hours.'

'Jools is right,' Lexi soothed. 'Come and sit down and try not to panic. I'm sure they'll be fine.'

'You don't know that though, do you?' Bella wept. 'How could you?'

'No, they don't,' Oliver said calmly, standing in front of the log-burner. 'But my brother was in the RNLI for a time. If anyone knows the waters around this island it's Marius and his crew.'

'Come and sit down,' Jools said, hoping to reason with her

friend before Claire got wind of their conversation and came to join them.

Bella stared at Jools, her eyes shiny with tears that ran down her cheeks. 'I don't know what I'd do without Jack,' she said.

Jools knew they were very much in love, but Bella had been so independent before she and Jack got together a few months ago. It was strange to see her friend so fearful of being without him. Not that she could bear anything happening to the lovely, fun man she had grown up with. She opened her mouth to say something when she noticed Bella's hands were resting on her flat stomach. She caught Jools's eye and instantly looked away before meekly sitting back down in front of the fire.

Jools's mind whirled. Surely, she was imagining things? Before she had time to think anything further, Claire entered the room looking slightly sleepy and rubbing her eyes.

'Why didn't you wake me?' she grumbled, giving each of them a shaky smile before noticing Bella was upset. She walked over to sit on the arm of the chair and put an arm around her daughter's shoulders. 'What's happened?'

Lexi explained about Jack. 'I'm sorry. We didn't know you were still here, otherwise we would have woken you,' she said. Jools wasn't sure she was being completely truthful. 'We thought Bella would want to know.'

Claire immediately burst into noisy tears and Jools was relieved they'd had a few minutes alone with Bella to speak to her in private.

'Hopefully, we'll have some news soon,' Oliver offered.

'Yes,' Jools said. 'I'm sure we'll hear something very soon.'

'Why don't I make us something to drink,' Lexi said, standing up.

Oliver followed her through to the small kitchen while Bella consoled her weeping mother and Jools desperately hoped they would hear something soon. If Bella was pregnant, as she suspected, the last thing she needed was to be in a state about Jack.

Did Jack even know? Maybe Bella hadn't had the chance to tell him yet. Should she say something? Maybe she should ask Bella outright if she was pregnant. All her friend had done was rest her hands on her stomach for a second or two. It was nothing much, but she had a feeling her suspicions were right. *Please bring them back safely, Marius.*

'Mum,' Bella said, leaning her head against Claire.

'Yes, sweetie?'

'I'm sorry for making a fuss about you wanting to marry Tony.' She gave a shaky sigh. 'I want you to know that I am happy for you both and won't do anything at all to stand in your way.'

Claire wiped her eyes on her sleeve and bent to kiss the top of Bella's head. 'Thank you,' she said. 'I appreciate you saying so.'

Bella slid an arm around her mother's waist. 'When the guys get back, I'm going to apologise to Tony and tell him I'm happy he's marrying you and that I'm looking forward to having two younger step-siblings.'

Jools watched Claire's mouth draw back into a smile. 'I know you are. We'll make this work somehow.'

'Talking of Tony's children,' Jools said, suddenly wondering where they were. 'Who's looking after them right now?' She hoped they weren't at home alone, forgotten about in the panic.

'They're at school,' Claire said. 'They only had yesterday off because it was Liberation Day but they're back in class again today. Thankfully.' She gave Jools a concerned look with red-rimmed eyes, then looked at the carriage clock on the mantelpiece. 'I'm going to have to collect them in a couple of hours, if Tony's not back by then.' She sat silently for a moment. 'In fact, I'll have to think about what to feed them tonight. I don't think I have anything much in the cupboards. I intended doing a food shop this morning but with everything that's happened I completely forgot about it.' She sounded close to tears again.

'It's fine,' Oliver said, coming back from the kitchen. 'I'm sure Lexi and I can look after them for a couple of hours. We'll take them to Sacha's café for supper, if that's all right with you?'

Claire's eyebrows almost disappeared into her messy fringe. 'You would do that?'

'We'd be happy to,' Lexi answered, following Oliver with a tray of steaming mugs. 'In fact, I'm sure you'll want to spend a little time alone with Tony when he gets back.' She put the tray on the coffee table and hesitated before adding,' We can pick them up from school too, then you won't have to worry about them until later. They're at the parish school, up the hill, aren't they?'

Claire nodded and gave a watery smile. 'Yes, that's right. The same place you girls and Jack went to.'

At the mention of Jack's name, Bella burst into fresh tears. 'Why haven't we heard from Marius yet?'

Jools wondered the same thing. She had no idea how long a rescue operation took, and doubted there was an average time. It would be longer when the weather was this bad. Worry coursed through her. She shook her head, pushing away disturbing thoughts. She had no intention of adding to the drama of the day. Instead, she would focus on being positive, for as long as she could manage. She picked up the nearest mug and took a sip of strong tea. Taking her cue, Oliver picked up another and handed it to Lexi before resuming his place in front of the fire.

'Has anyone heard if Barry is still with Betty?' Jools asked, wanting to change the subject.

'I sent her a message,' Claire said, one arm still around Bella as her daughter's sobs subsided. 'Just before going for a lie down. She said she's perfectly happy and cosy at home with her cat and not to worry about her.'

'Good.' Jools was glad she didn't need to go and visit Betty yet. The old lady knew her far too well and was too intuitive to not pick up on her concern for Jack. She didn't want to upset Betty by admitting Jack and Tony were missing – not so soon after the fun of Liberation Day.

Bella lifted her mug of tea and blew on the steaming liquid, then put it down with a wince. She caught Jools watching her and immediately looked away, and Jools knew for certain her friend was pregnant and didn't want to say anything until she had told Jack. She hoped fervently Jack would soon be home to enjoy this, probably, unexpected news. For now, though, she felt a burst of happiness for her friend, the first of them to fall pregnant.

She willed Marius to do all he could to bring Jack and Tony home again.

12

Bella and Claire insisted that they were fine to be left alone to wait for news of Tony and Jack. Claire gave Oliver the keys to Tony's house and the name of the teachers so he and Lexi could collect the children from the parish school. She promised to give the headmistress a call to let her know they were coming.

Jools, satisfied that there was nothing further that she could do for Bella and her mother, returned to the bookshop to have supper with her grandmother. As they sat down to a shepherd's pie, she finally told her grandmother what had happened.

'I did hear something late morning about a lost fishing boat from one of my customers,' Gran admitted.

'Why didn't you say anything?' Jools had been trying to protect her grandmother when all along she'd known that Jack and Tony were missing. Even though the bad weather had kept most people away from the shop, someone was bound to have mentioned it.

'Because I knew you were trying not to upset me and I was happy for you to carry on,' her gran said, serving more carrots and peas at the small kitchen table. 'I knew you wanted to support your friends and didn't want you feeling you had to keep popping back to check up on me.'

'Gran, really. I do wish you'd told me.'

Her gran pushed her fork into the meat and gravy on her plate. 'It's done now, so stop worrying about it.' After swallowing a mouthful of food, she added, 'No news in the last hour?'

Jools shook her head, trying not to give in to her fear. It had been hours since Marius received the emergency shout and she couldn't stand not knowing how he was faring. She looked across the table at her gran and saw that she wasn't the only one struggling to pretend that everything was all right. Jools forced herself to keep eating. Gran had spent a while cooking this delicious meal. The least she could do was appreciate her hard work and try to enjoy it.

Her phone vibrated against her hip. Jools gasped and almost dropped her fork. 'Sorry, Gran,' she said, aware how much her grandmother disliked people using their mobiles during a meal. 'You don't mind if I get this, do you?' She leaned back and extracted her still paint-smeared phone from her jeans pocket.

'Carry on. We're both desperate to hear news.'

Jools stared at the screen. She didn't recognise the number. With shaking hands, she answered the call. 'Hello?'

'Jools, hi.'

'Marius, it's so good to hear from you,' Jools had never been more relieved to hear someone's voice. 'You're okay?'

'I am. So are the others.' He sounded exhausted. 'I can't talk for long but wanted you to know that I was fine. Can you let Bella and Claire know that Jack and Tony are safe and well? There were a few issues, but nothing to worry about. Will you speak to them?'

'Yes, I'll go straight over.' Jools swallowed the lump in her throat determined not to cry. 'You're really OK?'

'I'm tired, but I'll be fine after a shower and a good night's sleep.' He was silent for a second. 'I'd better go now though. Lots to do.'

'Of course. Thank you so much for calling me, Marius. I really appreciate it.'

'No problem at all. I wanted to talk to you anyway. Bye, Jools. I'll speak to you again as soon as I can.'

She rang off and put her phone on the table. Her heart was pounding and tears were running down her face. 'They're all fine.'

Gran tore off a sheet of kitchen towel and handed it to her. 'There, there, lovey. I'm so pleased.' There was a tremor in her voice. 'Why don't you pop your supper in the oven and run over to let Claire and Bella know? It'll still be warm if you're not too long.'

'I will, Gran. Thanks.'

Moments later, Jools was knocking on Bella's front door. Within seconds it flew open and Claire stood there, an expectant look on her face.

'You've heard something?'

Jools nodded and stepped inside. 'They're both fine,' she said, not wanting to keep her in suspense for a second longer. 'Marius just phoned me. He didn't have time to say much but wanted me to let you know that Tony and Jack are perfectly fine. I'm sure they'll be home soon, but the most important thing is, they've been rescued and are safe and well.'

As Claire stumbled, Jools instinctively stepped forward to catch her. 'Come and sit down,' she said, leading her into the living room, to the armchair where Bella had sat earlier.

'I don't know what's come over me,' Claire said, blushing. 'I'm not usually this flaky.'

Bella ran through from the kitchen. 'What's happened?'

'It's fine, they've been rescued,' Jools said. 'They're both okay.'

Bella's hands flew to her cheeks. 'Oh, thank goodness.' A smile broke over her face as she looked at her mother. 'They're safe, Mum.'

Claire smiled back, colour returning to her face.

Jools hugged Bella and whispered, 'I'm so happy for you.'

'What a day.' Claire gave Jools a knowing glance. 'You seem pretty happy too,' she said, dabbing her red, puffy eyes with a tissue. 'You're quite taken with that glass blowing chap who went out to rescue them, aren't you?'

Jools gave her a sheepish smile. 'We don't even know each other that well, but there is something about him that I can't help feeling attracted to.'

'Good.' Claire said. 'He's a lovely chap from what I've seen and if he's brought back my Tony and Bella's Jack then he's got my eternal devotion.'

Bella laughed, her relief obvious. 'I think that might be a little of an over-reaction, don't you think, Mum?'

'Not at all.' Claire closed her eyes and sighed. 'Well, maybe just a little bit, but I am grateful to the lad and to the crew who were with him. They must all be exhausted.'

'So am I,' Bella said. 'But happy too.' She looked up at Jools and smiled. 'Thanks for coming over to tell us so quickly, Jools. We really appreciate it.'

'It was my pleasure.' After giving Bella a final squeeze, she walked to the door. 'I'd better get back to Gran and finish my supper. Try to relax tonight, if you can.'

As she walked to the bookshop, Jools realised how utterly drained she felt by the emotion she had been trying to suppress throughout the day, and from trying to remain strong when all she had wanted to do was sit at her living room window and watch out for Marius's return.

He was safe now though. All she needed to do was go home and enjoy Gran's tasty supper, knowing she would be seeing him again soon. She decided that whatever happened next, she was going to speak to Finn and tell him that there was no future for them. She would just have to find a way to let him down gently.

13

Jools was too busy the following day to think too much about Finn. While she had been out the previous evening, letting Bella and Claire know that their partners were safe, Gran had printed off an email.

'It came in yesterday afternoon.'

Jools read the message on the sheet of paper. 'It says I've to phone someone called Emma.'

'That's right. I called her and she told me it's about a book you've been searching for. I said I'd pass on the message and ask you to give her a ring, but I forgot in all the excitement.' Her gran raised her eyebrows. 'Am I right in thinking that this is Alan's book?'

'It is,' Jools said, placing the piece of paper on the kitchen worktop where she had been buttering her toast. 'I've been putting out feelers for a few weeks, hoping to locate a copy. I thought it would be a lovely surprise.'

When Gran didn't say anything, Jools stopped spreading butter and looked up at her, noticing her eyes were shiny. 'What?'

Gran shook her head and patted her chest a couple of times.

'It's just that you're such a kind girl. Your mother and father would have been so proud of you, do you know that?'

Jools put the knife on her plate and went to hug her grandmother. 'That's because I've had the best example to follow.' She took a steadying breath. There had been more than enough emotion over the past twenty-four hours, as far as she was concerned.

Gran stepped back and laughed. 'Honestly, we're so soft sometimes.'

Jools carried on buttering her toast, which had gone cold. 'We are, but we don't want people to know about it, do we?' she smiled.

'No,' Gran agreed. 'Our tough reputations would be ruined forever if that happened.'

Jools sat and ate her breakfast while Gran took the stairlift down to the shop. After she'd finished and washed up, she called Emma and explained who she was. 'Am I to understand that you've managed to locate a copy of Dan Blake's book, *Message for a Spy?*'

'Let me just check,' said the gentle voice at the other end of the phone. Jools heard some rustling and waited for the woman to speak again. 'That's correct. I was wondering if you'd like me to post it to you.'

'That would be amazing,' Jools said. 'Please let me know the cost of the book and postage and I'll reimburse you immediately.' It occurred to her that Alan might ask where the copy was found, so she asked Emma.

'In my shop,' she said simply. 'A friend of mine mentioned over lunch that he had seen a post online that said you were looking for a copy and to email you at Boardwalk Books.' Jools had almost forgotten she'd put out a plea on her Facebook page. 'I see it's a second-hand bookshop, like mine,' Emma continued. 'I had a look at your website. The shop looks very pretty and the location is lovely and I love that it's so close to the sea.'

'Thank you,' Jools said, pleased. 'We're very lucky to live here. It's my grandmother's shop really, but I live with her and help out when I can.'

'Is she the lady I spoke to yesterday?'

'That's right.'

'Well, I'm really happy to have been able to help you with this,' Emma said. 'If I visit Jersey, I'll be sure to look you up.'

'Please do that,' Jools said. 'It would be lovely to be able to thank you in person. It was such a long shot. I didn't really expect to find the book so quickly. Thanks again.'

Happy with her success, Jools ran downstairs to share the news with her grandmother.

'How did your call go?'

Jools leant across the counter and grinned. 'She's got a copy of *Message for a Spy* and is going to put it in the post. I can't wait to pass it on to Alan.' She picked up a pile of books and began sorting them before putting them back on the shelves. 'It's a shame I don't have it already. I could give it to him at book club tonight.'

Gran laughed. 'You're always such an impatient little thing.'

'Gran, I'm twenty-nine. I'm hardly little any more.' She pulled out a small stepladder to reach the higher shelves and put away the rest of the books.

'I didn't say young,' Gran teased. 'I said little. You are, but it suits you.'

Jools smiled as she stepped down. 'If you say so.' She wondered when her gran would see her as the grown woman she was. She was probably concerned about Jools moving out of the flat above the shop at some point, but she had no intention of going very far.

Right now, she wanted more than anything to see Marius but wasn't sure how he would feel after the rescue operation the day before. Should she call or send him a text? No. She wanted to see for herself that he was fine and uninjured. She decided to pay him a visit.

* * *

Jools caught the next bus, which took her up the hill and most of the way to Devil's Hole. She didn't want to bother Lexi by asking to borrow the car and it would do her good to walk through the lanes to Marius's workshop. *What if he's out?* If he wasn't there, she would simply have to walk back.

Grateful the weather was mild, if overcast, she arrived at the at the Devil's Hole car park ten minutes later, only slightly out of breath. It was silent apart from a rustling of leaves as a soft breeze pushed through the surrounding trees. She couldn't see if anything was open. There were no lights on in The Priory Inn. It was out of the way but popular with holidaymakers who would park up and walk down the many steps to where the devil's statue, that gave the place its name, rose out of the sea like an aggressive titan.

Jools walked to the wooden door of Marius's studio and stood for a moment before turning the handle and stepping inside. In front of her were shelves of coloured glass vases, ornaments and pictures; a treasure trove of beautifully crafted gifts. There didn't seem to be anyone around. Surely he must be here if the door was unlocked.

'Hello?' she said timidly.

'Jools.' Marius's voice came from behind her and was so unexpected that Jools jumped, her heart leaping to her throat in surprise. She spun around on her heels to face him.

Marius laughed, his eyes wide as he reached forward to stop her toppling against the display cabinet. 'Hey, steady on,' he said, wincing. 'I'm so sorry. I didn't mean to shock you. I thought you'd seen me.'

'I'm fine. I think,' she said with a laugh. 'But you did give me a start. I didn't think there was anyone here. It all seems so peaceful and quiet.'

'Until I bellowed your name,' he laughed.

'Yes,' she said, giving him a playful punch to his shoulder. 'Until you nearly frightened me half to death.'

'Look, why don't you come through to the back and we can sit in comfort, or if you prefer, we can go to the pub for a spot of lunch? Or I could make us something here. It would only be cheese on toast, I'm afraid. I don't have much else in.'

As if on cue, her stomach grumbled loudly. 'It seems that I'm hungry.' She patted her stomach. 'I'm happy to stay here, if that's okay. I quite fancy trying out your culinary skills.' She smiled at him, enjoying their comfortable companionship.

'I'll turn the sign to closed just in case someone arrives. They can always ring the bell if they want to see some glass work.' He locked the door and motioned for her to follow him through to the back of the workshop and up the narrow wooden stairs to his studio flat.

Jools was fascinated to see where he lived and wasn't disappointed. Compared to downstairs with its low ceiling, displays, furnace and working station, the flat was much brighter. The furnishings were sparse, with a table and four chairs next to a small window, a neat kitchenette and a corner with an overstuffed sofa and television in front of it. There was a curtained-off area that she presumed might be where he slept.

'This is it,' he announced. 'My living, eating and there is my sleeping area. The door we passed on the landing is my shower room. It isn't much, but I'm comfortable here and as you saw my commute to work is about fifteen steps, so I can't complain.'

Jools laughed. 'Your commute is similar to mine. It makes travelling to work, especially in bad weather, very much more enjoyable than if I worked in town.'

'My thoughts exactly.' He gazed at her thoughtfully. 'I can't imagine you working anywhere other than the bookshop, or doing your painting.'

'It does suit me there perfectly.'

'Right,' he said, pulling out one of the chairs nearest the window. 'You make yourself comfortable here unless you'd rather we sit on the sofa?'

'No,' she said, sitting and resting her hands on the old wooden table. 'This is a great vantage point to watch you cook.'

'Hah. Thankfully, it shouldn't take long so I won't have to worry about you judging me.'

'Cheese on toast isn't really cooking, is it?' she teased as he crouched to look for the cheese in a small fridge. She watched as he took a loaf of farmhouse bread from a wooden bread bin and a knife from the drawer.

'This could be the height of my cooking skills, for all you know,' he said, winking at her. 'How many slices would madam like, one, two, or maybe three?'

'Two please.'

As he worked, Jools took in the photos on a small bookcase. 'Are those of your family?'

He nodded. 'I have more packed away but wanted to keep this place as simple as possible. I think its lack of clutter helps keep my head clear to come up with new designs.' He turned on the grill and placed four pieces of bread and cheese on the rack. 'Does that make any sense?'

'It does,' she admitted. 'Although where I live with Gran has far too much stuff packed into it. She's lived there for decades. I should probably offer to help her go through it,' she said.

'Maybe she likes the clutter.'

Jools looked at his gentle face, so handsome and friendly. He had a calmness that gave her the sense that everything would be all right. His pale blond hair, which was longer than she usually liked on men, was somehow very masculine on him. She couldn't help thinking how the lightness of his hair accentuated his dark blue eyes. *Is this what Vikings looked like?* Her heart constricted to think that if things had turned out differently yesterday, she might not have seen him again. If it hadn't been for his bravery, and that of his crew, Claire would not now be planning her wedding and Bella ... her friend might have lost the love of her life.

Marius gazed at her and his mouth drew back slowly into a smile. He folded his arms across his chest, the amusement on his face suddenly vanishing.

'What is it?'

'You know, yesterday when we were battling to get home through that horrendous sea, I imagined you being here like this. It helped keep me going.'

'Was it dreadful?' She hoped it wasn't a stupid question.

'No.' Seeing her surprise, he added, 'Only because there were no casualties. That's always a good result. But it was a long and tiring day and for a time it got a bit hairy. Only for a short while though.' He shook his head. 'I shouldn't be sharing this with you, sorry.'

Jools got up and closed the distance between them. 'I've been wanting to do this for ages,' she said, wrapping him tightly in a hug. 'Ever since your phone call, saying that you'd been called out to sea.' She breathed in the freshly showered scent of his skin and closed her eyes, relishing the moment. 'I'm so relieved you're all OK.'

Marius slid his arms around her waist and pulled her against his firm chest. They stood in silence for a few minutes, breathing in sync until Marius kissed the top of her head. Jools leant back and looked up at him to check he was okay. He gazed down for a moment, before pressing his lips to hers in a passionate kiss.

Finally, coming up for air, they smiled at each other.

'I'm so happy you're here, Jools.'

'I wasn't sure if I should just pop in,' she said. 'But after what happened yesterday, I couldn't help myself.'

'I'm glad.' A smell of burning filled the air. Marius widened his eyes. 'I think I've just ruined lunch.'

14

The following afternoon Jools joined Bella, Sacha and Lexi on a beach walk. Lexi drove them to St Ouen's Bay, along Five Mile Road. Jools wasn't sure if the road was actually that long, but the beach certainly seemed to be when the tide was out.

Lexi parked her car at the bottom of L'Etacq hill. Jools got out and stood for a moment, gazing across the expanse of pale golden sand to La Pulente. She loved the wild bay with its sand dunes and the iconic La Rocco Tower, one of thirty coastal towers built around the coastline out of local granite, standing proudly on a tiny islet in the bay. People referred to them as Martello towers, despite them being a different design, and this incorrect naming was a bugbear of her grandmother's.

There were several cafés nestled along the sea wall, and across the bay, a view of the majestic lighthouse at Corbiere.

'I'm not sure Teddy will be able to walk all that way and back again,' Jools said quietly.

Bella nudged her. 'You mean *you* don't have the stamina, more like.'

Jools pulled a face, but her friend was right. After checking the time, she bent to unclip Teddy's lead and threw his tennis ball for him. He was used to being off his lead throughout the winter but the rules changed at the end of April. During the summer, he could only run free before half past ten in the morning or after six in the evening.

'How are you and your mum feeling after yesterday, Bella?' Lexi asked as they all slipped off their flip flops and began walking. Sacha went ahead, throwing Teddy's ball again when he brought it back.

'I kept waking through the night, needing to check that Jack was actually there and that I hadn't dreamt he'd been saved.'

Jools shuddered, recalling her friend's terrible fright the day before. 'You poor thing. How does Jack feel after everything that happened?'

'I was wondering the same thing,' Sacha said, joining them. 'Do you think he'll want to go out on Tony's boat again any time soon?' It was clear from her tone that Sacha was hoping her brother would decide to remain on terra firma for the foreseeable future.

Bella bent to pick up a yellow cockle shell. 'He insists he's fine and that he can't let Tony down if he ever needs him.' She sighed. 'He says, too, that the money comes in useful, though what for, I don't know.'

'Doesn't he make enough from his photo shoots?' Lexi asked. 'I thought he was doing so well.'

A red football rolled towards them and Jools ran forward, kicking it as hard as she could back to the group of teenagers playing on the beach. 'Ouch! That hurt more than I expected,' she groaned, rubbing her big toe for a couple of seconds before they resumed walking.

Bella smiled at Jools. 'I'd save kicking things for when you're wearing shoes.'

'I know that now,' Jools said, sticking out her tongue. 'Anyway, never mind my feet, what about Jack's photoshoots.'

'Well, he is booked in for quite a few, but you know Jack. He's not the type to enjoy standing still for hours in a studio.'

'Not that disciplined, you mean,' Sacha said. 'It isn't really Jack's thing, I know that, but surely the money he makes is worth it?'

Jools couldn't help feeling relieved that Jack, despite being semi-famous now, was the same local-surfer-boy and all-round chilled guy he had always been. 'What do you think about it, Bella?'

'I just want Jack to be happy. Obviously, I'd rather he was in a studio than on a fishing boat, but modelling has a short lifespan. As I know only too well, you have to keep yourself in top condition. I only have to think about my hands but poor Jack has to look great all the time.'

Jools and Lexi laughed. 'But he always does,' they said in unison, grinning at each other.

'I know,' Bella said, smiling. 'That's what I said to him.'

'If I know my brother, it's one thing to be in top condition because of his sporting activities, another entirely because someone *wants* him to look good.' Sacha rolled her eyes. 'He's a contrary devil when he wants to be.'

'That's it exactly,' Bella laughed. 'The first time they wanted to give him a spray tan at the studio, I thought he was going to have a fit.'

Jools pictured the look of horror on Jack's face and burst into giggles. The others joined in and for a minute or two none of them could do anything but fall against each other, laughing.

'I would have loved to have seen that,' Lexi giggled. 'Poor Jack.'

'Oi, Teddy!' Jools bellowed, spotting her gran's little dog running around the legs of the boys playing football. 'Sorry guys.

If you throw his tennis ball this way, he'll hopefully leave your ball alone.'

She watched as one of the boys ran and picked up the tennis ball and threw it in her direction.

'That little devil can be so naughty sometimes,' she said, relieved when Teddy came after his ball. 'Thank you.' she yelled with a wave.

'Who do you mean?' Lexi asked. 'The boys, or Teddy?'

Jools pulled a face at her friend. 'Oh, ha-ha.'

They began walking again.

'Never mind the boys and Teddy,' Sacha said. 'I want to know about Marius. Have you told him what a hero we all think he is?'

Jools looked from one face to the other as her friends waited for her to react. 'No.'

'I hope you told him how relieved Mum and I were though?' Bella asked.

'Yes, but I'm not going to say anything else, am I? I barely know him, and it would be odd if I was all gushing and telling him how wonderful he is.'

She felt Lexi's arm slip around her shoulder. 'Well, he is a hero,' Lexi said.

'He wasn't alone, you know. He was with a crew of other guys.'

'We know that, Jools. Look, we're only teasing.' Lexi narrowed her eyes. 'How are things going with the pair of you?'

Jools was used to hearing about her friends' love lives and wasn't used to talking about hers. She thought back to how Lexi and Oliver's relationship had begun and realised that, during the past year or so, they'd tended to be more private with their thoughts, especially at the beginning of the relationship. Jools hadn't been in a position to share much about her own partners, simply because there hadn't been much to share. She wasn't sure how much she should say now, but she was in a quandary about Finn and maybe her friends would have some useful advice.

She explained her concerns, detailing how she'd felt since Finn returned to the island. 'I don't want to let him down,' she explained. 'Not when he's come all this way to see me.'

Sacha frowned in her direction. 'I thought he'd come back because he promised Alessandro he'd be here to open the Isola Bella for the summer season.'

'Well, that too.' Sacha had a good point. He hadn't only come back for Jools, had he? 'But he was so upset when he saw me dancing with Marius.'

'Hey,' Bella said. 'You have every right to dance with whoever you choose and don't you think otherwise.'

'True,' Jools agreed. 'But don't you think Jack would be upset if he was the one to come back after a few months and find you having fun with someone else?'

Bella slowed down and gave Jools's question some thought. 'Probably. I suppose you and Marius did seem very happy in each other's company and there's a definite chemistry between you that I've never seen with you and Finn.'

Jools smiled to think that her friend had noticed. 'Do you really think so?'

'Which part?'

'About the chemistry.'

'Yes. There was a sort of brightness about you both.' She nodded. 'Don't you think that was why Finn reacted as he did? It makes sense to me, anyway.'

It made sense to her too, now she thought of it. Jools sighed. 'I think you have a point, Bella. And you, Sacha.'

'It's not as if you were in a relationship with Finn,' Lexi said. 'You don't owe him anything.'

'Still, I don't like to let anyone down.'

Sacha stopped walking and the others did the same. Jools watched as her three closest friends turned to face her.

'You're the most direct person out of the four of us,' Sacha said. 'It's a little disconcerting to see you feeling so ill at ease about saying what you want.'

'It is,' the other two agreed.

'But what should I do?' Jools knew she must seem ridiculous, asking her friends, but needed them to confirm that what she wanted to do was the right thing. 'Don't you think I should wait until Finn's been here a little longer before dumping him?'

Lexi winced. 'Wouldn't that be worse, if he has feelings for you?'

'You must do what you feel is right for you,' Sacha said. 'It's not for any of us to say. If your instincts are saying you should wait a little while, then do that. All I care about is that you follow your heart and don't end up with someone because it's what *they* want. You must do what is best for you, not anyone else.'

Bella nodded her agreement.

'Sacha's right,' said Lexi. 'Follow your heart.'

'OK. I will,' Jools said, happy that her friends wanted what was best for her. She needed to get things out into the open and have *the* conversation with Finn.

She heard yelling and saw Teddy running back and forth, trying to catch the football again. It was far too big for his mouth, despite him doing his best to bite into the plastic.

'Teddy, come here. *Now!*' The dog's ears pricked up when he heard his name, but although he hesitated for an instant, he continued to bite at the ball. 'Bugger! Now I've got to go and get him,' Jools said, breaking into a run. Why had she agreed to bring him? He was always so naughty. 'You're going on your lead now,' she said as she neared him. When he ignored her, she bent her knees and patted them to encourage him closer. 'Come on, Teddy.

Here, boy.' When he continued to ignore her, she rummaged around in the pockets of her shorts, hoping to find something to distract him other than a plastic bag and a square of kitchen roll. 'A-ha!' she shouted jubilantly, producing a bite-sized piece of one of his favourite treats. 'Look! What's this?'

Teddy immediately forgot the football and ran up to her, allowing her to clip his lead back onto his collar while he sat patiently, waiting for his treat. She popped it into his mouth and shook her head. 'Now we've got to find your tennis ball.'

'Here it is, lady,' one of the boys called, throwing it towards her.

'Thank you.' She picked up the ball and pushed it into her pocket, holding tightly to Teddy's lead. 'Right, now you're going to walk slowly next to me.'

Her friends caught up with her and they all linked arms.

Lexi grinned at Jools. 'We've all been saying what a lovely couple you and Marius make.'

'I hope when you break the news to Finn that he doesn't go back to the Caribbean, or wherever it was, before the season's over,' Sacha said. 'Poor Alessandro is busy on a dig and won't be too happy about having to start looking for a replacement to run the gelateria.'

'If he does though, let me know,' Bella said.

Jools felt a warm glow, sensing what Bella was about to say.

Sacha looked at Bella. 'But why would you be interested?'

'Because,' Bella said, winking at Sacha, 'If Finn *does* leave, I'm sure Jack would be the perfect manager for Isola Bella.'

'Are you?'

Jools wasn't sure why Sacha seemed so surprised by the suggestion, it was obvious to her and obviously to Bella.

Bella caught Jools's eye and grinned. Then turning her attention back to Sacha, said, 'He's great with customers, for one thing. Also, he has experience, having helped you run your café, so knows all about the money and ordering side of things. And if he worked for Alessandro it would mean he could forget about going out fishing with Tony.'

'Because he wouldn't have the time to do it, you mean?' Sacha looked thoughtful.

'Yes, exactly.'

'But what about Tony?' Jools said, feeling a little sorry for him. 'Who would help out on the boat?'

Bella frowned. 'Ah, I hadn't thought of that. No. Maybe we should leave things as they are for the time being.' She smiled at Jools, a mischievous twinkle in her eyes. 'Or at least until Jools finishes with Finn.'

'Maybe leave it for a little while then,' Lexi suggested. 'Surely there's no rush.'

'I'll have to think about it,' Jools said, a little confused by what she should do. 'And don't forget, Tony has a wedding to pay for, so he'll need all the money he can earn over the next few months. He's going to need Jack's help, or if not his, then someone else's.'

'True.' As Jools listened to her friends talking, she mulled over how her telling Finn they had no future as a couple might make things more difficult for Tony. She didn't want that on her conscience. Tony was a kind man who had gone through more than enough grief in the past couple of years. Losing his wife had nearly broken him, she recalled Betty saying the previous year. She remembered how he took his two children for supper at the café a few times in the week to try to cheer them up. It couldn't be easy being a single father when you were used to your wife being a stay-at-home mum.

Lexi turned to walk slowly backwards as she faced her friends. 'When are Tony and your mum planning on getting married? Do they know yet? Will it be soon?'

'You seem keen to know,' Sacha said.

'No, I'm just interested, that's all. We'll all be invited, won't we? We'll want to help Claire prepare for it, at least.'

Jools smiled and nodded with her friends, but couldn't help thinking that maybe Claire and Tony didn't need or want their help. 'Who knows?' she said. 'Maybe they intend to go away somewhere special, or have a small ceremony with just Bella and Tony's two children there?'

'Whatever they've decided, I've no idea,' Bella told them. 'All I know is that Mum is so relieved to have Tony safely home that if she doesn't get him down that aisle very soon, she'll explode. She was hysterical yesterday when she didn't hear from him. Then, when we found out that he and Jack were potentially lost at sea, I thought she was going to have some sort of fainting attack. My mum is always so chilled about everything. I've never seen her that way.' Bella sighed. 'At least I know without any doubt that she adores Tony and that she really does want to settle down with him. He's not one of her temporary fancies.'

'Poor Claire,' Jools said, recalling how terrified the poor woman had been the day before and how relieved she had been, almost to the point of collapse, when Jools had let her know that Tony and Jack were safe. 'I hated seeing her in such a state. I'd always thought her quite...' She didn't want to say the word *shallow* as it came across as mean and she liked Claire, very much. But she had always been a fickle person.

'Fickle?' Bella suggested, as if she'd read Jools's mind.

Jools smiled. 'That was your word, not mine.'

15

A few days later, Jools took the post from their regular postman, excited to see a book-shaped parcel with a Sussex postmark on it.

She still hadn't found the time to go and speak to Finn. She was unsure what to say and, as she hadn't heard from him, decided to leave it for now. After her lunch and kiss with Marius, she had been kept busy, helping Gran with the shop and working on the siren painting.

She had received a text from Sacha, letting her know that the mysterious buyer who had bought the paintings from the café wanted several more of the beach and the lighthouse. Jools wanted to make the most of having so much work, hoping it would lead to more commissions.

Now, she was sure she had received Alan's book and saw it as good reason to focus on something else for the time being.

'It's here,' she cheered, taking the post through to the shop and placing the rest of it onto the counter for her grandmother to look through. Jools waved the package in the air and then hurriedly opened it.

She gazed at the yellow front with its dark blue wording and the title *Message for a Spy* by Dan Blake at the bottom on the cover. 'I wonder why he's so intent on finding a copy of this particular book?'

'I've no idea, but it did seem important to him.'

'Let me have a look?' Her grandmother held out her hand and Jools passed the book to her.

She watched as Gran studied the book and turned it over to read the blurb on the back. 'I'm thrilled you've found the book, lovey, and I know Alan will be delighted to have a copy but if I'm honest with you, it doesn't look very intriguing to me. It's all about the cold war and I've never been remotely interested in that sort of thing, having lived through those dark times.'

Jools nodded. 'It's not really the sort of book I would be interested in reading either, but I think he'll be happy that I've managed to get this for him.'

She watched as Gran slowly opened the back cover. She stared at it for a moment and then gasped.

'What is it?' Jools asked anxiously. She waited for her grandmother to reply and hoped she wasn't in any pain. Jools knew only too well how much her grandmother hated it when she fussed over her.

Her grandmother shook her head slowly. 'Well, I never,' she murmured almost to herself.

Confused, Jools realised it wasn't pain that was causing her grandmother to react in this way but something else entirely. 'What is it, Gran?'

Her grandmother held up the book with one hand and pointed to the black and white photo on the inner sleeve of the dust jacket. 'Do you recognise that man?'

Jools had never heard of Dan Blake and couldn't see why her

grandmother would expect her to know what he looked like. 'What?'

'Just look at the photo and tell me if the man in it reminds you of anyone.'

Aware that it was easier to do as her grandmother insisted than waste time arguing with her, Jools bent to have a closer look at the photograph. 'No. I don't recognise him.'

She straightened up and frowned to notice her grandmother's eyes twinkling with excitement as she smiled back at her. 'What is it?'

'Look again. Properly this time.'

Jools held back a sigh. 'Fine, but I've already told you I don't know him.' As her eyes met those of the man in the photo it struck her how much like Marius's eyes they seemed. Then it dawned on her what her grandmother had noticed. 'Oh, Gran! It's Alan, isn't it?'

'It is. I'm certain of it.' Gran grinned at her and closed the book, resting her wrinkled hand over the back cover. 'You've done a wonderful thing finding this book for him, Jools. Well done.'

She was stunned. 'I'm so pleased I bothered to look for it.' She took the book from her grandmother's hand and had a quick peek at Alan's photo. 'He looked so much like Marius when he was younger, don't you think?'

'I do. Both are such talented men; being creative must run in their family.'

'It must,' Jools said slowly taking in the importance of her find. 'Don't you think it's exciting just to be able to hold a book that someone you know has written? I know I do. I think it's brilliant.'

'It is, you're right. Most of all though, I'm delighted you've found this copy for him. I can't wait to see his face when he discovers that you've found it.' She began sorting through the mail and opened the top letter. 'Will you give it to him at tonight's book group?'

'Yes,' Jools said, opening the book in a random place and sniffing gently. 'I love the smell of an old book,' she sighed, hugging the hardback briefly before holding it away from herself and studying it once more. Even its dust cover was intact. 'It's in almost perfect condition.'

After tidying up the shelves and serving a couple of customers, Jools was still buzzing with excitement at their discovery. Time was passing far too slowly and she needed something to take her mind off their plan for the evening. She asked her grandmother if she could go upstairs to paint for a couple of hours. 'I'll come back down to set up the chairs and refreshments for the book group before they arrive.'

'That's very sweet of you,' Gran said, waving her away as the bell jangled, and Betty walked through to the shop.

'Hi Betty,' Gran said.

'Good to see you both.' Betty took a seat in the worn leather armchair by the window that was kept for visitors. 'I've come to catch up on all the news about yesterday's dramas.'

Gran waved Jools away. 'I'm sure Jools will fetch us both a nice cup of tea before she starts her painting. Won't you, lovey?'

Jools could tell her grandmother was looking forward to a long gossip with Betty. 'I'll be happy to. Shall I bring a couple of biscuits?' she suggested. 'We have those digestives you particularly like.'

'Then how can I refuse,' Betty said.

Jools needed to press on and put the finishing touches to the siren painting if she was to be paid by the end of the month, so she hurriedly made two teas, adding a plate of biscuits to the tray before carrying it downstairs. She smiled to herself as her gran and Betty stopped speaking the moment she entered the room.

After thanking her, they started to chat again as soon as she reached the middle step on her way upstairs.

A few hours later, Jools was only vaguely aware that her gran was shouting up to her. She stopped working and opened the door, coming face to face with Marius.

'Oh! Hello,' she said, her delight momentarily outweighed by surprise at seeing him on the landing. 'I didn't expect to see you here.'

'Your gran said it was okay for me to come straight up.' He leaned forward and kissed her cheek. 'I think she was trying to get rid of me as quickly as possible. I suspect I walked in on an important conversation.'

Jools could tell he was amused and stepped back to let him into the bright room. 'Welcome to my studio.' For a moment she was tempted to share the news about his grandfather's book but decided to wait until the surprise had been revealed to Alan first.

'Is everything alright?'

'Yes, of course.'

Looking reassured, he stepped inside and bent to peer at the siren painting. 'It's almost finished now, isn't it?'

'Nearly. I just need to add a few finishing touches, let it dry and then varnish it a few times.' She narrowed her eyes trying to gauge his thoughts. 'What do you think? Is it good enough?'

'Hmm,' he said, before standing upright and turning to face her. 'It's brilliant,' he said with a smile. 'I still think the subject matter is a little odd, but she's getting her money's worth, Jools. You've done an amazing job.'

Relieved, Jools sighed. 'Phew, that's a relief. I'll be glad when it's done and I can start a new, more cheerful project.'

Marius laughed. 'I can imagine.'

'So,' she said, wondering if there was a particular reason he had come to see her. 'How are things with you today?'

'Fine.' He wasn't giving anything away. 'I was working earlier but had to deliver several pieces to one of the shops in town and thought I'd pop in and see you on my way home.'

Jools didn't bother mentioning that he had come out of his way if that was the case. She was pleased to see him and it made her happy that he'd come all the way to the boardwalk on his way back to Devil's Hole.

'That's kind of you,' she said. 'Can I offer you a drink, or anything to eat?'

'No, thanks.' He folded his arms. 'I don't want to disturb your work. I'm happy to stand here and watch you painting, if you don't mind.'

She smiled. 'I don't mind at all,' she said, thinking that if he had been happy for her and her friends to watch him at work then she really shouldn't have an issue returning the favour. Jools picked up her palette and exchanged the paintbrush she was holding for a smaller one. She squeezed out a small amount of her chosen paint and began adding strokes to an area of sky she wasn't quite happy with. 'Feel free to talk if you want, it won't disturb me.'

'I wasn't sure you would like me coming here,' he said quietly, as she put the finishing touches to the painting.

Jools frowned, confused that he might think such a thing. She turned to look at him quizzically. 'Why wouldn't I want you to visit me?'

He shrugged. 'I wasn't sure if I should stay away until you had spoken to Finn, or, you know, decided what you wanted to do about us, going forward.'

She wiped her paint brush and put it on her palette. 'I haven't spoken to him yet,' she admitted. 'I will though.' She hesitated. 'It's a bit complicated. I feel guilty, though to be honest I'm not sure why. Maybe because he looked so hurt when he saw us having fun together on Liberation Day.'

'Maybe.' Marius waited for her to remove her tunic. 'Will you let me know when you have spoken to him? I'd like us to go out for a meal, or on a date somewhere, but we can't do that until—'

'I'd like that very much,' she cut in.

'I feel a bit bad about last week, if I'm honest.'

'For burning the cheese on toast?' she teased.

He laughed and shook his head before becoming serious again. 'No, for kissing you.'

'Yes,' she said quietly, thinking of Finn. 'Me, too.'

They stared at each other silently for a moment. When she couldn't stand having him in the same room and not kissing him any longer, Jools walked to the door and opened it. 'Do you want to help me set the chairs out for Gran's book group? It's tonight,' she added. Then, recalling Alan's book, said. 'In fact, why don't you stay for this one?'

'Me?'

'You don't read?'

He pretended to be upset. 'I love reading, but I don't know what book they'll be discussing.'

'I don't want you here to discuss books,' she said, leading the way down the staircase.

'Then what do you want me for?'

She heard her gran and Betty laugh.

'Now that's a question only a brave man would ask,' Gran said as Jools entered the room closely followed by Marius.

'Gran!' She knew her grandmother thought herself hysterically funny and Betty obviously agreed, judging by her rosy-cheeked mirth. Jools couldn't help feeling a little embarrassed. She was about to mention that Marius was coming to the book group and was going to help her set it up when she saw the older ladies smiling at him. Turning, she realised he didn't seem bothered by their amusement and was smiling back at them.

'Shall we arrange these chairs?' she said to no one in particular.

Marius watched what she was doing then helped her bring the rest of the chairs from the storeroom and place them in a large circle. At one point, carrying a chair each and walking backwards, they slammed into each other and burst out laughing.

'We're closing soon,' she heard Gran say, and realised someone had entered the shop.

'I've been told that I'll find Jools Jones here,' said a female voice.

At the mention of her name, Jools spun round. She didn't recognise the woman, who looked to be around her own age, maybe a couple of years younger. 'That's me. How can I help you?'

Seconds later, Finn barged into the shop like a noisy toddler. 'Tamara, wait!'

'Finn?' They now had Jools's full attention. 'What's going on?'

Finn tried to take hold of Tamara's hand but she snapped it away. He then seemed to notice Jools for the first time and looked from her to Marius. 'Oh, what a surprise,' he said, sarcasm dripping from each word. 'He's here.'

'Yes, well, I...' Jools began before Marius stepped forward.

'Hang on a second, Jools. We need to hear what Tamara has to say, don't you think?'

He was right. There was something odd going on. Why had Finn barged into the shop after a woman Jools had never seen before?

'Hi Tamara. As you have probably worked out, I'm Jools. Would you prefer to talk to me in private? We can go upstairs if you'd rather do that?'

Tamara glared over her shoulder at Finn then focused her attention back on Jools. 'No. Thanks. I'm happy saying what I've got to say right here.'

'Would you like us to leave you?' Gran asked, reminding Jools that she and Betty were still in the room and that the book group would be arriving any minute.

'I'm going nowhere,' Betty said, not moving from her comfy armchair. 'You lot can carry on as you will though. Don't mind me.'

'Tamara, I won't tell you again,' Finn said.

Jools glared at him. 'She has something to say to me and I want to hear it. No one's keeping you here if you'd rather go. But if you're staying, you can stand there without speaking.' She looked at Tamara. 'I'm sorry but we have a book group scheduled to begin in five minutes, so we don't have long.'

Tamara shrugged. 'It will only take a couple of minutes.' Her tone wasn't exactly friendly.

'Go on then.' Jools was intrigued to hear what the girl had to say that was so important it couldn't wait.

'I want to know how long you've been seeing my boyfriend behind my back?'

For a second Jools thought she had misheard. 'What did you say?' Jools glanced at Marius, then realised Tamara was talking about Finn. 'What do you mean?'

'Finn told me that you've been contacting him constantly since he took you out a couple of times before he went travelling.'

'Did he now?' Jools shot Finn another glare, wishing she hadn't wasted so much time feeling guilty.

Tamara's hands clenched. 'Listen, Finn took you out, what? Twice?' Jools nodded. 'Right. Well, he met me in Sri Lanka and came back here with the intention of working out his notice but says you've been hounding him and crying so much that he hasn't felt able to do it yet.'

Was she in some sort of parallel universe? 'So, you thought you'd fly to Jersey and tell me what you thought of my behaviour,' Jools said, folding her arms. 'Is that it?'

'Yes, pretty much.'

'Leave it, Tam,' Finn muttered.

Jools was struggling not to laugh at his fantastical story. Stepping closer to Tamara, she pointed at Finn. 'He's delusional,' she said. Taking a deep breath to stop herself losing her cool, she continued, 'The only reason I haven't yet spoken to Finn about the relationship he led me to believe he wanted, is that he was so upset when he came back and saw me dancing with Marius, I didn't want to hurt him. I thought he had come back from the other side of the world especially to see me and couldn't bring myself to tell him that there was no future for us.' She turned to Finn, who was standing behind Tamara looking rather sheepish. 'Obviously, I was mistaken about your intentions,' she said. 'I think you have some explaining to do.'

He stepped forward, his shoulders stooped. 'I'm sorry, Jools…' he began.

'Not to me,' she said, irritated by his ego. A thought occurred to her about something he'd mentioned in his postcard. 'How did you two meet, by the way?'

Tamara smiled proudly. 'We were in a small group of people at the beach and when we all decided to go swimming, Finn confided to me that he didn't know how.'

She might have guessed. 'And you offered to teach him?'

'Yes.' Tamara frowned. 'How did you know?' She spun around to glower at Finn. 'You said you hadn't told anyone else that you couldn't swim.'

Jools almost felt sorry for the furious woman. 'I think that might be one of Finn's chat up lines.'

Finn came closer, puce in the face, sweat on his upper lip. Jools wasn't sure if it was because he was embarrassed, or furious to have been caught out. 'Listen, Jools, I'm sorry—'

Jools had had enough of the whole mess. 'You and Tamara need to leave now,' she interrupted. 'You should be talking to your girlfriend, Finn, not me.'

Tamara looked about to snarl. 'You can't dismiss us like this.'

'I think you'll find I can. I've said all I'm going to.' Jools didn't care what Tamara thought, but needed her calm enough to ensure she and Finn left the shop before the book club arrived. 'I'm not the one you should be angry with, Tamara. I think that when you've had time to calm down a bit you'll realise as much.'

Seeming confused by the exchange, and somewhat deflated, Tamara finally nodded. 'I suppose you're right.'

Finn didn't look back as he hurried out, closely followed by Tamara. With a shaky breath, Jools went to close the door, just as Alan arrived. He paused to watch the couple leaving, arguing as they went.

'Hi, Alan.' Jools waved him inside, excited to see him but trying not to show it. 'Don't worry about those two. Please, come in.'

She returned to the shop to find her grandmother standing with her cheeks puffed out.

'Well, that was odd. But at least we all know where we stand, don't we?' she said.

'We do?' Alan was holding an open book, looking bemused.

Betty chortled. 'Young love. I'd forgotten how trying it can be sometimes.'

'I was happy to see the back of all that nonsense, if you know what I mean.' Gran shared a knowing look with Jools. 'Is there anything in particular you're looking for, Alan?'

He shook his head and, closing the book, slipped it back into the gap between two other books where he had found it. He walked the couple of steps to the chair next to her grandmother and sat down.

'I never considered for a moment that Finn had a mermaid at his beck and call,' Jools said, trying to make light of her humiliation. Remembering the postcard Finn had sent her, she pictured Tamara teaching him to swim in the sea and sighed.

'Mermaid. Hah, that's a joke,' Gran said. 'Did you see the way she bared her teeth at you? That Tamara looked like one of those sea sirens you've been painting.' She shivered. 'I think he's got more than he bargained for with that one.'

Jools felt rather sorry for the girl. 'Well, it's not my business any more, thankfully.' She noticed Marius looking uncomfortable and wondered what he'd made of the exchange. 'I'll go and get the refreshments from upstairs,' she said.

'I'll come and help you.' Marius followed her out before she had a chance to respond.

In the kitchen, Jools filled the kettle and switched it on, then took out a tray and placed it on the worktop. 'I'm sorry about that,' she said, turning to face him. 'If I'd spoken to Finn sooner that drama downstairs probably would never have happened.'

'Don't worry,' he said with a shrug. 'It sounds like you had a lucky escape.'

'I thought tonight's excitement was going to be when I presented your grandad with his book,' she said, forgetting Marius didn't already know about her discovery.

'You've found a copy?' Now, Marius looked stunned. 'Jools, he's going to be beside himself when he sees it.'

'Shush,' she said, smiling. 'I don't want him to hear about it yet.' She gestured to the cupboard behind him. 'Could you pass me six cups and saucers, please?'

He opened the cupboard door and handed over the pretty cups and saucers, patterned with blue forget-me-nots, that Gran kept for guests. 'How did you find it?' he asked. 'I've been searching for a copy for years. It's the one thing he's desperate to get his hands on.' He beamed at her. 'You're so thoughtful, do you know that?' Before she had a chance to reply, he came over and kissed her on the lips. 'And clever.' He kissed her again. 'And pretty.'

'Pretty?' No one ever called her pretty. She had been referred to as looking like an angry doll, or a mischievous pixie, but never pretty. She liked it, she decided. 'Actually, thank you.' She let him take her in his arms and looked up into his blue eyes. Reaching up, she ran her fingers through his untidy hair. 'You're very hand-some,' she said. 'Or, as my friend Bella would say, you're hot.'

'You think so?' He grinned, clearly amused by the compliment.

She blushed. She'd never said anything like it before. 'Yes, I really do.'

He raised his eyebrows. 'Then I'm pleased. No, more than pleased.' He pulled her tightly to him and kissed her hard.

'If you two are finished up there,' Gran called, 'would you mind bringing our drinks? We're parched down here.'

Jools cringed. 'I wish she wouldn't shout like that. Gran can be so embarrassing sometimes.'

Marius grinned at her. 'You'd forgotten the orange juice, hadn't you?'

'Yup.' She returned his grin. 'Better get six tumblers and another tray while I make the tea.'

Finally, after waiting for Marius to take the orange juice from the fridge and pour it into a jug, Jools took out a bottle of red wine, knowing it was Alan's preference. She added a couple of glasses to one tray in case anyone else wanted a drink, and with the biscuit tin under her arm, she carried the tea tray downstairs.

'Here we are, Gran,' she said, indicating for Marius to put his tray on the counter. Satisfied that they had thought of everything, she turned to face the book group and smiled. 'Before you begin, I don't know if any of you knew, but Alan here is a published author.'

Betty gasped. 'You are? What an achievement. I've never met an author before.'

Alan smiled at her. 'I only wrote the one, I'm afraid.' He looked at Jools, his eyes wide. 'How on earth did you know that I'd written a book?'

Jools tapped the side of her nose.

'Why don't you tell us a bit about it?' Gran asked.

'I don't know that it's all that interesting.'

Marius stepped forward and rested a hand on his grandfather's shoulder. 'I'd love to know more, Grandad. Please tell us about it.'

Alan stared at him for a moment and then shrugged. 'Very well. It was many moons ago now,' he said, looking awkward yet proud. 'I don't even have a copy of it to prove it to you, but yes, Jools is correct. I did write a book once.'

Jools picked up the yellow-covered book where she had hidden it from view behind the counter and handed it to Marius with a smile. 'I'll let you do the honours,' she whispered.

'What's going on?' Alan asked, looking confused.

Marius beamed and mouthed a thank-you to her before turning to his grandfather. 'You do have a copy of it now, Grandad.' He held up the book to a ripple of surprise from the group before handing it to his grandfather.

Alan leant forward and peered at it, his mouth dropping open in surprise when he recognised the cover. 'But... *how?*'

'Jools put a post on social media,' Gran explained as Marius handed the book to his grandfather.

Alan held it as if it was a piece of fine china, stroking the front cover lightly. 'I can't believe this,' he whispered.

Jools had to take a deep breath to stop herself from becoming emotional. She watched as he lovingly opened the book and silently read a few lines, his lips moving slowly. The group seemed enthralled by the turn of events, watching with fond smiles and nudging each other delightedly.

He finally looked at Jools, his eyes filled with unshed tears. 'I can't believe you did this for me, young lady.' He paused to clear his throat a couple of times. 'But I'll always be grateful to you. Thank you.'

16

As she lay in bed that night it occurred to Jools that, rather than feeling miffed by Finn's underhand behaviour, she was relieved. She had no reason to put off speaking to him now that she knew he had a girlfriend. She wasn't even sure that a conversation with him was all that necessary now, but the following morning she waited until she had seen him open up the gelateria from her studio window and told her grandmother she was going out for a walk. Jools didn't need Gran asking awkward questions, but wanted to know what Finn intended to do about his job, so that she could tell the others. Also, she couldn't help feeling intrigued by what exactly had happened while he had been away.

Dressed in her favourite paint-spattered jeans and a t-shirt and trainers, she walked the short distance to the Isola Bella. She had a quick peek in the parlour window and seeing that there were no customers, quickly darted inside. She didn't want any of her friends spotting her going in and asking questions. She would tell them when she was ready to do so.

'I'm not quite ready to open yet,' Finn said, reaching down into the main cooler. 'Won't be long if you want to hang on a moment.'

'I'll wait, thanks,' Jools said, trying not to show her satisfaction when he raised his head in shock and banged it on the top of the cooler.

'Jools? What are you doing here?'

Was he worried about what she was going to say, or terrified of Tamara finding them speaking in private? 'I have something to ask you.' She pulled out a tall stool, set around a high metal table, and sat down.

'What is it?' He quickly washed his hands in the small sink behind him, and dried them before closing the glass over the cooler.

'Before we get into that, I'd like you to explain why you thought it necessary to make me feel guilty for seeing Marius.'

He looked surprised. 'When did I do that?'

'Liberation Day. All that fuss you made when you arrived and saw me dancing with him.' Another thought occurred to her. 'Then you kept yourself busy, no doubt wanting me to think that you were hurt.' He had the decency to look guilty and she was glad to be proved right.

Finn threw the hand towel on to the worktop. 'Look, Jools, I am sorry. I know I've behaved badly,' he said. 'You've every right to be confused. Especially now that you've met Tamara.'

Jools rested her elbows on the table. 'What *is* going on there?'

He sighed heavily. 'I did intend travelling with my mate, Mark, but a couple of weeks in we met up with two girls. Tamara and her friend.' He shrugged. 'I hooked up with Tamara and she and I went on together, leaving Mark and her friend to do the same.' He looked at Jools sheepishly. 'I know how bad it sounds, but at the time it didn't seem that way. I suppose it was because I was away from home and nothing seemed real. It was easy for me to pretend I wasn't doing anything wrong.' He pulled an apologetic face. 'I know it's no excuse.'

'Go on,' she said, not wanting to make it too easy for him.

'I didn't think it would go anywhere. You know, just a casual thing, but I fell for her.'

The fact he was being so open must mean it was serious. Jools was more relieved than ever that she didn't have feelings for him; she would have been heartbroken if she had. 'She obviously feels the same way if she turned up here to put me straight.'

His shoulders slumped. 'I really am sorry about that. I shouldn't have lied to her.'

'No, you shouldn't.' Jools felt a flare of anger. 'Letting her think I wouldn't leave you alone.'

'I don't even know why I said that. I thought it made me look good to have a girl crying over me.' He shook his head. 'I was hoping to avoid that particular conversation. I just hoped it would go away and things would carry on as normal.'

'With me, or with her?' Despite knowing the answer, Jools wanted to put him in the awkward position of having to be honest. If nothing else, it might teach Finn not to mess around with people's feelings.

'With her.' He gazed at the floor. 'Look, I really am sorry for the way I've behaved, Jools.'

She believed him. 'I thought better of you than this. I never took you for the type of guy to mess with someone's affections.'

He closed his eyes for a few seconds before looking at her. 'I know it's no excuse but I think the attention went to my head.'

'Why?' In spite of everything, she was intrigued.

'I was always the skinny kid, who never got the girl. The guy whose friends tried to set him up on dates only for the women to take one look at me and walk away.'

Studying him, Jools thought back to when they were younger, to seeing him around the island. He had been skinny and very shy. Things were starting to make sense. 'Go on.'

'A couple of years ago, my uncle took me to one side and told me he was taking me to his friend's boxing gym to train me up. He changed my diet and gave me a daily schedule to follow and over the months I built up muscle and somehow my physique changed. It helped my confidence no end, and then I met you and you agreed to go out with me.'

'I liked you,' she said. 'And then you went away and met Tamara and she liked you, too.'

'I'm sorry,' he said again. 'As I said, the attention went to my head.'

'It's fine,' she said, relieved to find that she meant it. 'We'd only been on a couple of dates. I was keeping an open mind and looking forward to you coming back, but then I met Marius. I kept him at arm's length because I didn't know which one of you I wanted to be with, but soon realised it was him. Then you came back unexpectedly and acted all hurt and devastated, which was confusing.' She shrugged. 'You're not the only one with little experience of relationships.'

'I know. I'm sorry.'

'Stop saying sorry, Finn. My ego isn't battered and I'm happy to be with Marius. Although I still don't get why you acted the way you did at the Liberation Day event.'

'Because when I saw you having fun with him, I was jealous.' Jools opened her mouth to ask why, when he'd already fallen for Tamara, but he raised his hand. 'I know,' he said. 'It was ridiculous of me. When I thought about it the following day, I realised I only wanted you because you clearly wanted someone else.'

'Seriously?'

He looked her in the eye. 'What can I say? I'm an idiot.'

'Yes, you are.' She smiled, relieved to finally have the truth. 'Let's call it quits and move on. I hope you've found what you're looking for with Tamara.' She slid down off the stool 'I'll get going and leave you to it.'

'Thanks, Jools.'

Remembering Jack, she turned. 'I meant to ask... have you decided what you'll be doing next? I mean, are you going travelling with Tamara? Or do you think you'll stay here for the summer season?'

He seemed confused by her question. 'I'm not sure yet, if I'm honest.'

The door opened and Jools spun round to see Tamara.

'What's she doing here?' she asked Finn.

Finn's face paled. 'It's not what it looks like.'

'It's true,' Jools said. 'I wanted to clear up a few things with Finn, that's all. In case you're wondering, there really was nothing much between us. We went out a couple of times, but it was hardly Romeo and Juliet. I'm glad he's found you.' She smiled the friendliest smile she could muster. 'You've nothing to worry about.'

Tamara looked doubtfully at Finn. 'You led me to believe that she was in love with you.'

'We talked about this last night,' he said quietly. As he crossed the floor and took Tamara's hands in his, Jools slipped out and closed the door behind her.

If it was true love, they'd work it out. It was none of her business now. Jools was glad her connection to Finn had been settled and was behind her without either of them getting hurt.

'Thank heavens that's over and done with.'

'You talking to yourself again?' Sacha asked, catching up with her.

'I just had a conversation with Finn and his girlfriend, Tamara,' Jools said. 'Apparently, they met up when they were travelling.' She shrugged when Sacha opened her mouth to speak, sensing her friend was about to offer some platitude. 'It's fine. I mean, I was annoyed that he'd been seeing someone when I was building myself up to ending whatever it was we started before he went away, but that's all. Tamara had a go at me because Finn told her I'd been hounding him.' She sighed. 'Anyway, we've sorted it out and I'm fine.'

Sacha hugged her. 'I have to admit, Finn isn't the man I had assumed him to be. I thought he had more about him, but I suppose it takes all sorts.'

'Don't think too badly of him,' Jools said, amazed to hear herself defending his actions. 'He had his reasons and no one was hurt in the end.'

'You're too nice.' Smiling, Sacha linked arms with Jools. 'Right, what are you going to do for the rest of the day?'

Jools wanted more than anything to visit Marius at his studio but didn't like to disturb him if he was busy. 'I have a lot of work I should be getting on with,' she said, trying to talk herself into it.

Sacha grinned. 'I sense a *but* coming.'

'You're right, of course,' Jools said with a smile. 'What I really want to do is take the bus up to Marius's studio.' As she spoke an idea began forming in her mind. 'I could take Teddy. He'll need a walk and there are places around there I can take him.'

'So, why don't you?'

Jools glanced at her friend. 'You know what? I'm going to do just that.' She nodded. 'Thanks, Sacha.' It occurred to her that she hadn't asked her friend about her day. 'Were you on your way to speak to Alessandro? He's not in the gelateria, if that's where you were going next.'

Sacha smiled. 'I gathered as much. No, I was on my way to find Jack. I need him to help me pack away some heavy stock.'

'I haven't seen him for a while, but he's probably at Bella's if he isn't surfing.' Since Jack had got together with Bella, spending time with her was becoming his favourite pastime.

'He's been surfing at least once today, so I reckon he's at her cottage.' Sacha gave Jools's arm a squeeze. 'I'd better get a move on. I've left Lexi and Oliver watching the café and have been out longer than I intended.'

Jools widened her eyes in mock horror. 'Sorry about that.'

Sacha gave her another hug. 'Not at all. It was good to have a quick catch-up with you. Now go and find that gorgeous Norwegian you seem to be so taken with.' She giggled. 'I can't imagine why.'

Jools pulled a face. 'I think you can,' she said as she walked away and smiled to hear Sacha chuckling.

She only had a few minutes before the bus arrived and would have preferred to get changed and put on a little makeup. All she had on was her customary flick of black eyeliner and a touch of mascara, but it would have to do. Jools arrived at the bookshop and grabbed Teddy's lead, calling out to her grandmother, 'I'm going to take the little terror out for a walk.'

'Good!' her Gran called from upstairs. 'He's been a pain for the past few hours. I think he spotted another dog out of the window. Which means he's been jumping up onto my armchair again.'

Teddy came bounding down the stairs, barking as he spotted his lead, and bounced up and down as though he had springs instead of feet.

'Calm down, Teddy.' She bent to take hold of his collar so that she could clip on his lead. 'I might be a couple of hours,' she shouted, not wanting her grandmother to worry if she was late.

'Where are you going, lovey?' Gran appeared at the top of the stairs.

Jools knew that she wouldn't get away with pretending. Her grandmother knew her even better than her three best friends did.

'I was thinking of taking the bus up to Devils Hole.' She didn't elaborate but noticed the slow smile on her grandmother's face as she worked out what, or rather who, she was going to see.

'All right, my lovey. Have a good time,' she said. 'At least you can carry that little devil if he gets too tired to walk.'

'Bye, Gran.' Jools smiled down at Teddy, who was turning in excited circles. 'You love the bus, don't you?' she said, suspecting he understood far more than they imagined.

She reached the top of the boardwalk and walked the hundred metres to the bus stop on the main road, getting there in time to stick out her arm as the bus approached.

There were only a few people on board but it seemed that all of them knew Teddy.

''Ello little chap. 'Ow you doin' then?' an elderly man asked as his wife stopped to stroke Teddy's furry head. ''E's such a good boy, that one.'

'Don't be fooled by this angelic behaviour,' Jools teased. 'He's only sitting still because he knows I'll take him home if he's naughty.'

The couple laughed and made their way to their seats.

The journey only took a few minutes. Jools wished Teddy's fans goodbye as they got off the bus, waving at the old man and his wife as the bus carried on down the road.

'Right, come along then, little man.' They walked for a couple of minutes before reaching the granite buildings. 'I wonder if he'll be in,' she said to herself. Her stomach clenched as nerves kicked in. Maybe this wasn't such a great idea, after all. Then she pictured her friends, encouraging her to take a deep breath and go inside.

'Don't be such a wuss,' she mumbled. She reached the door and, turning the handle, pushed it open and stepped inside, pinning a smile on her face in an attempt to look confident.

She couldn't see Marius. Lifting Teddy to keep him from knocking any of the glass ornaments over, she took the opportunity to have a closer look at his work. He really was exceptionally talented. She was studying a blue and white vase with a smattering of silver running through it when she heard Marius laughing.

Jools's heart contracted as she followed the sound to the opposite end of the studio, ready to let him know she was there. She froze, her smile fading when she saw a beautiful woman with long blonde hair like a shimmering waterfall down her back, leaning forward to whisper something to Marius, making him laugh again. She had her hand on Marius's shoulder and he was obviously comfortable in her presence. Jools swallowed. She had obviously walked in on an intimate moment between them.

She retraced her steps as silently as she could, desperate to leave before her appearance was noticed. As she reached the door she stumbled, shooting out a hand to save herself. Teddy, ever alert to the unexpected, barked.

'Shush,' she hissed, quickly opening the door.

'Hello?'

Jools cringed at sound of Marius's voice. Putting Teddy down so it was easier to run, she took off around the side of the building, hoping Marius hadn't spotted her. She heard him call out a couple of times but kept moving. If she stopped, Teddy would no doubt bark again and she had no intention of letting that happen.

She ran through the small yard of the shop next door, Teddy straining at his leash. Once they'd reached the main road and were far enough away, Jools slowed to a walk, panting.

'You little bugger,' she grumbled as Teddy wagged his tail, trotting happily beside her, oblivious to the embarrassment he had almost caused. 'There isn't a bus for an hour, so we're going to have to walk home.' It wasn't far, and she could probably make it in under an hour, but she hoped that Teddy wouldn't want to be carried.

As they walked, she had time to think about what she had seen. Tears burned her eyes and, relieved to not have anyone to hide them from, Jools let them fall.

Served her right for letting her guard down and allowing herself to like someone, just because she'd been kissed a couple of times. Only yesterday, she had thought two men were interested in her. Now, it seemed, neither of them was. 'Stupid woman.' She had been single for long enough to know that she wasn't the typical girly girl a lot of men were attracted to, with her pink spiky hair, boyfriend jeans and untidy ways. She was hardly the sort of girl men fell for in romantic novels or movies. The thought brought on a fresh bout of crying.

By the time they were walking down the hill towards the boardwalk, Jools could almost wring out the crumpled tissue grasped in her hand.

'Jools! Hey, Jools!'

Lexi was calling her. Angry with herself for wallowing in self-pity, Jools wiped her nose and attempted to dry her eyes with her fingers. She turned to her friend with a smile fixed on her face.

'Bloody hell, what's happened?'

Jools knew by the shocked expression on her friend's face that she looked a fright. 'Nothing,' she lied. 'I'm fine.'

'You're not.' Lexi ran over to her. 'You can't go back to your gran looking like that,' she said, taking Teddy's lead from her and linking an arm through hers. 'You're coming inside with me.'

Jools cringed. She loved her friend but, right now, all she wanted to do was wallow in the peace of her own bedroom. Lexi did have a point though. She couldn't go home looking dreadful. The last thing she wanted to do was worry her grandmother.

'You don't have to tell me anything,' Lexi said as they reached her front door and she opened it, waiting for Jools to lead the way inside. 'We'll soon have you tidied up and ready to go home. But first, I'm going to make you a hot drink while you wash your face. You can use my make-up to freshen up.' She closed the door and bent to unclasp Teddy's lead. 'And I've got a lovely, cooked sausage in my fridge that I know this one will enjoy.'

'Thanks, Lexi.' Jools indicated the staircase. 'Is it okay if I use your bathroom?'

'Take all the time you want,' Lexi said. 'I'm going to thoroughly spoil my little pal here.'

'What? For a change, you mean?' Jools managed a smile, already feeling calmer.

She ran upstairs and into the bathroom, gasping in shock at the state of her puffy eyes in the mirror above the sink. Thank heavens her friend had insisted she come inside and fix herself. She looked horrendous. Leaning forward, she cringed at the remnants of eyeliner smudged onto her cheeks, the mascara down her face. Lexi was right, she would have given her grandmother a fright if she had seen her looking like this.

She washed her face and dried it on a few tissues, not wanting to dirty Lexi's pristine towels. After smoothing on some face cream, she added a little foundation and tried to replicate her eyeliner flick and mascara with Lexi's makeup. She studied her reflection. 'Much, much better,' she said, deciding that no man was worth looking as hideous as she had on arrival at Lexi's. She added pink lip gloss, then dampened her hands and ran them through her hair, spiking it up.

Downstairs, she stopped in the living room doorway and held her arms wide. 'Ta-dah!'

Lexi looked up from feeding Teddy and smiled. 'You look great. Do you feel better?'

'Yes, thanks.'

'Good. Do you want to tell me about it?'

Jools gazed at her friend, knowing she wouldn't judge her.

'Okay.'

They sat in the comfy armchairs and Jools told Lexi about seeing Marius at his studio with the woman. 'I'm mortified to think that he might have caught me watching.'

Lexi nodded. 'And, if you don't mind me saying, I think you've just realised how deep your feelings for him go.'

Jools pictured his strong face and pale golden hair. It hurt to think of him being with someone else. It was her own fault. If she'd sorted things out with Finn sooner, maybe Marius wouldn't have found another woman to spend time with. 'You're right,' she said. 'It was like a sucker-punch to the gut.' She took a shuddering sigh. 'Oh, Lexi, I've been such a fool.'

Lexi walked over and wrapped her arms around Jools. 'These things happen to all of us.'

'They do?' She couldn't help thinking that her lack of experience had played a big part in hindering whatever it was that had begun to blossom with Marius. 'Has it happened to you then?' she asked, unable to recall when it might have.

Lexi smiled. 'You don't think that my relationship with Oliver has been an easy one, do you? We had all sorts of issues. I mean, think about how it all began.'

Jools thought back to when Lexi's dad had sold her cottages to Oliver. 'True. And you both worked through that, didn't you?'

'Exactly,' Lexi reassured her. 'And it's not as if you and Marius have anything like that going on.' She patted Jools's leg. 'It'll be fine. You mark my words.'

'Thanks, Lexi.' She kissed her friend on the cheek, grateful for her support. 'I suppose I'd better get Teddy back to Gran. I don't want her worrying about us.'

'You do that. And, Jools,' Lexi said, wagging a finger. 'No unnecessary worrying, OK?'

'I promise.'

17

That afternoon, after spending a few hours painting, Jools's grandmother asked her to fetch a bag of old books from Betty's that her friend wanted to sell. She set off, feeling much better after spending time with Lexi and losing herself in work. She was beginning to think that if Marius hadn't seen her at his studio, she could forget it ever happened. Although, she thought as she walked, forgetting what she had seen was going to take some doing. And if she was honest, she didn't want to forget. Then again, if he was the type of person to see two women at the same time then he wasn't for her. She remembered kissing him when she was supposed to be waiting for Finn and wondered whether she was being a little hypocritical.

Hearing footsteps coming up behind her, she presumed it was one of the other villagers and took no notice. 'I need to concentrate on things I can control,' she murmured, trying to persuade herself. 'Like my paintings.'

It dawned on her that the person behind her hadn't overtaken and when Jools turned, she was started to see that Marius had joined her. 'Oh, it's you.'

'Were you talking to yourself?' He grinned. Then, noticing they were steps away from the Isola Bella, added, 'Been to see Finn?'

'That's the second time someone has caught me talking to myself,' she admitted. 'And, yes, I've been to see Finn, but that was this morning.' She realised she shouldn't have added the last part. Now, if Marius suspected she was the person who had run away from his studio, she wouldn't have an alibi. *Alibi?* What was wrong with her today?

She discreetly studied his face, searching for something that might give away that he knew. Finding nothing, she relaxed slightly. 'No work today?' She wondered why he wasn't with the blonde she had seen earlier.

'I had a demonstration for a client, but not much else.'

Had the woman been the client? They'd looked too intimate, somehow. The thought of him lying to her and of them being together made her heart ache.

'Where are you off to?' he said.

'Why?' It came out snappier than she had intended. 'I'm on my way to Betty's to collect some books for Gran.'

'I was wondering, if you're not busy, whether you'd like to join me for a stroll.' He glanced at her, seeming unsure of himself.

She wanted to, very much, deciding that it might be the perfect time to muster up the courage to ask him about his visitor. Then again, she wasn't sure how she could do that without admitting to being at his studio and running away. *Bugger.* It wasn't as if he had done anything wrong, as far as she knew.

'Come along then,' she said. 'We can go down by the light-house and sit peacefully for a bit.' She looked up at him. 'I can't be too long though, or Gran will wonder where I've got to and I don't want to keep Betty waiting.'

'Great.' He grinned at her. 'I was hoping I'd get to spend some time down here with you.'

She couldn't help smiling. 'Are you trying to tell me you came to the boardwalk specifically to see me?'

He pulled a comical face. 'It seems that I have.'

Jools raised her eyebrows. 'What if I'd been busy?'

He reached over and tickled her waist. 'Then I would have had to sit somewhere quietly by myself and wait until you were free.'

She wriggled out of his grasp, giggling. 'Stop that! I hate being tickled.' She was irritated that he had made her laugh when she was trying to be cross with him.

Bella stepped out of her cottage as they were passing. 'Where are you two love-birds off to?'

Jools gave her friend a deadpan look, wishing she hadn't used the words *love-birds*.

'We're off to the lighthouse for a chat,' Marius said, seeming unbothered by Bella's question.

Bella stepped aside to let them pass. 'Well, I won't hold you up,' she said. 'Have a lovely time.'

They walked on for a few metres and then Marius laughed.

'What's so funny?' she asked.

He stepped in front of her and walked slowly backwards. 'You. Your expression when Bella made that comment. I thought you were going to kick her in the shins, or something.'

Jools gasped. 'I'd never do that.'

'You weren't tempted?'

'Maybe,' she giggled, unable to help herself as she was taken off-guard when he grabbed her hand and ran along the promenade towards the lighthouse. 'Hey,' she shouted, trying to keep up. 'What are you doing?'

He slowed slightly. 'You'll see.'

They reached the lighthouse and he slowed to a walk, then pulled her to him and kissed her.

Jools was taken by surprise, but as his lips pressed hers she became lost in the kiss before remembering the woman at the studio and pulling away. Marius looked surprised and confused by her reaction and the rumbling of a feisty car engine was a welcome distraction. They looked around as its engine was revved before slowing to a gentle purr.

'I say, darlings?'

Jools smiled at Sacha's eccentric Aunt Rosie. 'Hi there. I haven't seen you in a while.'

'Nice car,' Marius said, moving closer with Jools for a better look. 'Red, too. Perfect colour for it.'

Rosie seemed to preen herself and gave him a sultry look. 'Why, thank you. And you are?' She smoothed her immaculate silk headscarf with a manicured hand.

'Marius Arnesen,' he said.

Jools heard the smile in his voice and could tell he was as impressed with Aunt Rosie as they all were whenever she appeared. Rosie locked eyes with her and raised her eyebrows minutely. There would have been more movement in her forehead if she had left her looks to nature.

Rosie returned her gaze to Marius. 'Why have I never seen you around here before now, Marius Arnesen?' She batted her false eyelashes flirtatiously.

Marius laughed. 'Probably because I've only recently been coming down here more often.'

'Because of our lovely Jools, I presume?' She reached up and rested her hand on Jools's cheek. 'Our beautiful little artist.'

'He came down here because his grandad moved back to the island and likes to walk on the beach and has joined Gran's book group,' Jools explained.

'That was before I got to know this young lady' He exchanged a glance with Jools that made her blush.

'Can we help you with something?' Jools asked. There had to be a reason Sacha and Jack's aunt had driven down to the board-walk. Most people didn't bother as cars weren't encouraged on the quiet road which was usually swarming with people. Then again, Aunt Rosie wasn't most people.

'I'm looking for Claire,' she said. 'Have you seen her anywhere today?'

Jools shook her head. 'Afraid not. Can I pass on a message for you? Or, I could leave one with Betty. I'm popping in to see her.'

'That would be kind of you. Please let her know I was here and that I'll—'

'Rosie?' Claire called, coming out of Betty's front door. 'I thought I saw you from the living room window. Are you looking for me?' She had an expectant expression on her face. Rosie was known for her elegance, eccentricities and penchant for younger men, but also for her kindness, and willingness to help people when they needed it.

Rosie smiled over at her. 'Yes, darling. I saw your message and thought there's no time to waste. I've come to talk weddings with you.' She waved Jools and Marius away from the car. 'Let me park this beast and we can get started.'

Jools looked at Rosie, immaculate and loving all things expen-sive and chic. She was the opposite of Claire, who could easily pass for someone in her twenties still making the most of a lengthy gap year from university.

Jools watched Rosie park her car and step out, wondering how anyone could manage to walk in such high heels, let alone drive in them. Rosie caught her eye. 'You're welcome to join us, if you wish,' she said. 'I'm sure Claire won't mind.'

'Please, go with them if you'd like to,' Marius said quietly. 'We can catch up later, if you'd rather.'

'No, I'm fine thanks.'

'Sure?'

She nodded. 'Thanks, Rosie, but I'll leave you two to chat in private. Let me know if there's anything I can do to help though, won't you?'

Claire opened the gate at the end of Betty's pathway to let Rosie through. 'Thanks, Jools.'

Jools turned to Marius. 'I'll explain in a minute,' she whispered.

He looked confused. 'OK. Come on. Let's get away from here.' He led her up the few granite steps behind the lighthouse and down to a small, secluded cove on the other side. Then, taking hold of her hand, he walked her up against the rocks and away from prying eyes. 'Before we're spotted by anyone else you know, I want to do this.' He placed a hand on her cheek then slid it gently behind her head, pulling her slowly towards him and lowering his lips onto hers.

His kiss was unlike any other, the sensation sweeping through her body more intense. She wound her arms around him and allowed herself to get lost in the blissful experience.

Eventually they came up for air and Jools, feeling a little light-headed, ran her fingers through her short hair for want of something to do. She stared at him trying to think what to say next. 'That was nice.' *Talk about understatement of the year.*

'Yes,' he smiled, looking a little dazed. 'Wasn't it.'

They gazed at each other for a little while and then Marius said, 'I forgot; you were going to tell me something.'

'I was?' She tried to think back to the conversation before their kiss, but couldn't remember.

'About why you didn't want to stay and help Claire and Rosie.'

'Ah, yes.' She took him by the hand. 'Let's go and sit for a while.' She knew she should be going to Betty's to collect the books she'd promised her gran, but couldn't drag herself away from Marius.

'It's a long story then, is it?' he teased.

'No, but I need to sit.' Her knees were still jelly-like and she hadn't completely recovered from the pleasure of kissing him. In fact, she would rather do it again than talk about Bella's mum.

They sat next to each other and Jools pushed her fingers into the soft, pale golden sand, lifting her hands and letting the tiny grains flow between her fingers. She thought about the blonde women in Marius's studio and stiffened.

'What's the matter?'

'Before I tell you about Claire, I want to be clear about something.'

He frowned, looking concerned. 'Go on.'

'I know we barely know each other but I want to be sure that you're not...' she hesitated. 'Not seeing other people.'

His frown deepened. 'What makes you ask?'

Damn. How could she tell him without giving away that she had seen him earlier. She would have to own up to what she had done. 'There's something I need to tell you first.' She cringed inwardly.

He took her hands in his. 'Go on.'

'I wanted to surprise you earlier, so I came to the studio with Teddy and saw you with that woman. The one with the lovely hair.' Mortified, she stared at the waves rolling onto the sand in front of them, feeling his gaze on her.

'You mean, it was Teddy who barked?'

'Yes,' she whispered, turning her head to look him in the eye. 'I ran off like a coward instead of confronting you.'

He sat for a moment then threw his head back and roared with laughter.

Jools was flooded with indignation. Here she was, opening her heart and admitting something horribly embarrassing, and he was mocking her. She made to stand up, but Marius put a restraining hand on her arm. 'Please. Don't go. I wasn't laughing at you, Jools, I promise.'

'Well, what's so bloody funny then?'

He leant forward and kissed her on the nose. 'I thought I was going mad when I couldn't find a dog. I was certain I had heard one barking but Sophie insisted that I was mistaken.'

'Sophie?' Jools tried to keep her flare of jealousy under wraps.

'Didn't you see her there with me?'

'Obviously. That's why I ran away,' she said, embarrassed.

'She's my cousin. She's over for a few days and came to the studio to watch me working and to collect a gift I made for her parent's anniversary.' His frown was back. 'What a shame you didn't come in properly. I could have introduced you. You'd get on well with her. She's great fun, too.'

His cousin? Jools recalled her long, pale golden hair and wondered why she hadn't seen the likeness. Of *course* they were related. 'That's such a shame,' she said, keeping her voice light. 'I would love to meet her.'

'Then I'll have to introduce you to her when she's next here.'

'She's gone?'

'I dropped her off at the airport on the way here.' He pulled her to him and kissed her again. Still stung by the humiliation of mistaking his cousin for another woman, it took a moment for the caress of his lips to make her relax and forget everything else.

They finally drew apart, breathless.

'You still haven't told me about Claire,' he reminded her.

Happy to change the subject, Jools nodded. 'One night, a few weeks ago, I couldn't sleep so decided to come for a walk out here and came across Claire and Tony.' She hesitated, thinking back to the romantic moment that she had interrupted.

'What were they doing?'

'He was proposing.'

'Sounds romantic.'

'It was. The moon was shining down on them. It was like watching a scene from a romance on the TV. I tried not to let them see me, but they did.'

'Were they upset?'

'No, but I knew that Bella, Claire's daughter, might be. Their relationship is a bit of a strange one. Claire left Bella to be raised by her grandmother while she went travelling. She was still a teenager when she had Bella.' Jools lowered her voice in case someone was on the other side of the wall and might hear. She didn't want to risk upsetting Bella or Claire again. 'They've only recently become close again. I think Bella feels responsible for her mum. I think she worries Claire might mess things up for Tony. She can be a bit fickle.'

She couldn't help feeling a little guilty for saying these things about her friend's mother, but wasn't saying anything that was untrue. 'You won't repeat any of this, will you?'

'No, of course not. We all have the odd family secret, Jools. I think it makes people more interesting. The secrets that don't hurt anyone, that is.'

She gave his comment some thought. 'I agree.'

'Go one.' He nudged her gently with his shoulder. 'I'm intrigued. Why, or how, could Claire mess things up with Tony?'

'He was only widowed a couple of years ago.'

'Poor man,' Marius said, frowning. 'That's tragic. And he has children?'

'Yes, a boy and a girl. Claire's never been known to stay in one place for long and she's only been back on the boardwalk for a few months, so there's still time for her to get fed up and change her mind. I think that's what Bella's wary of.'

'Understandable, I guess.' He thought for a moment. 'And how does this involve you?'

'Because I found out before Bella that Claire and Tony were engaged.' When he didn't look any the wiser, she added, 'Bella should have known before anyone else. Her relationship with her mother is tentative enough without me knowing before she did.'

'I sort of get that. What did she say when she found out? Was she happy for them?'

'Eventually. I think she worries that Tony's children will get used to having her mum around and then if she leaves the island again, they'll be upset.'

'Hmm, that would be awful for them. What do you think will happen then?'

'I think that Claire's finally matured, and I do believe she's very much in love with Tony. You should have seen how devastated she was when he and Jack were missing. I think that if she wasn't 100 per cent sure of her feelings for him before then, she certainly was when that storm sprang up.'

'Right. And you decided that you shouldn't help Claire and Rosie with wedding arrangement because it wasn't your place?'

'Got it in one.' She smiled and put her arms round his neck, drawing him close so she could kiss him. It felt a bit forward but she couldn't resist feeling that perfect mouth on hers again.

He eventually pulled away to take off his denim jacket and spread it out on the sand. Then, taking her in his arms, he lowered her down and lay beside her. 'Do you mind if I kiss you again?'

'What, as a prize for being so clever?' she teased, only too happy for them to kiss for any reason at all.

'Yes, if you like.'

'Oh, go on then,' she giggled.

18

First thing the next morning, Jools was polishing the shop floor with her grandmother's ancient pale blue floor polisher. She was humming to herself as she concentrated on not missing any areas when the power died. 'What the hell?'

She pressed the machine off and on a few times and then kicked it. 'Ouch! Bloody thing.'

'You won't get it to work that way,' Bella laughed.

Jools shrieked with shock to discover she wasn't alone. Turning to face her friend, she scowled. Bella was holding up the plug she'd taken out of the wall socket.

'What are you doing?' Jools was frustrated to have been disturbed when she was doing such a good job. 'Gran's expecting this to be finished in the next half an hour before we open.'

Bella had the grace to look shamefaced. 'Sorry, Jools. I won't take up much of your time.'

'That's fine,' she said. 'Sorry to snarl. What can I do for you?'

'Please come with me to Betty's?' It occurred to Jools that she never did pick up the books she was supposed to have collected the day before.

'What for?' she asked, suspecting she already knew.

'Aunt Rosie is helping Mum plan the wedding.' She narrowed her eyes. 'You don't seem surprised.'

Jools realised she had been caught out, again, and grimaced. 'Sorry. I just happened to be at the lighthouse with Marius when Rosie arrived.'

Bella sighed. 'Not your fault. I'm never in the right place.'

'Yes, you are. Stop moaning and tell me what you want to do.' She had had enough of apologising for not doing anything wrong. 'Then I can get on with what I'm supposed to be doing.'

'I want you to come with me. I've asked Sacha, but she's busy, and Lexi is cooking something special for a lunch she's giving for her dad and Gloria.'

Jools knew she should probably feel offended to be the last of Bella's friends to be asked but couldn't help seeing the funny side. 'Have you asked me last because you think I'm not girly enough to help with a wedding?'

'No, of course not.' Jools could see her friend was doing her best to look shocked by the suggestion. 'Oh, fine. Yes. But you must admit you're not the flowery type and let's be real, my mum is. In fact, if she had her way her wedding would be all incense, petals dropping on water and floaty dresses, with flowers in her hair. You're more fifties-American-art-chic.'

'Thanks, I think.' Jools couldn't help laughing. 'Don't look so worried, Bella. I'm happy to help. But first, you can push that plug back into the socket and let me finish this job before Gran starts complaining.' Bella obliged. 'What time do you want me at Betty's.'

'As soon as you're free. Say, nine thirty?'

'Nine thirty it is.'

Jools switched the polisher back on and soon it was chugging with a life of its own. 'See you later,' she shouted over the noise as Bella left the shop.

* * *

An hour later, Jools left the shop to see Bella walking up to her. 'Hello there,' she called. 'Great timing.'

'Did you finish your chores?' Bella fastened a clip in her hair with difficulty.

'You'll probably find that a bit easier if you take those cotton gloves off. Have you got another hand-modelling job?'

Bella glanced at her gloved hands and grinned. 'Yes, I have. They wanted a female hand to rest on Jack's shoulder during a shoot he's got in a couple of days and he mentioned my name. I didn't expect them to sign me, but they did, so that's great for the coffers.'

Jools could imagine. 'It must be nice being able to work with him. Is the shoot on the mainland?' she asked as they began walking to Betty's.

'It's in Cornwall. All our travel costs are covered, so we're going to stay for an extra couple of days so that Jack can do some surfing and I can mooch around the shops and generally take it easy. I can't wait. He loves Cornwall, as we all know, but I've never been there with him. It should be fun.'

'And rather romantic, I imagine.' Jools wondered what it would be like to spend a few days away from home with Marius.

They stopped to speak to a few of the locals along the way and had just reached Betty's gate when Bella stopped. 'I was thinking that if you were with Marius when Rosie turned up, things must be going pretty well between you? Are they?'

Jools smiled, thinking of the couple of hours they'd spent at the beach. It *had* been romantic. 'Yes, it seems to be,' she said. 'I'm so glad I've sorted things out with Finn. To be honest, it was a bit of nonsense we had going on there. He seems happy with Tamara.'

'Well, Marius and his crew will always be heroes to me,' Bella said, opening the gate, waiting for Jools to walk through. 'I think he's lovely. And, although I know you're not one for relationships, I think that you and he could be very happy together.'

Jools smiled as they approached Betty's front door. She'd spotted Aunt Rosie's bright red sports car, the roof still down, no doubt to make the most of the sunshine and let everyone see her as she drove by, just as she was always perfectly turned out as if expecting someone to take a photo of her.

Jools turned and smiled at her friend. 'Before you get carried away, it's early days for Marius and me. Remember, we're here to help plan your mum and Tony's wedding, not mine.' She gazed at her friend, trying to read her thoughts. 'Or yours and Jack's.'

Bella gasped. 'I wasn't thinking any such thing.' She pushed Jools gently out of the way. 'Come on, they'll be wondering where we've got to.'

Jools knocked on Betty's door and stepped into the tiny hallway. 'Hellooo. It's only us!'

'We're in the living room,' Betty called. Not that they could have been anywhere else. The cottage was one of the smallest with a cosy living room at the front, a tiny kitchen and bathroom at the back, and two small but adequate bedrooms upstairs. It was a good thing Betty was still able to use the stairs, Jools thought as she walked through to see the old lady. She was sitting in her favourite armchair, her neatly trimmed and curled white hair tidy, as always. Claire and Rosie were sitting next to each other on the two-seater sofa.

'One of you can sit on the foot stool,' Claire instructed. 'The other will have to perch on the sofa arm, or bring in a chair from the kitchen.'

Jools motioned for Bella to take the footstool and brought through a painted pine chair from the kitchen. She hadn't given much thought to how she could contribute and as she sat down, decided to wait to be told what her role would be.

Claire tapped the notepad she was holding with a biro. 'We've been writing bits down that we think we'll need.'

'Brainstorming,' Rosie added. 'We've done quite well so far, I believe. It's going to be a simple affair,' she said, shaking her head slowly. 'Or that's what Claire intimated when she asked for my input. Isn't that right, Claire?'

Claire grimaced. 'Well, I thought it would be quicker and easier to arrange.'

'Why?' Bella frowned. 'I thought you were having a small wedding on the beach, then either something to eat and drink at my place, or a reception at the café if more people were coming.'

Claire moved slightly in her seat. 'Yes, and that's still the plan. Sort of.'

'So, what's the problem?'

Jools didn't want Bella to fall out with her mother so soon after their arrival. 'I think what Claire's saying is, although the wedding is a small affair, there's more to arranging it than she realised.'

Rosie nodded. 'That's it exactly. Firstly, although Claire and Tony can't legally be married on the beach—' she ignored the collective groan, '—I've checked it out and they could be married up at Grantez.'

'You mean that beautiful area surrounded by pine trees overlooking the whole of St Ouen's bay?' Bella asked. 'Where they hold the Sunset Concerts each year?'

Jools recalled attending a concert the previous year, when they'd driven up to the Neolithic site and walked through the field with a couple of thousand other concert goers, carrying their picnic blankets, food and drink to the natural amphitheatre surrounded by tall pines. It was a magical place. 'That would be such a romantic setting,' she sighed.

'Hold on,' Rosie said, interrupting the flow of approval. 'It was a good idea of mine, but Claire thought it might be too difficult to get to for some of the older villagers. She wants everyone to come to her wedding, or at least be able to see it from their windows.'

Thinking of her grandmother, who would hate to miss out, Jools was grateful for Claire's thoughtfulness.

'But what about the beach?' Bella asked.

'Rosie has arranged for Tony and I to be married in private, earlier in the day, at the Registry Office in town.'

'What?' Bella's voice rose. 'But you'll hate that, won't you?'

'Not really,' Claire said. 'Not if we can have a ceremony on the beach afterwards, which is what we're going to do.'

'Sounds good.' Bella shot her mother an approving glance and smiled at Rosie. 'Thanks for helping with this. I wouldn't have known where to start.'

Rosie preened. 'Please. It's no problem at all.' She smiled, a cheeky twinkle in her eyes. 'In fact, it's all online. All I had to do was look it up and take it from there.'

'So, what do you need us to do?' Jools wished she'd found an excuse not to come. She had no idea about weddings, had only been to two in her entire life. She listened as the obvious things were read out from Claire's list: flowers for her, Bella, and Tony's daughter, Jessie; a buttonhole for Tony and his son, Alfie; booking a celebrant for the beach event.

'We won't need a car, obviously,' Claire said. 'Tony and I will drive his into town and have a quiet lunch together after the legal wedding, which I'm told takes only a few minutes.' She looked at Bella. 'I'm presuming you'll be my witness? We're going to ask Jack to be Tony's.'

Bella beamed at her mother. It warmed Jools's heart to see them being nice to each other. 'I'd love that, Mum.'

'Thank you.' Claire's face lit up at her daughter's response. 'For the beach event, or the wedding proper as I like to think of it, as Tony lives up the hill and I only need to cross the road, we won't need transport.'

'You're assuming the weather's going to be fine?' Jools wasn't sure whether she should mention such an obvious concern. 'When is the wedding being held?'

'Early June,' Rosie said. 'D-Day.'

'Isn't that the sixth of June?' Bella groaned. 'You mean, we have less than three weeks to arrange this event, Mum?'

'If you must know, Tony wanted that date. He thinks it's the best way to commemorate his grandfather, who was killed on that day. He says it'll make the date a happy anniversary for his family instead of a sad one.' Claire stood, her gaze darkening. 'I shouldn't have to explain myself to you, Bella. This is my big day and you should want to help me in any way you can.' Without warning, she swept out of the cottage, slamming the door on her way.

'Well, that was rather uncalled for,' Rosie said, turning to Bella. 'Wedding planning is stressful for the bride. She needs our support, especially yours. Why don't you go after her and apologise? We'll stay here and think of anything else that needs doing and I'll give you each something from the list. The best thing we can do for Claire is to be sensitive to her needs.' When Bella didn't move but simply stared at her in silence, Rosie said, 'What are you waiting for? Go on, get after her.'

Bella widened her eyes at Jools, then rose. 'You're right,' she said to Rosie. 'I'm sorry.' Without another word, she hurried from the room.

Jools couldn't help feeling sorry for her friend. She wasn't used to being part of her mother's life in such a close-knit way and she was obviously finding it a challenge.

'Right,' Rosie said, once Bella had gone. 'Let's have a think. What did you say about the weather being inclement?'

Jools suddenly realised the other significance of the wedding date. It was the day after the exhibition. She was going to have to get more organised if she were to finish her paintings by then.

'Jools?'

She snapped out of her reverie when Rosie repeated her name and sat up straighter. 'I was thinking that if it rains, we'll need some sort of cover for people to shelter under.' She thought about the logistics of a beach wedding. 'And what about the tide?'

'The tide?' Rosie looked alarmed.

'Heavens, yes,' Betty said, smiling at Jools. She'd been sitting silently in her rocking chair by the window, probably listening to everything while looking out at the boardwalk. 'That's a good point. We need to check when it's high tide.'

'That's not difficult though, surely?' Rosie looked as though she was trying to frown.

'We need to work out when it will be on the day,' Jools said. 'Jack's the one to ask. He always knows what's going on because of his surfing. Then we'll need to arrange for the ceremony to take place as the tide is going out, to allow as much time as possible before it comes back in.'

Rosie sighed. 'I thought this was going to take an hour at the most to sort out. I didn't expect to be learning about the tides.'

'It's fine, really,' Jools reassured her. 'I don't think there's anything else to consider.'

'No one's going to get washed out to sea,' Betty said, adding with a chuckle, 'Though, you could always ask the guests to bring their swimming costumes.'

Seagulls squawked outside. The front door opened and Jools heard Bella shooing them away. She tensed, hoping her friend had managed to smooth things over with Claire.

'We're back,' Bella said, stating the obvious as she came in, followed by her mother. 'I'm sorry for having a moan. I'm aware you all have places to be and don't want to hold everyone up.'

'Same here.' Claire's cheeks were flushed but she looked calmer.

'Sit down, dear, and finish up,' said Betty.

Claire crossed the room and rested her palm on Betty's liver-spotted hand. 'Thank you,' she said. 'You're never flustered by anything. I wish I were more like you.'

Betty smiled. 'You're fine as you are, Claire. Now, tell us how we can help.'

Rosie clasped her hands together as they regrouped. 'You were saying earlier about outfits, Claire. You and Bella should pop into town and find something to wear.' She looked to Bella for dissent, and finding none, continued. 'Tony's little girl can wear a pink cotton summer dress, with a little cardigan should it be chilly on the day, and her flip flops, and the little boy will need a pair of light-coloured or navy trousers to wear with a simple shirt and trainers. It's all about being casual, as if it's been thrown together at the last minute.'

Jools didn't like to mention that they weren't far off doing that. Instead, she waited for Rosie to work through all the things that needed arranging. 'That leaves Jools to help organise the beach setting. You'll need a wedding arch with flowers and shells. Jack can help. I'll speak to him shortly.'

Jools stiffened. She had little experience of making things look nice, unless they were in a painting. 'What else should I get?'

'Sweetie, you need lots of jars with tea lights for when it gets darker. They should outline an imaginary aisle for the bride, groom and attendants to walk down. The rest of the guests can stand either side.'

'Right. Tea lights in jars.'

Rosie swung her arm back and forth, like a cabin attendant

pointing out the floor lights on a plane before take-off. 'Those without tea lights should have shells in them, and some should contain wildflowers.'

Jools pictured the scene. 'Exactly how many jars?'

'About forty-eight.'

'Forty-eight?' Where was she going to get that many jars? Then it dawned on her that she would also need to source the shells and flowers. The shells she could collect from the beach and tip back on the sand after the wedding. 'Inspired,' she said, 'I'll ask Tony's children to help me collect the shells.'

'What a clever idea,' Claire said, looking happier. 'I'm sure they'll want to feel involved in the planning. Well done, Jools.'

'Thank you.' She was relieved to have been useful. 'I suppose Sacha can help with the jars. Do they all have to be the same?'

Rosie shook her head. 'I'm sure between us we can find plenty. We can ask around for donations.'

Reassured by Rosie's suggestion, she said, 'What about the wildflowers?'

Rosie shrugged. 'You can take the children to pick those too.'

Bella clapped her hands, which meant she had come up with an idea she thought was brilliant. 'You don't want any wedding presents, do you, Mum?'

Claire shook her head. 'We've got everything we need already. Why?'

'Maybe we could ask the guests to bring a small posy of wild-flowers in lieu of a gift.'

Jools's heart leapt. 'I love that.' Now she wouldn't have to worry about what to buy the happy couple. 'What do you think, Claire?'

Claire patted her daughter's arm. 'I think it's perfect. Well done, Bella.'

It was a relief to see mother and daughter happy in each other's company. This should be a happy time, Jools thought.

'We'll also need pretty throws, colourful towels. They can be placed in neat piles and rolled out if people want to sit down after the ceremony.'

'What about fairy lights?' Betty asked. 'I think we need as much light as possible, especially for the older ones, like me.'

'We can buy solar ones so we don't need to worry about electricity,' Jools suggested. 'But we must make sure they're charged before the big day.' She was starting to enjoy herself. All this talk of a beach wedding and the thought of two people in love, making their vows with the sea as a backdrop, warmed her heart. 'I'm getting excited about this,' she admitted.

'Me, too.' Claire said, clasping her hands together as she looked at each of them in turn. 'Thank you for helping me, I really appreciate it. I want us to focus on the beach event because that's where we'll be sharing our big day with everyone close to us. I'm not worried about what I wear to the Registry Office, but I want my wedding dress to be the one I wear on the beach.'

They all spoke at once, eager to reassure her that whatever she wanted, they were happy to help with.

A short while later, Bella and Jools said their goodbyes and left.

'Thanks for coming, Jools.' Bella closed the gate behind them. 'I know it's not really your thing. It's not mine either, if I'm honest.'

Jools tried to picture her friend and mother going clothes shopping together. 'When are you intending to go into town for your outfits?'

Bella groaned. 'I don't have much time to waste,' she said. 'But we can't order anything online in case it gets here too late or doesn't fit.'

'You'll have to go before you and Jack go on that photo shoot.'

'I know.' She sighed. 'I want to get everything for Mum's big day out of the way so I can forget about it and focus on being with

Jack. It's so rare we have time away from this place and everyone else.'

'It's nice to help your mum though, too.'

'You're right,' Bella said. 'It's good to see her happy.'

They walked on in silence for a few steps.

'Do you know what you want to wear?' Jools asked.

'Something simple.'

'Really?' Jools was surprised. 'Strangely enough, I think this type of wedding would be perfect for you and Jack.'

Bella gave a little smile. 'I was thinking the same thing. But I can't copy what my mum is doing, if Jack and I ever tie the knot, can I?'

Jools wondered whether her friend trying to tell her something. Did she want to get married? She didn't ask, knowing Bella would tell her when she was ready. 'You could have a version of it,' she said. 'Everyone associates Jack with the surf. Where else would any of us picture him getting married?'

Bella slipped her arm around Jools's as they strolled towards the bookshop. 'You see? I knew you'd find a way to make me feel better.'

'I try.' Jools smiled. 'And now I'd better go and see Sacha about those flipping jam jars.'

19

'Your gran said you'd be here.'

Jools looked up to see Marius running down the granite steps to join her on the beach, a large bucket in one hand and a can of drink in the other.

'I thought you could do with some help collecting those shells.' His eyes twinkled in amusement when Jools pulled a face at him. 'I also bought you some lemonade. I suspect you might need it on a warm day like today.' He handed her the can and waited while she opened it and took a few gulps.

'Thank you,' she sighed. 'I feel like I've been doing this for hours.' She indicated the two full buckets at her feet. 'I'm going to have to wash and set them out to dry once I finish collecting them.'

'It'll be quicker now with the two of us.'

'I was going to ask Tony's children to help but they're at school and I thought I'd better make a start. They can help fill the jars instead.'

Marius gazed down at the shells. 'Are we looking for any in particular?'

Jools smiled. 'I was initially only collecting the prettier ones but as long as they're not broken and are small enough to fit quite a few in a jar, I pick them up.' She held out the can. 'Want a drink?'

'Not for me thanks. I had one earlier.'

She finished the lemonade and put the can in the recycling bin before running back to join Marius. 'Thanks, that was delicious.'

'My pleasure.' They set to work and after a few minutes, Marius dropped two handfuls of shells in his bucket. 'How's the painting going for the exhibition? I should imagine you'd rather be inside working on those than doing this. He picked up several more shells, studied them and wiped off some sand. 'Although, I'm finding this strangely therapeutic,' he added, dropping the shells into the bucket.

'I have to admit the same thing.' She added a few more to his collection. 'I was a little panicky when it dawned on me how many shells I'd need to find. If I'm honest, I'm a little behind on my paintings, but I'm doing a bit of this every morning and evening and so far, I'm liking it.'

'If you need any help with your paintings, or this, do let me know. If I'm not busy I'm more than happy to come down and help.'

'Thanks.' She smiled at him, her stomach contracting lustfully as his eyes caught hers and held her gaze for a couple of seconds. Jools pushed her hands into her jeans pockets. 'Your grandad seems to be enjoying visiting Gran and his new book club pals.'

Marius smiled. 'He said only last night how much happier he is here than he had imagined he would be. I think it's because your gran and everyone else on the boardwalk has made him so welcome, giving him things to do to fill up his days.'

Jools was glad. She knew her grandmother would be too when she told her later. They hated to think of anyone feeling lonely, especially when there was an entire village of people keen to make someone feel part of their community. 'That's good to hear. He's a lovely man and I'm relieved he's happy here.'

She picked up another handful of shells, discarding several that weren't up to the standard she was looking for. The jars had to look as perfect as possible and she wasn't going to be the one person to let Claire down when it came to her role in the wedding preparations.

'You said you were behind on your paintings for the exhibition,' Marius said.

She stopped and looked at him. 'I promised to paint nine canvases to complement your glass designs and, so far, I've done seven. I'm a little stuck on the final two. I know you sent me pictures of the glassware you've designed, but I can't quite figure out a painting of the landscape to go with it. I suppose I need a little more inspiration.'

Marius began working again, but slower this time, and Jools realised he was thinking. 'Why don't you come to the studio with me today.' He smiled at her. 'After we've filled this bucket. I can show you what I've done so far and maybe talk you through the two final pictures. I haven't produced the glass works yet, but I can show you something similar and talk you through my thought process. Who knows? It might help.'

She liked the idea, very much. She realised that although she liked Marius and they had spent quite a bit of time together, they still didn't really know each other very well when it came to their work. Maybe that was why she was finding it difficult to come up with the look she wanted for the paintings.

'What do you think?'

Jools smiled. 'I think it's a great idea. If we get a move on now, we should be able to finish in an hour or two.'

Marius laughed. The deep, rolling sound made her smile more broadly and she wondered whether he was ever anything but relaxed and friendly. Nothing seemed to faze him, she realised as she picked up another handful of shells and wiped the excess sand off them. He was such good company. She watched him work and forgot what she was doing until she noticed him staring back at her.

'Is something the matter?' His fair eyebrows lowered. 'Was it something I said?'

She shook her head, turning away to carry on collecting shells before he noticed how pink her cheeks were. 'No. It was nothing.'

'Are you sure?'

She could hear the concern in his voice and wanted to reassure him. 'I was just thinking how kind it is of you to want to help me.'

'Kindness has nothing to do with it.' He smiled, lifting his bucket and giving it a gentle shake.

'It doesn't?'

'Well, not totally.'

She was intrigued. 'Then, what?'

'I was hoping that once I'd got you to agree to come to the studio I might entice you to eat lunch with me.'

'What, again?' She tried not to show how delighted she was at the prospect.

Marius narrowed his eyes. 'Do you think you could be persuaded?'

'Maybe,' she giggled, bending to gather more shells. 'If you ask me nicely.'

Putting down his bucket, he turned her slowly to face him and kissed her. 'Was that nicely enough?' His voice was deep and slightly husky.

Jools blinked a few times, struggling to compose herself. 'Um, yes. I think that maybe you've managed to persuade me to accept your invitation to lunch.'

He dropped a kiss on her nose and smiled. 'Good. Now all I have to do is come up with something tasty to make you.'

All she really needed was a piece of toast or a cheese sandwich and more of his kisses. She made a pretence at checking the time despite not wearing a watch. 'You have about an hour to come up with something tempting.'

'Right,' he said, laughing. 'Then I had better get thinking, hadn't I?'

* * *

An hour and a half later Jools accompanied Marius to his studio.

'I won't switch on the lights down here,' he said. 'Even though we're pretty much off the main road, there always seems to be someone around when you want a lunch break.'

'That's a problem?' Jools was used to Gran opening the shop at all hours if someone wanted to drop off their unwanted books, even on a Sunday and, on one occasion, Boxing Day. She'd forgotten that most people stuck to rigid opening times.

Marius grinned at her, the glint in his electric blue eyes seeming to send a message. When she didn't pick up on it, he said, 'It is when you've been been looking forward to spending time alone with someone special.'

His words produced a warm glow in the pit of her stomach 'I assume you mean me.'

Marius laughed. 'Well, who else could I mean?'

She didn't like to think about there being any other women in his life. It had been hard enough to see him with his cousin, Sophie, before she realised she was his cousin.

Jools smiled at him, happy he was as interested in her as she was in him. 'I'm glad.'

'Oh?'

'That you want to spend time alone with me.'

He stepped closer, pulling her out of the view of the studio window, and his kiss took Jools's breath away.

Later, dishevelled and slightly giddy with excitement, Jools tried to gather herself.

'I suppose I should show you the pieces I've already made for the exhibition, seeing as that's the excuse I came up with to bring you here,' Marius said, smoothing his ruffled hair.

'Yes, you should.' Being with Marius was turning out to be more fun than she had ever had with any other man, even though they had done little more than walk, chat and collect shells. Oh, and kiss, she reminded herself, happily.

'I've kept them together at the back of the studio,' he said, leading the way. 'Over here.'

She followed him to a large mahogany cupboard, the doors of which were locked. He took a key tied with string from the back of the cabinet. 'I think it's best to lock them away from prying eyes. I don't want to have to explain to people that these pieces aren't for sale.'

'I suppose you would rather they were bought at the exhibition?' she asked, wanting to learn how these things worked.

'That's right. It's all about self-promotion really. Something I have an abhorrence for. I think most creative people do, don't you agree?'

She hadn't thought about it before. 'I haven't ever promoted my work before,' she admitted. It occurred to her that, until recently, she had only ever considered her art as an extension of herself, rather than something she needed to advertise.

'But you've sold quite a few paintings, or so Sacha said.'

'When did she say that?' Jools couldn't imagine how it had come up, but loved Sacha for showing off about Jools's art whenever she got the chance.

'I asked her about them at the café.'

He stepped towards the cabinet and pushed the key into the lock then gently pulled back the doors, exposing his brightly coloured, intricate pieces of artwork.

Jools stared open-mouthed. 'Marius,' she said, walking closer to have a better view. 'These are magnificent.'

His shoulders relaxed as she studied the pieces of glass. She wondered why he'd asked Sacha about her paintings, but there would be time to ask him later.

He reached forward and lifted out a tall, thick vase spiralling gently to the top in delicate shades of red and white.

'The lighthouse?' She wished she could afford to have something this beautiful one day.

'I decided I couldn't do work for an exhibition with the boardwalk as a subject, and not have a piece that depicted the lighthouse.' He hesitated, glancing at her. 'It was also somewhere we've spent time together. It makes me happy to think of being there with you.'

Jools swallowed at the emotion in his sentiment.

'It's beautiful.' She pointed at another, larger, piece in varying shades of blue from the palest turquoise to marine, pierced with shards of silver. 'That looks familiar,' she said, gazing at it.

He replaced the red and white vase and slowly lifted the blue and silver piece from the shelf it was standing on. 'You tell me,' he said. 'You're the artist.'

She stared for a few seconds longer, trying to visualise what the glass scene brought to mind. Finally, it came to her. 'It's the view from my grandmother's living room window, isn't it? The waves, and the splashes of silver the sun casts on the sea towards evening.' She pressed her hands to her cheeks. 'Oh, Marius, it's stunning.' She turned to see what he thought of her suggestion

'What?' His face was unreadable. She hoped she hadn't got it wrong. He was so talented; far more than she felt herself to be.

He slowly placed the vase back in the cupboard and turned to look at her. 'I'm stunned you can read me so well,' he said. 'You've described exactly what I was trying to achieve.'

Jools let out a sigh of relief. 'Thank heavens for that. I thought for a moment that I'd upset you.'

'Not at all. I'm just amazed, that's all.'

Smiling with pleasure, she let him show her the rest of his exhibits. 'These are amazing,' she said, proud that her work was going to be displayed alongside his. 'I'm not sure my paintings are up to the mark,'

'Rubbish,' he said at once. 'Your paintings are wonderful.'

She arched an eyebrow at him. 'Is that something you discussed with Sacha?'

He carefully folded the cabinet doors closed, locked the door, and hung the key back where he'd taken it from. 'Maybe,' he said, mysteriously.

'Do you mind if I ask you something?'

'Ask away.'

'Why were you talking to my friend about my work?'

'Why do you think?'

She gave a mock-stern frown. 'You tell me.'

'Let's go and sit in the flat and I'll make you some lunch.'

'Marius!' She playfully slapped his arm. 'Just tell me.'

'It's nothing underhand, if that's what's worrying you.'

Something occurred to her. 'Are you the mysterious buyer?'

'Sorry?' He innocently widened his eyes.

'Marius, did you buy the paintings from the café and commission me to paint four more?'

He stared at her thoughtfully. 'Would it be such a bad thing if I had?'

'Yes, if you thought you were doing me a favour.' She took a step back. 'I wanted someone to buy them because they loved them, not because they thought it would make me feel good. There's no creative satisfaction in that.'

He gave her a reassuring smile. 'Then it's a good thing it wasn't me, though I do love your paintings and definitely wouldn't have bought them just to make you feel good.'

'So, why the chat with Sacha?'

'I'd gone to pick up drinks for you and your gran a while back. Sacha happened to point out your paintings and said how well they sold.'

'And you didn't offer to buy them?'

'Looks like I can't win,' he said, picking up on her teasing tone.

'Oh, you can,' Jools said, following him up to his flat. 'You can make me cheese on toast without burning it.'

He grabbed her hand and pulled her close, burying his face in her hair. 'No promises,' he growled.

20

Jools was chatting to Lexi as they sat at the metal table on Lexi's front lawn. It was a warm, still, perfect spring day. Jools couldn't help thinking that even though she, Sacha and Bella lived directly above the beach, Lexi's view from up on the hill was the most perfect.

'I love it up here,' Jools said after taking a sip of the wine spritzer Lexi had made for them. 'I always forget how magnificent the view is.' She shot to her feet. *This view.* It was exactly what was missing from her exhibition pieces. 'Lexi?' she said, sitting down again. 'Can I ask you a favour, please?'

'Fire away.'

She explained that she needed two more paintings. 'The others are of smaller areas, the lighthouse, the cliffs, the sand, the sea, different weather and times of day. There's one of the board-walk and the cottages, and one with Sacha's café in it, but I need to paint two more views and one of them could be a larger painting encompassing the entire place.'

'I'd love you to paint this view,' Lexi said, smiling her approval. 'I'm sure Oliver would love to see it as part of the exhibition, too.'

'He's not here today?'

Lexi shook her head. 'He had to go into town for a meeting, but he'll be back in a couple of hours.'

Jools opened her mouth to ask how they were getting on when a car pulled up on the road in front of the cottages. They sat silently, watching as Gloria stepped onto the pavement.

'Gloria, is everything all right?' Lexi asked.

Jools knew that the two of them had made amends but doubted they were close enough yet for unannounced visits.

Gloria waved and then lifted a bundle of what looked like towels from the back of the car. 'Mrs Jones put the word out that you wanted brightly coloured blankets and towels for the beach wedding, Jools.'

Jools shot a surprised glance at Lexi and then smiled at Gloria. 'That's right,' she said, standing up. 'Are those for me then?'

'They are.' Gloria carried the items over and placed them on the table. 'I called at the bookshop and your gran told me you were here,' she said. 'Do you think these will do? They're only on loan for the day, but Jeff and I thought that they would do nicely.'

Jools smiled gratefully at her. 'They'll do very nicely, thank you.'

'It's kind of you to bring them, Gloria,' Lexi said.

Gloria seemed pleased with their reaction. 'I've got a lot of making up to do with you, Lexi.' Her smile disappeared. 'I know people around here are suspicious of me and I've given them good cause, but I want to change their opinion. I love your father and will do anything to make him happy. And if this helps, then I'm delighted.'

Jools could see that Lexi was at a loss for words. 'Thank you, Gloria,' she said. 'I'll make sure to let Claire know these came from you. I'm sure everyone will be grateful.'

'Would you, Lexi?' She seemed genuinely relieved. 'Thank you very much. Right,' she said, clapping her hands. 'I won't disturb you any longer.' She turned and began walking to her car. 'See you both soon, I hope.'

'Bye,' they replied, staring after Gloria as she drove away.

'Do you believe her?' Lexi asked as the car disappeared up the hill.

'I think I do,' Jools said. 'I mean, would you want to make an enemy out of the village?' She giggled. 'Especially Betty.'

'No, I would not.'

They gave each other horrified smiles at the thought.

'I'd better get on with some typing I promised Oliver,' Lexi said, standing. 'Why don't you go home and get your paints and easel and get to work on the painting for the exhibition. May as well make the most of this perfect weather.' She smiled again. 'And the peace. When Oliver gets back, he'll probably forget you're here and start singing.'

'Singing?' She couldn't picture the tall, handsome Scot singing for some reason.

'Yes,' Lexi smiled. 'He's taken to singing about the place.'

'Bless him,' Jools said, thinking how wonderful it was that her friend had found a man who made her smile so often. 'He's obviously happy, like you.'

Lexi sighed and looked skyward; an expression of utter contentment etched on her face. 'I really can't imagine being happier right now.'

Jools hugged her friend. 'I'm so thrilled for you both. You deserve all the joy in the world, do you know that?'

Lexi hugged her back. 'Thank you. That's so sweet of you.'

* * *

An hour later, as Jools rubbed away a few pencil strokes on her sketch pad, the sound of Oliver singing reached her before his car slowed to a stop by the cottage. She smiled to herself and continued working. She didn't want to embarrass him by letting him know that she had heard.

The car door clunked shut and his footsteps came across the path. 'Hey, Jools. How are you?'

She turned to face him, acting as if she hadn't spotted his arrival. 'Hi, Oliver. Lexi said I could work on a painting here, for the exhibition.'

He walked over to look at her drawing and then down the hill at the vista in front of them. 'I love that view,' he said, almost to himself. 'I think you've caught it very well. I look forward to seeing the final piece.'

'Thanks. I hope I do it justice.'

'You will. You always capture the essence of this place in your work. You're incredibly talented, do you know that?' Before she could think of how to respond to his compliment, he smiled. 'I have a feeling that you don't. I hope you will one day.'

Jools was taken aback by his praise, but delighted. 'That's very kind of you, Oliver. I appreciate it, really I do.'

Lexi had joined them and studied Jools's sketch. 'Oliver never says things he doesn't mean. He's right, too,' she murmured. 'This is going to be wonderful. Will you manage to finish it in time?'

Jools tried to ignore her rising panic. 'I'll have to. I still have to come up with a final painting after this one's finished.'

'Blimey,' Lexi said with a wince. 'I'll fetch you another drink and we'll leave you in peace.'

'Great, thanks.'

'Come on, Oliver.' Lexi kissed his cheek and took his hand. 'I had a visit from Gloria today.'

'Gloria?'

Jools smiled to herself. He sounded as shocked to hear it as they'd been to see her.

'Come inside and I'll tell you all about it.'

* * *

Jools worked for the rest of the day, forgetting the time and everything else apart from the view that had captured her focus and the oils she was working with. She loved times like these, when the rest of the world ceased to exist while she put colour on her canvas. As the hours wore on the light changed. A couple of times, she was tempted to alter the sky to fit in, but stuck with her original vision.

Finally, she stepped back from the painting and studied it. It wasn't bad, she decided, after adding touches of colour to several areas. She had enough to work with to finish it off. Hearing a gasp behind her, she turned to see Lexi staring open-mouthed at the canvas.

'Oh, Jools.'

Jools hoped her reaction was one of joy rather than horror. 'You like it?' she asked, mentally crossing her fingers. 'It's not finished yet,' she added. 'Not by a long way, but that's the bare bones of it.'

'It looks finished to me.' Lexi stepped forward to study her work more closely. 'You're so talented, Jools. Each time I see a new painting of yours, I'm taken aback by what you can achieve with a paintbrush and some oils.'

'That's kind of you, thanks.'

Lexi shook her head. 'My father would be so proud if I'd become an artist, like him.'

'Didn't you ever want to try your hand at it?' Jools wondered why this conversation had never cropped up between them in all the years they'd been friends.

'I did try when I was much younger. Dad gave me lessons.'

Jools was surprised. 'I never knew that.'

Lexi nodded wistfully. 'However, I was completely talentless.'

Jools hated to think of anyone being described that way, especially her good friend. 'I doubt that very much.' She thought of how amazing Lexi's father's paintings were. It must be difficult to have a parent who was so accomplished in something that you weren't. 'You shouldn't compare yourself to your father and his work. He's had a lifetime of experience.'

Lexi smiled. 'It wasn't just that,' she said quietly. 'I really was hopeless. Me painting was like a hippo trying to do ballet. I really have no skill whatsoever.' She laughed. 'Don't look so troubled, Jools. It's true. And what's more I don't mind. And thankfully, after seeing how hard I tried to paint, my father was relieved when I decided to give up.'

'He's proud of you anyway,' Jools said.

'I know.' She felt Lexi's hand on her back. 'I came out to ask if you'd like a lift home. You can't carry a wet painting and all your gear.'

'That would be great.' Jools hadn't given a thought as to how she was going to carry everything back. 'We can take the blankets that Gloria brought,' she suggested, carefully unclipping her canvas from the easel. She placed it on the table while she packed away her paints.

'Only if you have somewhere to keep them. Otherwise, I can drop them off at Betty's, so Claire can keep tally of how many things have been collected for her big day.'

They agreed that Gloria's offerings could be taken to Betty's and after Lexi had parked outside the bookshop, she turned off the ignition and stepped out to help Jools unload her things. 'Have you thought about what you'll paint for the final picture?'

'Nope. I have no idea. Although...'

'What?'

'Do you think the café might be a good topic? It's the heart of the boardwalk, after all, and everyone loves it. It's also quirky to look at and sums up the vibe of this place.'

Lexi nodded. 'I think that's a brilliant idea. Sacha would love it.' She thought for a second. 'The best viewpoint would be from down on the sand looking up at the café, don't you think?'

'Yes. Yes, it would.' She punched the air. 'That's a brilliant suggestion, Lexi.'

'Well, I didn't think it was that clever.'

'But it is. Don't you see?' Jools words came out in a rush of excitement. 'All my other paintings are from the boardwalk, looking out to sea. Even the one I've done today has the sea in front of me. It makes perfect sense to paint the last picture looking into the heart of the village with the sea behind me.' She grinned. 'I love it.'

Lexi laughed. 'I'm thrilled to have been such a help, especially when we know that I'm not at all creative.'

'Nonsense,' Jools said, carefully taking her canvas from the boot of Lexi's car. 'You just haven't discovered where your creative talents lie yet.'

'I wonder if I ever will?' Lexi gave Jools a wink, suggesting she was happy as she was.

21

THE EXHIBITION

Jools spent the following few days keeping as busy as possible, finalising her paintings, running around collecting things required for Claire and Tony's wedding and helping Gran when she could.

'Don't worry about me,' her gran had said a couple of days ago, when Jools was beginning to panic that she wouldn't have time to get everything done. 'Alan has offered to help in the shop and I was happy to accept.'

Jools suspected that Alan was thrilled to have something to do, but he got on well with Gran and Betty and the three of them seemed to enjoy spending time together.

She looked over at the cotton dress she had bought online for the wedding and hoped the weather stayed warm. If it didn't, she would have to rethink.

She carried the final two paintings down to Lexi's car. Her friend had kindly offered to give her a lift to the Exhibition Centre in the next village. Jools was excited to discover what Marius had planned for staging their pieces. He had said he would meet her there and she was looking forward to seeing him since the last time they'd been together was at his studio flat.

'All ready?' Lexi said as they set off. 'You're looking a little anxious, but you shouldn't.'

'What if no one comes to the exhibition?' Jools didn't mind people not turning up if it was only a small event. She had heard on the village grapevine that the local newspaper was sending a reporter to interview her and Marius, together with a photographer to take pictures to go with the feature. She had never been in the paper before and the thought of it terrified her.

'Most of the locals from the boardwalk will be there,' Lexi said, waving at Oliver as he drove past them the opposite way.

'I hope so.'

'Most of them are too nosy not to be,' Lexi joked. 'No, really. Everyone loves your paintings and they'll be a resounding success, you mark my words.'

Jools took a deep breath and tried to calm down. She didn't need her hands shaking if she was to carry paintings into the centre. What if she dropped one? She tried not to think about it.

Lexi patted her leg. 'Hey. Stop fretting. You will be brilliant. If you worry too much you are going to end up not enjoying the evening and that would be a terrible shame. Imagine if you never get to do one of these events again and you wasted it by worrying about everything.'

Jools thought that made sense. 'I'll try,' she said. 'Is your dad coming with Gloria?'

Lexi nodded. 'He can't wait.'

'But he's so talented. He'll think my paintings are amateur compared to his work.'

'Stop it. He won't. He'll be proud that he knows you and that you're following your dream. Now, enough stressing. You are going to promise me that you'll focus on having a lovely time. Agreed?'

'Okay.'

Lexi drew up in the small car park and helped Jools carry her canvases into the building. Jools was relieved to see Marius already there, chatting to the manager. He looked up and smiled, saying something to the immaculate woman before hurrying over to greet them.

'Here,' he said, leaning forward to kiss her and then Lexi on the cheek. 'Great to see you both.' He reached out to take the canvases from Lexi. 'Jools, follow me and I'll show you where to put these. We're almost ready to hang them but I wanted to be certain you were happy with what I had in mind.'

She followed him to the back of the studio, passing his coloured glass-work pieces set out on individual plinths and display shelves which were stark white to contrast with the colours. 'They're stunning,' she said, impressed by how beautiful everything looked under the bright lights.

'Thanks.' He leaned one of the paintings carefully against the wall, before taking the other to where one of his pieces was displayed. 'You see these hooks on the wall?' Jools nodded. 'That's where we'll hang this painting. I think it complements this piece really well, don't you?'

She nodded and smiled, delighted with how the very different pieces of artwork balanced each other. 'You can tell they're of the same scene but from a different perspective using different formats.'

'Exactly,' Marius said. 'That's what we were hoping to achieve.'

'And we've done it.' The relief that her painting looked so impressive alongside his work was overwhelming. For the first time in days, she began to feel a little more confident that she knew what she was doing, and that Marius had been right to persuade her to take part. 'You are very clever,' she said honestly.

Lexi stayed to help set up the rest of the exhibition and eventually, tired but happy, Jools asked Marius if she could go home and change.

'Yes do, and don't forget to have something to eat before coming back later. I know we're having canapés and drinks, but you'll probably find that you're either too nervous to eat, or too busy speaking to attendees to have a chance to eat anything at all.' He gave her a peck on the lips. 'You've done brilliantly, Jools. I know this is going to be a perfect evening.'

'It's down to your hard work, setting this up, not me,' she said. 'And I'm grateful for your encouragement.' She smiled. 'I'd better get going.'

'I'll see you at seven o'clock.'

'Thanks for waiting, Lexi,' she said, when they were in the car. 'I'm sure you have lots of other things to be getting on with.'

'Nothing this important. Anyway, I couldn't leave you to walk home, now could I? You've got to conserve your energy for your big event this evening. Oliver and I will come to collect you and your grandmother later and take you back. Dad and Gloria are going to meet us up there.' She gave a little squeal, crunching the gears. 'I'm so excited, Jools. This is such a big deal for you and I just know it'll be the first of many. The exhibition and the newspaper article will help get word out about your paintings to the general public.'

'I suppose so,' Jools agreed, not quite as sure as her friend that she was ready for the rest of the island to see her work.

Two hours later, wearing a smart pair of black trousers that Bella had lent to her, and a sparkly top that Jools wasn't sure was really her, she checked her hair was perfectly mussed up and her eyeliner and red lipstick just right, before giving Teddy a quick cuddle.

'Wish me luck, little buddy.' He sat back on his haunches and raised his front paws. 'Thank you.'

She blew him a kiss, and stepped outside to join her grandmother, Lexi and Oliver in the car.

Jools took her gran's hand and gave it a squeeze. 'Thanks for coming. I know you don't really like going out at night.'

'Nothing was going to keep me from joining you this evening,' she said, smiling. 'Not even *Eastenders.*'

'Ready?' Lexi asked, eyes sparkling with excitement.

'As I'll ever be.'

After parking the car and walking into the hall, Jools gasped. 'Who are all those people? Surely they're not all here to see my and Marius's work?'

'Of course they are.' Oliver rested a hand on her shoulder. 'And they're very lucky to be here.' He gazed around him, taking in the displays. 'These really are excellent,' he said. 'Maybe after tonight you'll realise how talented you are.'

'I hope so,' Lexi said. 'By the end of this evening she might have a glimmer of understanding about what we see in her work.'

Jools scanned the room for Marius. She hadn't expected him to greet her, knowing he would be far too busy speaking to people, but she wished she could spot where he was and say hello.

'Where's Marius?' Gran asked. 'I can't see him anywhere.'

'Neither can I.' Jools was beginning to feel a little unnerved. 'I wonder where he's got to?'

'Hello, lovely ladies,' Alan said, hurrying over to welcome them. 'Isn't this splendid? You young people are incredibly talented, I must say.'

'Thank you,' Jools said. 'Do you know where I can find Marius? I haven't seen him yet.'

'Ah.' Alan did a little side-shuffle in his shiny shoes, looking rather shifty.

'He's not here, is he?'

Alan shook his head slowly.

'Not here?' Gran cried, causing a few heads to turn and look in their direction. 'Why ever not?'

Alan looked around him briefly before lowering his voice. 'There's been a shout, I'm afraid. Just after you left earlier. He's still not back.'

Jools couldn't believe what she was hearing. 'But why was he on duty when he knew he had to host this event tonight?' She felt suddenly breathless with panic.

'You know Marius,' Alan said. 'Maybe he's stepped in to take someone else's place on the boat.' He laid a hand on her shoulder in a comforting gesture. It didn't work. While she was here, nice and safe around people she loved, Marius was out at sea, attempting a rescue. *Please, let him be safe.*

She looked around, panic flaring. 'I've never done this sort of thing before.'

'Have you attended an exhibition like one this though?' Alan asked. 'You know, someone else's?'

She thought of the few times Lexi had invited her, Bella and Sacha to attend events for her father and nodded. 'Yes.'

'Then just remember how they went and you'll be fine. Just say a few words to everyone to welcome them and thank them for coming and make your way around the room chatting about your work. It won't be too bad.'

'You don't think?' she grimaced. 'That's my idea of hell.' She took a deep breath in an effort to control her nerves.

'You'll be fine. We're all friends here and no one has come to find fault.'

'But what about the newspaper journalist?'

He gave a reassuring smile. 'I'll accompany her around the room. I can fill her in on some of the thought processes behind Marius's work. We've discussed it enough times.' He widened his eyes and nodded. 'Remember to try to enjoy yourself this evening.'

'Thank you.' Jools couldn't imagine she would be doing anything apart from putting on a brave face and gritting her teeth until the event was over. She hated being the centre of attention and had only agreed to take part because Marius was the main attraction. Now she was going to have to step up and give the speech that she had expected him to do. She hadn't prepared anything. And on top of that, she couldn't help worrying about Marius. *He knows what he's doing,* she reminded herself. The sea wasn't as rough this evening as it had been during his previous rescue mission. The least she could do, for Marius's sake, she decided, was look as if she was enjoying herself.

'Hi, Jools!' Bella arrived with Jack and Claire, Tony and Betty followed them in. Jools relaxed slightly and went over to greet them.

'It's good to see you here. Thanks so much for coming,' she said, practicing her welcome. She watched them gaze around the room at the exhibits.

'This looks amazing,' Jack said. 'Well done, you.'

Jools smiled gratefully. 'It was Marius who put everything together, so he's the one who should take the credit for that.'

'But your paintings,' Claire said, stepping closer to inspect the nearest one. 'They're so good.'

'They are,' Tony agreed. 'You're really talented.'

Jools couldn't help blushing at their kind comments. 'That's nice of you to say so.'

She spotted more people arriving and glancing over at the hall manager saw that she was being given a very pointed look. 'I think I'd better go and welcome the next arrivals. Help yourselves to something to eat and drink and I'll catch up with you as soon as I can.'

After she had chatted briefly to the next group of people and another couple after that, Jools realised that she was coping far better than she could have hoped. How long was Marius going to be? She hoped he was able to get back and enjoy a moment in the spotlight before the event was over. Overwhelmed, she took a moment to stand in a quiet corner and watch the proceedings. Excited chatter filled the room, people were clearly enjoying themselves. A crowd had gathered around her grandmother, who looked to be in her element, holding court. Gran caught her eye, placed one hand on her heart and smiled. Emotion caught in Jools's throat as she realised her grandmother was telling her how proud she was. For the first time, she allowed herself to relax and enjoy the moment. She searched the room for Marius, hoping he might turn up, but realised that she couldn't put off making a speech any longer. She clenched her free hand to stop it from shaking and closed her eyes for a couple of seconds. Then she accepted a microphone from the immaculate woman she'd seen earlier, her hair slicked back into a neat French pleat.

Jools grabbed a glass of champagne from a passing waitress and swallowed it in one gulp, then tapped the microphone to see if it was on. An echo of feedback filled the room. Everyone stopped speaking and turned to face her with expectant expressions. Jools's breath seemed to leave her as she stared at the sea of faces.

She took a deep breath and braced herself. 'Firstly, I'd like to thank you all for coming,' she said, trying to calm down and stop her voice from shaking. 'When Marius asked me to take part in this exhibition, it never occurred to me that I would be the one making the speech, so please bear with me.'

'You're doing brilliantly, Jools,' Bella cheered.

'You've got this,' Sacha called, as a few of the audience clapped.

Jools cleared her throat again. 'Thank you. As you can tell, my friends are here to support me. Unfortunately, Marius has been called away. I know a lot of you are here for him and and I'm sure he'll get here as soon as he possibly can. For now, I'd like to say how grateful we both are that you've all taken the time to come this evening and we hope that you like the exhibits we've prepared.'

Unable to think of what else to say, she scanned the room and was about to thank them once more when Marius hurried in through the front door. Her heart soared at the sight of him. He looked windswept and flustered, but he'd made it. When he spotted her, microphone in hand, he gave an apologetic wince. She knew he would understand her anxiety at being left to host the evening on her own. Not wishing to worry him further, she gave a reassuring smile and held out her arm in his direction. 'Talk of the devil and he appears,' she said with a laugh. 'Here's the man of the moment. Marius, we've been looking forward to your arrival,' she smiled to show she was teasing as he rushed towards her, pushing his hands through his hair in an effort to tidy himself up.

'Everything okay,' she murmured. He looked tired.

'I'm good.'

She handed him the microphone. 'Would you like to say a few words?'

Putting his arm around her shoulder, he smiled down at her. 'I'm sorry I'm late,' he began. 'But I know my co-exhibitor, Jools, will have been the perfect hostess in my absence.' Everyone cheered and clapped. Jools felt her cheeks redden. 'I'm sure she's already thanked you for being here, so I'd just like to tell her how grateful I am that she agreed to take part this evening and bring her beautiful paintings to your attention...'

Jools didn't hear anything more. She watched his mouth moving, his animated speech entertaining everyone, but all she could think was how exhausted he must be after preparing for the event for weeks, setting up earlier and not having a chance to rest or even eat or drink anything since she had left him earlier, not to mention getting an emergency call from the RNLI at the las minute. No wonder he looked worn out, his happy expression forced. She slipped her hand into his and focused on listening, copying everyone else's reactions as she smiled and nodded, willing the evening to be over so they could talk.

Once he'd thanked everyone again, he switched off the microphone and handed it back to the waiting manager. Immediately, people began crowding him and he was led away to talk through his exhibits. He glanced over his shoulder and mouthed an apology and Jools gave a small wave to let him know it was fine and not to worry.

By the end of the evening, as groups of people began leaving, Jools wondered if she would be able to catch a moment alone with him. They'd been interviewed by the charming journalist for the paper and had their photo taken but hadn't been able to speak privately.

'I'm off now, lovey,' Gran said. 'Lexi and Oliver are going to give me a lift home.'

'That's great, Gran,' she said. 'Thanks, all of you.'

Lexi hugged her. 'It was a brilliant evening, Jools,' she whispered. 'You should be proud of all that you've achieved. I know we're all impressed with what you've done.'

'Thanks, that's really kind of you.'

She saw Jeff and Gloria walking in her direction. Nervous to hear what Lexi's talented father thought of her work, she braced herself. 'We're going to get going too,' Jeff said, shaking her hand. 'Your paintings are excellent, Jools.' She was relieved at his verdict and touched that he'd taken the time to let her know. 'You have a real talent there, young lady. You need to try to look at them as if they were someone else's. Maybe then you would see how good they are.'

'Thank you,' Jools said, feeling her face heat up. 'And thank you both for coming. I really appreciate it.'

'No problem at all,' Gloria said. 'I've enjoyed myself. In fact, I was saying to Jeff that he should think about putting together an exhibition of his own.'

'You should, Dad,' Lexi said, beaming at him. 'I'm sure it's the perfect incentive to get back into painting.'

Jeff smiled at Jools. 'Maybe we could do one together?'

She gasped. It was a dream come true to be asked by someone with such a wonderful reputation. 'Really?'

He nodded, obviously warming to the idea. 'Let me have a think and make a few calls and I'll get back to you in a few weeks with some dates. How about that?'

Lexi hugged her dad and pressed a kiss on his cheek. 'Oh, Dad, that's the best news I've heard for ages. You're always happiest when you're creating something.'

Jools watched as they hugged again, happy to see that despite the difficulties they had gone through in the previous months, they were back on good terms. Seeing the two of them close again made her heart sing. She would happily agree to whatever dates were suggested if it meant Lexi's proposition to get her father painting again came to fruition.

'Arrange whatever you like,' she said to him. 'I'm just grateful you've asked me to take part.'

'Good, then that's what I'll do.'

She watched them leave and felt a hand rest lightly on her shoulder. Jools turned to face Marius. 'Hi.'

'Hello, you,' he said. 'Do you forgive me for leaving you in the lurch this evening?'

She pretended to consider his question. 'Let me see...' She motioned for him to come closer and when he bent his head, kissed him lightly on his mouth. 'There's nothing to forgive,' she said. 'It was just bad timing that you were called out.'

His shoulders relaxed and he smiled and pulled her to him.

'I'm so sorry that I wasn't here. I know this whole thing was my idea and when I saw you standing there with a microphone in your hand, addressing everyone, I knew how difficult it must have been.'

She rested her hands on his chest and pushed him back gently. 'Hey, I might not choose to be the main focus of everyone's attention, but I'm not a delicate flower who needs to be cosseted. I was fine,' she laughed at the memory of how nervous she had been earlier. 'It just took a little bit of Dutch courage, that's all.'

'That's a relief.'

'And anyway, you were the one out doing important work.' She gave his hand a gentle squeeze. 'How was your shout?'

'False alarm,' he replied wearily.

'*What?*' Angry that he'd to miss their special night for no reason, Jools frowned. 'I thought...' she shook her head. 'I imagined you out there, risking your life,' she shuddered. 'I can't believe someone would make a false call.'

He shook his head. 'It's annoying, but I would rather that than it be someone in difficulty,' he said. 'Although I'm sorry that I wasn't here, at least no one was hurt, or worse.'

'How do you know when there's an emergency?' She hadn't thought to ask before. 'Do you receive a text?'

'We have pagers that are activated by the coastguard. The launch authority then pages the crew members and the crew message to advise if they're able to attend the shout.'

'It's all done so quickly.' She tried to imagine the scenario.

'It has to be,' he said, kissing the tip of her nose. 'Thank you for caring.'

22

THE WEDDING DAY

Jools covered her mouth as she yawned. It was the day after the exhibition and she wasn't sure which was more exhausting; recovering from the stress of the previous evening, or the pressure of carrying out her tasks for the wedding. Claire and Tony had left for the Registry Office an hour ago with Bella, Jack and Tony's children, and Jools wanted to get as much done as possible before they returned after their celebratory lunch.

She puffed as she carried yet another box of jam jars down the steps onto the beach, ready to set up where Claire and Tony were to hold their ceremony. She had already carried down the tea lights and strings of fairy lights once she'd checked the tide was far enough away from the sea wall.

'Holding a beach wedding where the tide can move twelve metres twice a day probably wasn't the best idea,' Jack grumbled, having raked the sand to make it neat and removed seaweed from where Alessandro and Marius were helping him erect the archway that Rosie was attempting to decorate with flowers, shells and strings of tiny white fairy lights.

Jools couldn't have agreed more but kept her thoughts to herself. Jack might get away with riling his aunt, Rosie, but Jools didn't want to get on the wrong side of her, especially when she still had so much to do before hurrying back to the bookshop to freshen up and change for the evening ceremony.

'Aunt Rosie,' she called, after placing jam jars in parallel lines to make up the aisle. 'How do they look? I don't want to do any more until I'm sure I've got them in the right place.'

Rosie turned to look at Jools's work and gave her a thumbs up. 'Good work. Now you'd better get a move on and get the rest in place. We are still going to need to light the tea lights. Where are the posies of wildflowers to go in the empty jars?'

'Sacha has kept them in water at the café. We thought it was cooler in there. She's going to send someone out with them soon, I'm sure. If not, I'll go and get them.'

She'd already positioned the jars with the sea shells in, filled by Tony's children who'd painstakingly worked on them all weekend.

Gran opened her living room window and leaned out. 'Is someone going to collect the blankets from Betty?' she bellowed. 'She'll need to get herself ready and I don't want her having to worry about them.'

Jools wondered how anyone could have imagined that a beach wedding would be a simple event to organise. There was so much to do, and so little time in which to get it all done. 'Will do, Gran,' she replied, unsure who to ask.

'I will go,' Alessandro called. 'Finn, he will come with me. Please, do not worry, Mrs Jones.'

Jools gave Alessandro a grateful look as he ran past her. She straightened, arching her back to ease her aching muscles, and sighed wearily. Remembering her paintings were still hanging in the hall of the Exhibition Centre, she asked Marius to check when they had to be taken down and removed.

'I've explained about the wedding,' he said, sounding tired. 'They're happy for us to collect them sometime tomorrow, so there's no panic.'

'That's a relief.' Like Marius, she was too tired this morning to have to worry about them on top of everything else. 'See you later.'

She decided to walk up the lane, turning right at the top of the boardwalk to pick a handful of wildflowers for her own posy. Then, returning home, she popped them in a small vase and made her and her grandmother a sandwich and sat down to eat it.

'You're looking very pale, lovey,' Gran said, frowning at her across the kitchen table. 'You must be careful not to overdo things. You don't want to be ill.'

'I'm fine, Gran. It's nothing an early night won't put right. I think I'm tired after weeks with so many pictures to paint, not that I'm complaining. I've never been so busy, I've loved finally selling my work and the exhibition was really exciting.'

After lunch, she washed up and helped her gran change into her smart, two-piece outfit.

'I know Claire said that the wedding was a casual event, and I'm not even going down to the beach, but I will be watching from the living room and I don't want anyone thinking I haven't bothered.'

Jools smiled. 'You look lovely,' she said. 'I'm just going back to finish putting the jars and blankets out. I shouldn't be too long. I'll come back for a shower and make sure you're ready to watch everything as it happens.'

Back on the beach, Marius joined her. 'That looks wonderful,' he said as she finished lighting the first row of tea lights. 'You've made a brilliant job of that, Jools. Let me do the ones on the other side.'

Jools gratefully passed him the long-handled lighter she had borrowed from Jack and watched him working before noticing that Jack was carrying a couple of small buckets with posies in them.

'Here you go,' he said. He had a plastic jug in one hand. 'Sacha said I'm to half fill the jars with water before putting the flowers in.'

'Great. You do the water; I'll do the flowers.' Jools was relieved to be almost finished. 'We'll get this done in no time.'

'I'll rake the sand down the aisle once you're done, so it's perfect for Claire and Tony,' Marius offered.

'Typical artist,' Jack said. 'Worrying about the detail.' He laughed and flicked some of the water in Marius's direction.

'When you've both finished larking about,' Jools said, giving them a mock-serious glare. 'We've still got the blankets to arrange and to get changed before we can relax and have fun.'

* * *

To save time, Jools had asked Marius if he wanted to bring a change of clothes to the bookshop. She also liked the idea of them arriving at the wedding together, even if it was a short journey along the boardwalk and down the steps to the beach. It felt grown up to have a proper date for the special occasion.

Gran was already positioned at her prime viewing place in her chair at their living room window. She had insisted that with the window open and the wedding taking place below it, she would probably have a better view than anyone else. Jools thought she might be right.

'I'll be like one of those drone things you sometimes see on the television.'

Jools also liked to think that when the sun went down, Gran

would be warm in the flat and able to take herself off to bed when she got tired and had had enough of the celebrations.

'I'll make sure to bring you up something to eat and drink,' Jools promised.

'You'd better had,' her grandmother said. 'Otherwise, I'll call out of the window to remind you.'

Half an hour later, Jools dried her hair and peered out of the window to see Marius alone on the beach, finishing his raking. She smiled to herself. He was such a kind man. So thoughtful and willing to help others. He seemed to sense her watching and stopped what he was doing. Leaning on the handle of the rake he looked up and smiled at her. 'You look lovely.'

'I will when I'm dressed up,' she insisted, but knew that he truly meant what he said. She didn't have to put on airs and graces for him. He seemed very happy with her just as she was.

A few minutes later he arrived at the bookshop. 'Everything looks great out there. I'm sure Tony and Claire are going to have a perfect evening. At least the weather's held and we don't have to worry about it raining.' He glanced over at the window as if to double-check. 'Hello, Mrs Jones. You look very nice.'

'Thank you,' she said, tapping her wristwatch. 'I think you need to get in that shower and hurry up if you're not going to be late to the event. They're going to be here soon.'

Jools hadn't realised how late it was. 'I've left a fresh towel in there for you.'

'Thanks,' he said. 'I'll only be five minutes.'

Jools grinned at her grandmother as he left the room. 'Shall we time him, do you think?'

'I will,' Gran laughed, looking down at her watch and tapping her foot.

Jools could feel the excitement in the air as they waited for Marius.

'I told you I would be five minutes,' he called out triumphantly, walking into the living room. His hair was still damp but he was already dressed, smart and handsome in a pale blue shirt and navy chinos.

'You were six and a half minutes actually,' Gran said, giving him a wink to show she was only teasing. 'Right, you two, get a move on.'

Jools left her grandmother sitting in her armchair at the living room window with a glass of wine and a plate of sandwiches in case she needed a snack.

'I'll come and bring you some nibbles from Sacha, as well as something else to drink a bit later,' she said as Marius took her hand in his.

'Good girl. Now, you go and enjoy yourself and stop fretting about me. I'm perfectly happy as I am.'

Jools kissed her gran. 'Have fun,' she said, letting Marius lead her to the door.

As soon as they were outside, he kissed her quickly and then whistled through his teeth. 'How lucky am I to be partnered with the prettiest girl on the boardwalk? You look stunning.'

'Flatterer,' she smiled, loving every second as she smoothed the skirt of her pink dress.

'I don't think I've ever seen your legs before.' He winked at her.

'And you might never see them again if you keep doing that,' she laughed. She heard Tony's voice, speaking to his son and daughter. They were at the top of the steps, about to walk down onto the sand. 'We'd better hurry,' she said, tugging Marius's hand. 'If Tony's here, Claire and Bella won't be far behind.'

As they followed them onto the beach, Jools looked at Tony's daughter. She was seven years-old, her wavy fair hair held back from her face with a pretty head band. Her pink cotton dress had an orange flower on the skirt, which looked as if it was a pocket, and on her feet were pink flip flops. Jools smiled. It was typical of Claire to want the little girl to feel relaxed, yet special. Jools wondered which of them had chosen the outfit. Tony's son wore chinos, like his father, and a short-sleeved shirt in pale grey. The trio looked incredibly happy and her heart swelled to see the little family. This was a new beginning for them and Jools felt sure they would all be very happy together.

The celebrant was waiting under the flower-covered archway and everyone who had been invited was standing next to their designated towel on either side of the aisle which was softly lit by the flickering tea-lights.

'You were right, it does look amazing,' Jools whispered.

Marius lifted her hand to his lips and, turning it over, kissed her palm. The feel of his mouth on her skin sent shivers down her spine. She couldn't believe how happy she felt. 'This is your doing.'

'We all did our bit,' she said, not wanting to take too much credit.

A man Jools didn't know, but suspected was a friend of Tony's, positioned himself by the archway and began playing a guitar. As he strummed the wedding march, everyone turned to see Claire, standing at the bottom of the steps to the beach, holding a larger wildflower posy and looking beautiful in her wedding dress. Bella, beside her, kissed Claire's cheek.

'Go and marry your lovely fiancé, Mum.'

Jools caught the words on the breeze and almost gave into the emotion that had been building inside her for most of the day. Everything was so beautiful. She dabbed her nose with a tissue, relieved to have remembered to bring one with her. Jools listened to the celebrant guiding the couple through the vows they had written for each other, lulled by the distant sound of waves and the fairy lights that shone brighter as the sun slowly set. She glanced up at her grandmother and gave her a discreet wave. It had been a long, and sometimes stressful, year for all of them, but one that they would remember fondly.

23

Everyone clapped and cheered as the celebrant invited Claire and Tony to kiss.

It had been a perfect day in the end. Jools smiled to herself, recalling how happy Claire had been to be marrying Tony. Jack and Alessandro began pouring drinks for everyone and Jools and Lexi helped Sacha serve plates of food.

Two hours later, a taxi arrived to whisk Tony and Claire to one of the island's coastal towers, where they'd booked a short stay. After several minutes of hugging and kissing and cheering, the happy couple waved goodbye and left their guests, ready to start their marriage.

A little while later, Betty said her goodbyes. 'I'm taking Jessie and Alfie back to my cottage to stay the night,' she said to Bella. 'Your mum made up their beds this morning, so they're all set up.'

'Brilliant. Jack and I will come and collect them in the morning,' Bella said, ruffling her new step siblings' hair and causing them to grumble at her. 'They'll stay with us until Mum and Tony return, as arranged.'

'Perfect,' Betty said. She was about to leave the beach when something seemed to occur to her and she turned, facing Bella, Jools, Sacha and Lexi. 'I gather from Claire that the four of you are concerned about what will happen to me now that Claire will be moving out and going to live with her new husband.'

Jools glanced at her friends and back at Betty. 'We thought we might take it in turns to stay in your spare room,' she said. They hadn't actually discussed it but, knowing her friends, they would have the same mindset as far as Betty's welfare was concerned.

'Nonsense,' Betty said. 'You'll do nothing of the sort. I'm not incapable of taking care of myself just yet.'

'But you don't want to go back to living alone, do you?' Jools asked, concerned.

'No, and I don't have to. Barry and I have spent a lot of time together since Lexi and Oliver introduced us,' she explained. 'He's very lonely in his house up at Les Landes, so we've decided that he's going to move into my cottage with his little dog and we will keep each other company.'

'He is?' Jools wondered how many more surprises Betty had up her sleeve.

'We have much more in common than either of us realised. We like the same television programmes and food. We love your café, Sacha, and your gran's bookshop and book club, Jools. I think we're going to have fun.'

'Then that sounds like the perfect arrangement,' Lexi said. 'If Barry wants any help packing up his bungalow and moving down here just let us know, won't you?'

'I'll be sure to tell him. Thank you.' Betty blew each of them a kiss. 'Right, now I'd better get these children home to bed before they get over-tired and I end up missing something on the television.'

Jools and her friends dropped down on the various blankets and towels lying on the beach.

'I am dying of exhaustion,' Bella groaned, flopping back theatrically next to Jack. 'I don't think I've ever felt so drained, both emotionally and physically.'

'But your mum is happy,' Lexi laughed. 'So, it's all been worth it, surely?'

'I do hope so,' Bella said through a yawn. 'Jack, I need a lemonade if there's any left. I'm parched.'

Jools caught Jack gazing lovingly at Bella. Her friend's face was glowing, despite her tiredness. Her little secret was making her happy. It wasn't just that she had come to terms with her mother being married to Tony causing her to look so serene.

'Who else wants refreshments?' Jack asked, getting to his feet. Once everyone was holding a drink, he sat back down next to Bella. She straightened and shuffled closer and he wrapped his arm around her waist. 'Now we're all comfortable, Bella and I would like to share something with our closest friends, and—' he winked at Sacha, '—my twin sister.'

'Ooh, what?' Sacha knelt beside Alessandro, as if it might help her hear the news more quickly. 'Get on with it, Jack.'

'You'd better hurry up and tell them before your sister bursts with frustration,' Bella said.

'Maybe you should do it.' He grinned.

Jools knew Jack was using delaying tactics to irritate his sister and had to stifle her giggle.

Sacha groaned. 'I don't care who tells us, but one of you has to before we all go mad with the suspense.'

'We're expecting a baby,' Jack announced.

Jools did her best to look surprised. She was delighted for her friend who seemed more content and in love than she had ever seen her before. 'What amazing news,' she said, blinking away tears. 'Congratulations, both of you.'

Sacha leapt up and hugged Bella tightly. 'I'm going to be an auntie?'

Jack nodded. 'Before you get too excited, it means that you'll be first on our list for babysitting duties.'

'I don't care. I love babies.' She pressed her hands to her heart and spun around on the sand. 'I'm so happy for you both.' Swaying slightly, she looked at Lexi. 'I don't know why, but I suspect they're not the only ones with news.'

Jools stared. Surely Lexi wasn't pregnant too? She hadn't been with Oliver long, but then again, that probably didn't matter. 'Lexi?'

Lexi took Oliver's hand and smiled up at him. 'Shall I?'

He looked at her with such devotion Jools felt a lump constrict her throat.

'Yes, why not?'

'Oliver's asked me to marry him,' she announced, looking as happy as Bella did. 'And, I said yes.' Everyone looked stunned. 'I know it's very quick,' Lexi added, pulling a face at her friends. 'But we're not going to rush the wedding. We've decided to wait until next year, but wanted to make a commitment to each other.'

'That's wonderful news.' Jools couldn't be happier for her friend. Lexi had been through so much and anyone who knew her could see that she was desperately in love with Oliver.

Smiling, Lexi added, 'Not only that, but Dad has agreed to give me away. When we went up to his bungalow to ask him, Gloria made a point of apologising for being such a cow.' There were murmurs of approval from her friends. 'She explained that she'd felt threatened by my close relationship with Dad and thought I didn't like her.'

'Which you didn't,' Bella said dryly.

'No, I didn't. But only after I discovered what she'd done. I didn't mind her before I knew how devious she had been.' Lexi shrugged. 'Anyway, she's apologised for thinking that I might try to split them up. She assumed if there was a disagreement, Dad would take my side.'

Nobody mentioned that he had done the opposite because Lexi knew that only too well.

'She's lucky you're not a mean person,' Jools said, unable to picture Lexi being cruel to anyone without exceptionally good reason.

'I try not to be.' Lexi smiled. 'Anyway, she apologised, and I've accepted her apology. We all agreed to move on from what's happened and start again.'

'I'm so pleased,' Sacha said, crawling across the sand to give Lexi a hug. 'You've always been so close to your dad and it was horrible seeing you estranged from each other. I'm really happy you've made it up and everything's going to be fine.'

'Thanks, Sacha.' Lexi leaned into Oliver. 'It was Oliver who made it happen, so I've got him to thank.'

'I was the one who inadvertently triggered their issues,' he said. 'I felt it was down to me to find a way to bring them closer together again. I can't expect Lexi to be happy with me if she's missing her father. This way everyone's happy and I know that my future wife will be happy, too.' He gave her a kiss.

'I've got no news,' Sacha said with a pout. 'I feel a little left out.'

'I am happy to be married to you, if you wish,' Alessandro said with a smile.

Sacha shook her head, then, taking his face in her hands, planted a kiss on his lips. 'No chance. We haven't even tried living together yet, plus, you're my competition on this boardwalk.' She gave him a wink.

What about me? Jools thought. She didn't have any exciting news to share either. She realised Marius was watching her silently. 'What?' she whispered, wondering whether she had food on her chin or something.

'I've got some exciting news for you,' he said, his voice low. 'I can tell you later when we're alone, or I can tell you now in front of your friends if you don't mind.'

'You have to tell us now,' Lexi said, overhearing. 'Don't leave us hanging.'

Jools shrugged. 'Why not?'

Marius put down his glass and turned to face her. He cleared his throat. 'I phoned the woman who organised the exhibition earlier today and she had news for us.' Jools bit her lip in anticipation. 'She said all your paintings have sold.'

'All of them?' Jools whispered. 'Every single one?'

'Yes, every single one.'

'Do you know who the buyers are?'

'I do.' He smiled at Sacha and then Bella. 'Do you want to tell her, or shall I?'

Sacha grinned. 'I bought the one of the café to hang in pride of place.'

'Oh, Sacha, that's so extravagant of you. Thank you.'

Sacha shook her head. 'Not at all. It's perfect. I always thought there was something missing in there and as soon as I saw the painting, I knew what it was.'

Bella took a sip of her lemonade. 'I bought one for Mum and Tony as their wedding gift. The one of the lighthouse in the moonlight.'

'You did?' It was the perfect gift. 'To remind her of the night Tony proposed?'

'Exactly,' Bella said. 'And to prove that I really am happy about her marrying Tony.'

'Thanks, Bella. I'm so happy that they have that painting.'

She realised that there were seven other paintings to account for. 'Do you know who bought the others?'

'I bought the one of the two dogs on the beach.' Marius gave her an embarrassed look. 'I thought they looked like Teddy and Grandad's Jarvis.'

'That's because they are.'

He gave her hand a gentle squeeze, obviously understanding that she had painted that picture with the day they met on the beach in mind. 'Thank you. And does that mean that the man and woman in the painting are you and me?'

She nodded. 'They are.'

He stared at her silently for a few seconds. 'Thank you.'

'I'm the one who should thank you,' she said. 'For buying it. At least this way I'll be able to see the two of us whenever I want to.'

'You can do that anyway,' he said, leaning over to kiss her.

'Hey,' Jack said. 'When the two of you have finished can you tell us who bought the other six paintings?'

'Ah,' Marius said, looking very pleased with himself all of a sudden. 'Now we get to the exciting bit.'

Jools couldn't work out what he was leading up to and then it dawned on her. 'Have you discovered who my mysterious buyer is?' When he didn't answer immediately, she nudged him. 'Please say you have.'

'Maybe.' He tilted his head. 'In fact, I have two pieces of news.'

'Get on with it,' Jack laughed.

'Your mysterious buyer is… drum roll please.' Her friends patted the sand in front of them in a rapid tattoo. 'Aunt Rosie.'

'Aunt Rosie?'

Jools's mouth dropped open in surprise. She turned to Sacha. 'Did you know?'

Sacha looked as shocked as Jools felt. 'I didn't, I promise you.' She frowned in confusion. 'Did she say why the elaborate secrecy Marius?'

'Apparently, she bought the initial paintings because she decided they would be perfect reminders of Jersey if she hung them in her new flat in London.'

'How lovely,' Jools said, touched by the idea. 'Why didn't she want me to know?'

Sacha smiled. 'I imagine it's because she didn't want you to think she was buying them because she knows you.'

Wasn't that what Jools had practically accused Marius of doing? 'I can understand that,' she said though, secretly, she couldn't help being a tiny bit disappointed that a stranger hadn't swept in and snapped up one of her paintings, impressed by her genius.

'That's not all,' Marius said. 'She had the first four paintings sent over and has a friend with an art gallery somewhere in Knightsbridge. She showed them to him, along with a vase of mine she bought a couple of months ago, and apparently, we've been offered a month-long exhibition in his gallery. Rosie is sending over the paperwork tomorrow.'

Jools was momentarily speechless. It was more than she could have hoped for. 'That's amazing news,' she said, as her friends chimed in their congratulations. The idea of producing work for another exhibition was daunting, but she knew how lucky she was to have the opportunity and was determined to make the most of it. 'I can't believe it.'

'The exhibition isn't until September, so we have plenty of time to get to work.'

Excitement building, she laughed. 'Oh, Marius, this could be our lucky break.'

'My lucky break was meeting you on this beach that day.' He drew her to him and kissed her.

'Do you know what?' She pulled back and looked into his eyes. 'It was mine too.'

ACKNOWLEDGMENTS

Thanks, as ever, to my wonderfully supportive husband, Rob and to my children, Saskia and James for their constant support.

To my wonderful editor Tara Loder, to Rose Fox for her proofs and to the entire team at Boldwood Books for being so amazing.

To Karen Clarke, an early reader of this book, I know it is much better thanks to your invaluable input.

To Nigel Sweeny MBE, a long-time member of the St Catherine's RNLI here in Jersey for his help with my research, any errors are mine alone.

I am grateful to glass artist, Glyn Burton, for being so welcoming and showing me the exquisite glassware in his shop and describing how various metal oxides are used to produce the different coloured glass he uses to make a range of beautiful products from seascapes to pendants and earrings. Also, to his colleague, Jodie Carney, who kindly let me watch her in her workshop as she heated glass rods to a soft malleable consistency to make gorgeous earrings. If you're visiting Jersey their workshop/shop at Devil's Hole is well worth a visit.

To my three rescue dogs, Jarvis, Claude and Rudi who, regardless of whether I want to step away from my work in progress, always insist on their daily beach walk and ensure I get some fresh air and exercise.

And most of all to you, dear reader. I hope you enjoy this latest visit to the boardwalk.

A LETTER TO MY READERS

Dear Reader,

Thank you for choosing to read Jools's story, I hope you enjoyed getting to know her, Marius, and Mrs Jones and spending time with them on the boardwalk.

One of my favourite pastimes when I'm away from the island is visiting second-hand bookshops and so I had to include one in this series. This is where Jools spends most of her time and I hope you enjoyed visiting Boardwalk Books too.

If you enjoyed this book, I would be very grateful if you could give it a rating on Amazon, or even a short review because these go a long way to helping other readers discover an author's books.

Until next time,

Georgina x

MORE FROM GEORGINA TROY

We hope you enjoyed reading *Sunny Days on the Boardwalk*. If you did, please leave a review.

If you'd like to gift a copy, this book is also available as an ebook, hardback, paperback, digital audio download and audiobook CD.

Sign up to Georgina Troy's mailing list for news, competitions and updates on future books.

https://bit.ly/GeorginaTroyNews

Explore more wonderfully escapist fiction from Georgina Troy...

ABOUT THE AUTHOR

Georgina Troy writes bestselling uplifting romantic escapes and sets her novels on the island of Jersey, where she was born and has lived for most of her life. She has done a twelve-book deal with Boldwood, including backlist titles, and the first book in her Sunshine Island series was published in May 2022.

Visit Georgina's website: https://deborahcarr.org/my-books/georgina-troy-books/

Follow Georgina on social media here:

[f] facebook.com/GeorginaTroyAuthor

[twitter] twitter.com/GeorginaTroy

[instagram] instagram.com/ajerseywriter

[BB] bookbub.com/authors/georgina-troy

Boldwood

Boldwood Books is an award-winning fiction publishing company seeking out the best stories from around the world.

Find out more at www.boldwoodbooks.com

Join our reader community for brilliant books, competitions and offers!

Follow us
@BoldwoodBooks
@BookandTonic

Sign up to our weekly
deals newsletter

https://bit.ly/BoldwoodBNewsletter

Printed in Great Britain
by Amazon

40380014R00139